I0633310

What Was That?

What Was That?

Katharine Haviland Taylor

RAMBLE HOUSE
2018

First American trade paperback edition

Ramble House
10329 Sheephead Drive
Vancleave MS 39565 USA

www.ramblehouse.com

Originally printed in six parts in *Argosy – All-Story Weekly*,
beginning in Vol. CXXVI Number 2, October 9, 1920

This work is in the Public Domain

This edition © 2018 Ramble House

ISBN 13: 978-1-60543-922-8

Preparation: Jim Weiler & Gavin L. O'Keefe
Cover design © 2018 Gavin L. O'Keefe

CHAPTER I.

HOW IT STARTED

I ENJOY SEEING the works, particularly that one small wheel, without which nothing would go. Now that it's all over, I like to recall that cold March afternoon when I saw a bomb floated on the English Channel. I was painting in Paris when the war broke out, and at once hurried home. On the way I encountered an English boy I'd met at Le Monte Dore, and, of course, I fell on his neck.

He was a touch of something known, and I did feel lonely, for "home" was a pretty general term then. I didn't know where it was going to be, nor—how nice it would be, which was worse.

He took me down below Dover, where, with some other men, he was experimenting with bombs under government control. They launched one of the affairs so that I could see it.

"Look at the little beggar!" said my friend, in a tone that was almost caressing. "A bit calm, isn't she? But—she'll make some jolly hell when she 'up and busts.' "

And the suggestion of Nan Severance was quite as innocent in appearance as that bomb, and it acted quite as that bomb was meant to; so—it isn't strange that the remembrance of the start of our plan and that bomb launching should hold hands in the store-house of my mind. I never think of one without the other.

It happened this way: Nan blew in the nine-by-twelve cupboard I call my "Studio" when I write home—Ohio—and said: "Lord, but I'm tired of life!"

"I'm with you," I replied, surveying my canvas.

"Painting an omelette?" she asked, as she sank down on a box-couch.

"Tulips," I answered, "background for a girl in white—string of amber beads—trying to be a magazine cover—this morning I thought it was all right, and then I ran out of yellow ochre and by the time I'd fussed around getting it I was all out of tune."

I didn't get much sympathy. "Well, at least you can do what you want to—or *try* to," she said, looking at my canvas between narrowed eyelids, "while I have to correct proof or starve, and what ideas I have—things that really might work up, go stale. I know I could write if I ever had a chance."

"I know, Nan," I answered, as soothingly as I could.

"You don't," she answered viciously. "I just wish that I could have a whole summer to write in, a whole summer in which I wouldn't have to read proof, worry about rent, think of food, or—"

At that moment Midgette Grant, who isn't quite one of us, came in.

For one thing, her dad supplies her with lots of the cold hard, and we struggle for it—that makes a divide. Then she bobs her hair and does all those things artists of any sort who live below Fifteenth Street are supposed to do and very often don't, which is another divide. She had been crying.

"Dearest boy from home," she explained, "really *was* lost. I had hoped every day to hear that he wasn't. Now after a lapse of two years he would have turned up if he had been alive, wouldn't he?"

"War?" asked Nan, a little contemptuously. Midgette's sentimentalities and wanderings annoy her.

"Yes, and he didn't care whether he was killed or not. That's what makes it sad."

"Oh, stuff!" said Nan. "Never knew anybody who didn't really want to live. Hand a pistol to any conversational suicide. He'll scream and say, 'Don't point that thing at me!' "

"You don't understand," said Midgette hotly. "This was different. This boy *didn't* talk. He was only silent. And before it happened, he was simply a darling. He could have had me any time, and I tried to let him see it every time we met—"

"Before what happened?" asked Nan, this time with real irritation showing in her voice.

"Before his father was murdered," replied Midgette.

"Murdered?" repeated Nan. She likes things of that sort. She says they stir her plot sense into more active being. "Tell me about it," ordered Nan.

Midgette shook off her furs and settled. And then she told the story—told it well, which was unusual for her. Here it is:

"The whole thing was strange," said Midgette, settling herself with Nan on the box-couch. "It has never been explained, which keeps it alive in the small town where I lived. The facts are these: Rudolph Loucks, the father of this boy who has failed to turn up, was murdered on the hillside above his bungalow which lies close against a creek. Rather romantic, the way it was done; very strange. And, as I said, never explained—"

"Go on," said Nan.

Midgette picked up a glove, fingered it, then resolutely put it down, after which she drew a deep breath and proceeded. "This Rudolph Loucks had a great deal of money, controlled almost every business enterprise in the small town, was bad, vicious in some ways—but for some reason liked by men. I think he had a gift for comradeship.

"Anyway, his bungalow was a resort for all sorts—some of them first families, some of them otherwise; and the entertainment varied with the caliber of his guests. He lived in town, but kept old Nathan Greenleaf, a woodsman, untaught naturalist and carpenter, in a cabin near by to keep the fires of his bungalow going in winter, and the road to it cleared.

"Rudolph, senior, liked to motor out there in the dead of night with a crowd, skate to music, have a hot breakfast, and motor back to town after hours of daylight asleep. He looked like a heavy-jowled, too-well-fed satyr, and I have often thought that some of his more inky affairs were only the fruit of imagination, turned sour.

"The night of his murder showed one of them, when he persuaded the daughter of a hotel-keeper of the flats to go with him to his bungalow. She was only seventeen, but a clear-eyed youngster that a man, even a bad one, would think twice about hurting. I suppose he liked her freshness, and did not care much what he hurt.

"Somehow he persuaded her—for all she would babble was, 'I didn't wanta, but he made me—oh, Gawd, oh, *Gawd!* I didn't wanta!' She started with him up the long road that winds around Greyson's Hill. On the other side of this lie his bungalow and the creek, I think about three miles from town. The night was stormy, a heavy snow was falling, and a wind made it drift. No one but Rudolph Loucks would have tried so long a trip on that wild night.

"I think you can see it, if you try; the plodding horses—a motor would have refused to travel those heavy roads—the jaded man beginning to feel the stimulus of a new drink, the frightened girl. He knew the game, and he wanted to win this one, so he narrowed his little pig eyes, bit his lips, and feigned a careless air. And here's the mystery. Halfway up the hill he stopped his carriage, looked back of him, and waited; something was behind them; after a moment the little girl heard it.

" 'G'wan,' she whispered, 'Can't yuh g'wan? *Some one's coming!*' He gripped her arm so cruelly that he left a black mark on her flesh, and with a word silenced her; and then he went on at a furious rate, now and again looking into the swirling snow behind them. Again they stopped, again he listened. Then he lit a cigarette, and Vera Struthers saw that he was white and that his hands shook.

" 'Get out,' he ordered. She did, sinking to her knees in the snow, and he followed her. He puffed at his cigarette a moment, staring toward the town from which they'd come.

" 'You heard something?' he asked in a whisper.

"She began to speak, but paused, for through the heavy air came the muffled sound of a plodding horse and the sharp crack of a whip.

"Then Rudolph Loucks did something which has been explained only by guesswork. He quickly tied her hands behind her with a muffler and directed her to a farm-house, and said: 'Send some one after me—' She stepped to the roadside, lurching miserably, and he started on, faded from sight and hearing, and the wind was the only sound.

"Then again came the sound of horses' hoofs, and a sleigh flashed by. Vera said there was only one person in it. But the light was dim, the snow thick and no one ever really knew how much she had seen and heard or how much she imagined.

"Two hours later she reached the farmhouse. Half frozen, and almost speechless, she told them to look for Rudolph Loucks.

" 'Some one followed us,' she said. 'He tied me, I dunno why. He says fer youse to follow him!'

"Over and over she repeated her injunction. I suppose the night with its horror had left her numbed, and the pressure of his curt order was the only one which she could feel. The farmer's son, a pathetic wreck of a boy with a clouded mind, took up the refrain and chanted it: 'Some one followed us,' he sung, 'he says to follow *him*. Some one followed *us,* he says to follow *him*—'

"In the middle of this dirge news came that Rudolph Loucks had been found, shot in the back, face down on the snow, in a rolling field which lay above his bungalow. It was about four when they came upon him. The snow had drifted over tracks, and the horses stood, heads drooping, too near to freezing even to tremble from the horrible cold. The snow lay in uneven little heaps, where it had drifted over footprints, and a great, scarlet blotch colored the snow which was below Rudolph Loucks's head and chest.

"Twenty feet away lay a pistol which belonged to the town banker, and in a pocket of the dead man's coat was a jagged piece of paper torn from a corner of the *London News,* the only subscription to which is taken by our local clergyman, and on this was written in the clear, bold unmistakable writing of Judge Harkins: 'I'll get you so—' and the rest was gone. It was supposed that the entire word was 'soon.' "

"Who did it?" asked Nan, reaching for a match box and lighting up. "That judge?"

"No, he was in New York."

"The clergyman?"

"Lord, Nan, certainly not! He couldn't have hit him if he tried!"

"The banker?"

"Hardly. He had pneumonia, and there were two trained nurses to testify where he was that night."

"Well, how'd they get his pistol?" asked Nan, sitting forward.

"No one knows," replied Midgette. "No one knows anything, no one was convicted; every man in town was suspected, every motive on earth thought of, every reason on earth investigated."

"Why did he tie that girl's hands?" I asked.

"I suppose," answered Midgette, "so that she wouldn't be suspected. Perhaps he was sorry for some of the things he had done. People have a way of being sorry when it's too late, you know. If she had been found with free hands she'd have been thought guilty, of course."

"Where is she now?" I asked.

"Haven't the least idea," said Midgette. "I know she left town. Had to; the trial was thrilling."

"I should think so!" said Nan. "And it's his son who's among the missing?"

"Yes."

"Did he have a wife?"

"Certainly not! That dear, innocent boy who—"

"I meant the father," said Nan.

"Why don't you say what you mean?" asked Midgette, but slightly mollified. "Of course he once had a wife, but she died when Rudolph, junior, was about eighteen. I suppose she was too wearied by her husband's ways to go on."

"Any women who might have wanted to hurt him?" I asked.

"Thousands, I imagine; but how would any one of them get hold of Frank Lethridge's pistol? He is an absolutely confirmed woman-hater. Won't even have one in his house as a maid. Keeps a Jap.

"No, you can't solve it, Nan. Better detectives than you are gave it up. Why, that famous man from Pittsburgh, what's his name? Wonderful head—he frankly acknowledged it had him going. There were so many chains of evidence, each one leading to a different person. There was the pistol, the *London News,* the judge's writing; there was the sleigh, and the man who had hired it for the evening—"

"Who was he?" asked Nan.

"A Norwegian draftsman who had just come to town. He was found blindfolded and gagged in an up-stairs room of the Struthers Hotel, the very one which Rudolph Loucks had persuaded Vera Struthers to leave that evening."

"Didn't her father know how he had got in?" I asked.

"No," Midgette replied. "He didn't. The room opened on to the roof of an adjoining building, and the Norwegian had been dragged in through this. He said he had been gripped by some one who had crept up back of his sleigh, blindfolded, gagged, and hauled him up innumerable stairs, and tied him in this room. It was hours before they found him."

"Whom was he going to take out?" Nan asked, flicking the ash from her cigarette on top of my best hat, which was lying on the floor at the end of the couch.

"I don't know," Midgette answered. "But that had nothing to do with it, nor had he. They—who ever they were—simply wanted a sleigh, and didn't dare hire one. Rather slick, wasn't it?"

"Where did this happen?" Nan asked.

"Just at the beginning of Greyson's Hill. Probably the murderers were waiting there, and decided it was too near town to fire a shot with safety."

"Seems funny that they couldn't find any one, any reason," I said. I laid down my palette, lit a one-plate gas burner, and began to heat water as I spoke.

"Tea?" said Midgette. "Good! Yes, doesn't it? But, as I said, the evidence was confusing. Every one was suspected, and no one could be condemned, or whatever it is you do to 'em. Sandwiches? Oh, April, don't bother!"

I am April Barry.

"What happened to the son? You said he was lost?" Nan asked. She was full of questions.

"Yes—" Midgette wiped a tear away, and went on: "Father wrote me about it to-day. Said that the cousin had taken over management of the estate, and that the bungalow was for rent at an absurdly cheap figure because no one seems to want it. Rudolph, junior, had rented it before the war to some one who used it only for business—boat-house business. *That* fellow was shot at the battle of Chateau Thierry, and Rudolph's cousin bought the boats from his mother. Wonderful business opportunity for any one who wanted it, but the spot is too much for our neighborhood."

Nan sat up, jammed out the light of her cigarette on the window sill. "April, you told me last month that you were hard up; I know I am. Why don't we take over that place for this summer? Run a tearoom, rent the boats, make a little, and have our mornings free for work?"

Something cold gripped me. That shiver must have been sent by the little star that backs my safety. It made me say: "Oh, Nan, I don't—*know*—"

"My dear," she persuaded, "why not? Get a crowd if you like. Safety in numbers. Say we take Laurence O'Leary—he has to move soon. Probably Jane Hoyle would go; said she wanted to rest for a while this season; I would—you *must*—this infant" —she waved at Midgette—"would be with us—and perhaps Gustave Gerome, that is, if Jane goes."

Midgette looked doubtful. "Look here," she said, "I've got to tell you something else that keeps that place from being rented. I don't care whether you believe it or not, but Rudolph Loucks has been seen more than once—Rudolph, Senior, I mean—lying on that hillside just as he lay after he was shot, and one skeptic started to go up to the spot, and the ghost slid away from him into a wood of fir trees that edges the field."

"Stuff!" Nan and I howled in chorus.

Midgette did not join our laughter.

"Enjoy yourselves," she said easily; "my best friends have seen it."

"Well, they won't any more," said Nan.

"People don't avoid the place in the daytime, do they?"

"No," replied Midgette.

"And there's good boating?"

"Oh, yes. It's awfully pretty—willows, little bridges, a mill about a mile down stream. Cows standing at the water's edge to drink."

"You," Nan said to Midgette, with an understanding smile, "have said that your chief ambition in this world is to do something that would jar your home town; here's your chance; crowd of young people, unchaperoned, living together for the summer in a bungalow. It'll be about as tame as a bed-room farce, but it will advertise in wonderfully dark tones!

"And for you, April" —Nan turned to me—"a whole summer for painting, without any push for money; wonderful opportunity—unless you feel that Billy would object?"

That rather decided me. Billy is an admirer of mine, who irritates me, and nothing so enrages me as to have people think he influences me, or that I care for him.

"You should know," I replied, "that Billy doesn't swing my ballot. Whatever I decide is my own deciding."

Nan only smiled. "Horrify him, wouldn't it? This mixed affair for the season?"

I admitted it would.

"Well, then, I suppose that counts you out," she said.

I felt myself grow pink, and I heard myself say, "If you get the crowd to agree, I'm with you. It is an opportunity, I can see that—" and I turned to make the tea, for the water was boiling.

And that's the way it all started. Simple, wasn't it? And so was the launching of that bomb. It slid in place so gently that the water hardly rippled, and, as I said, the memory of that and that blustery day in March, are clamped together in my mind—quite naturally!

CHAPTER II.

PRINTED IN RED

BILLY WAS HORRIFIED. I met him while I was out hunting a meat-grinder and some individual tea-pots.

"You mean to say," he demanded, "that Gustave Gerome and that ass, Laurence O'Leary, are to go with your crowd?"

I nodded.

"Nice to have O'Leary reading free verse aloud before breakfast," he said, through set teeth. "I suppose he will. Never met him when he didn't read aloud something he wrote. Who started this? I call it disgusting!"

"Oh, we all thought it a good idea," I replied. I didn't want to blame Nan. Billy doesn't like her.

"Why you won't marry me—" he said, with a baffled shake of his head.

"Is a great mystery," I admitted. He grew pink.

"You can be a spiteful little cuss," he said. "You know perfectly well what I meant. I didn't mean that I was a drawing card. I only meant I'd die for you, and that's something, isn't it—dear? And that I have enough money to make you entirely comfortable, and that I'd give my life to make you happy, and—"

"I know," I replied. "There are the very tea-pots I want! *Sweet, ducky* things—"

"Oh, damn!" said Billy. In that mood he assisted me to make my purchases, and in that mood he left me.

"If you want me," he said, as I fitted my key in my lock an hour later, "wire me." I smiled a little. I was awfully mean at that time, I know it now. Billy put his hand over mine, held it closely, and made me look up at him. "Some day," he asserted, "you'll know how cruel you have been. And you'll be sorry. I love you, April, and the sort of stuff I offer you no woman should laugh at, for—it's the best I can give, you know."

I was enough softened by that to say I was sorry I couldn't take it, but softening didn't help Billy. It only made him hopeful, and a little masterful.

"My *soul,* how I care!" he declared after he had kissed me, and stood looking down at me. I was angry, and when I looked up and saw the man who has the studio on the next floor, I was more so. I always borrow paint from him when I run out of it. He believes in mutual consent, but said he would marry me if I was narrow enough to prefer it. I said I'd consider it. He buys very good paints, and I have never seen the necessity of facing issues unless one is forced to. I thought that probably by the time he realized that my heart wouldn't warm for him, I would find another lender. But Billy spoiled it.

"He loaned me paints!" I said angrily.

"Damn him!" said Billy.

"And you had no right to do that!"

"I know," he agreed, miserably.

"And I hope you won't bother me this summer," I went on. "I am going to work hard. I don't want to be troubled."

"You won't be," said Billy. "I'm through." And then he turned and left. And although I didn't like him then, something did ache inside. I went in, and cried a little. I tried to imagine it was because the fountain of free paint was clogged, but it wasn't. It was really Billy's saying he was through.

After I'd had my dinner, I got out the tea-pots, and decided that they were worth all I'd paid for them. I was counting the vast sums we would make, when Midgette came in and told me about how she was going to use her dad's last check.

"Wicker furniture," she said, "on those broad porches—won't it be *sweet,* April?" Then she went on to explain how she had told her father that she'd have a darling surprise for him if he'd only finance it.

"He may not quite understand Laurence and Gustave being with us," she went on, speculatively. "He's been an elder in the church for years, and that is sort of narrowing, isn't it? I think too much religion always makes people believe the worst. Where'd you get the fudge; can I have some? And then his business hasn't made for soul growth—"

"It would be frightful if he cut your allowance, wouldn't it?" I asked.

"I've been thinking of it," she admitted, and none too happily. "But of course I'll see it through. I promised Nan I would, and I *do* want to show those people what life *can* be, and as she says, my opportunity is here. But speculating about things and doing them is so *different*."

I agreed.

"Well, no doubt it will be entirely pleasant," she said, as she stood up. "I don't see why it shouldn't be, and it is a pretty spot, though the mosquitoes are thick and terribly active. I think June is a little *early*—"

I saw she regretted the whole affair, but I didn't think she'd be able to get out of it, for Nan has a powerful will. When Midgette left I wrote nine notes to Billy, all of which I tore up. At the moment there was nothing to say to Billy P. Watts, who'd made a fortune in the rise of leather. I hadn't reached the point where I realized what I wanted to say. *That* came later.

It came when every one began to scream *"What-was-that?"* It came when we all began to spend so much time in town, and Midgette threatened to go home to her father; it came when we had to stick it out, and needed some one to stick with us. Then and then only I began to realize that there is something real and something very cheering about a man who honestly deserves to be called "Billy," and who will let you call him that—or anything —whenever you need him.

The place had not been opened, and the air was stale. The care-taker, old Nathan Greenleaf, unlocked it for us, and his matter-of-fact manner and rustic look was reassuring.

"Don't you be skairt if there's noises," he said, "water's high from that there last rain, and she's carryin' driftwood. That bumps the landing in the night. But don't you young ladies be skairt."

Nan, taking the burden of the crowd on her shoulders, went out to inspect the kitchen, humming a little tune on her way. When she had unbolted the heavy shutters out there and light flooded the place, she stopped singing. I hurried out to her and found her staring at something on the wall. She gulped a little as I drew near, and pointed. I looked, and saw the print of some one's fingers on the woodwork, and these were marked in red, fresh red, which smelled as only one thing smells.

"You know," she said, *"it is."*

"Yes," I agreed, "but some one cut his or her hand while they were cleaning here. It's nothing to be excited about—" I tried to believe it. Then I took a frightfully gray rag which swung from a pipe below the sink, moistened it, and wiped off the stain. "The others mustn't know," I said; "Midgette's nervous now. There's no use of starting this with hysterical notions."

"No," Nan agreed, but she stood staring at the spot until I shook her, scolded her, and warned her against spoiling everything before anything had started. And then Gerome appeared at the door, his palette already over his thumb. "It's simply ripping," he announced. "Most wonderful bits for work. Nan, I love you!"

She managed to laugh at him, and then she sobered, for from below us came the sound of breaking glass, and after it deadly, awful silence.

"What-was-that?" screamed Midgette, her words tangling in their hurry. And that started them. Every one said those words, rather screamed them, and when they didn't, they thought them.

Laurence went down cellar, from which one could walk into the boat-house; this was under the porch, which was high and overhung the creek. "A dog," he announced when he returned, "jumped through a window, I suppose. Darn the beast." But later he singled me out for confidence, as had Nan. I was not grateful for this mark of trust in either case.

All the others had turned in; I was cleaning paint brushes and he was locking up. "There was a dog," he said slowly, as he picked off some hardened tallow which had dripped down the side of his candle, "but—the mongrel wasn't scratched. Hadn't a spot of blood on him—but—" He paused.

"Go on!" I said. I was nervous.

"There were finger prints by the door, in—in blood." Laurence coughed. "Couldn't quite understand," he went on. "But I washed 'em off. Didn't want Midgette to have hysterics. I went down to see Greenleaf just before dinner. I told him to keep an eye out. He said he would. No doubt there's some perfectly logical explanation," he ended.

"No doubt," I said, looking around behind me and wishing that the candlelight I'd once thought so picturesque could be replaced by ninety horse-power mazda stuff. Then we heard a bumping, that sort of muffled bumping which only something floating on water can make.

"Driftwood," said Laurence, nervously.

"Certainly," I replied.

He picked at his candle for a few minutes more with absolute absorption, fussed with it until I was ready to scream, so—when something was flung against the hard wood of the door, and fell to boom on the hollow floor of the porch, it was no wonder that I did scream.

"Shut up!" said Laurence, who with that sudden noise had abandoned his candle researches. "Shut up! Can't you see you've got to be calm? My God, April, *what was that?*" Laurence took down a lantern, lit it, and opened the door. There was no one in sight, but a brick lay a foot or so from the door on the porch floor.

"What *was* that?" called Midgette from the stairs. At least she put a different accent on it, for which I was grateful.

"Dropped one of the bags," Laurence answered, and we heard soft scuffles, the closing of doors above and quiet. "It gets me," whispered Laurence, picking up the offending brick, and studying it. "But I guess"—he peered into the dark with his words—"I won't investigate to-night. Don't want to leave you alone. But to-morrow," he said, as he carefully closed and locked the door, "we'll track this thing to earth."

With a good-night I turned toward the stairs. My knees shook a little and I took hold of the bannisters. My room was three steps higher than any of the others and at the end of a passage. The railing felt a little sticky. I was not surprised when I gained my room to find that my palm was sticky with blood. I didn't bother Laurence about it. There was no use of doing so, but I lay wakeful for a long time—shivering a good deal in that pitchy dark which the close-set trees made—and I thought of Billy.

CHAPTER III.

COMPLICATIONS

OUR LITTLE PARTY consisted of myself—April Barry—illustrator; Laurence O'Leary, who does free verse; Gustave Gerome, who did the backgrounds for those tableaux Grant Philip's posed; Jane Hoyle, who dances and poses; Nan Severance, who corrects proof and longs to write; and Midgette, who tries to do everything and does nothing. There had been a light rain in the night; the sun shone in that thin, golden way it sometimes does in the early miming, and every cobweb on the grass glittered with thousands of tiny, flashing drops of wet.

I met Laurence O'Leary on the porch. He had been sent out to get kindling, but had forgotten his errand, because the rising mists of the creek had sent him into a free verse. I was dispatched to speed the muse and hustle the fuel. Gustave Gerome at that moment stuck his head out of the door, and simply yelled, "If I don't get some breakfast I'll wither, and some one else will die!"

"Food!" said Laurence, scornfully, after Gustave had withdrawn. "God, what a carnal thought for the start of this bright, jewel day!"

With the poetry look still in his eyes, he bent over to pick up the wood. "Chill mist is dead," he muttered, "and naked day stands forth, alone, ungirt, for rains or sun to clothe; chill mist is gone and—damn!" he ended, for he dropped a big fire log on his foot.

We managed to get breakfast after two hours' fussing with the stove, but everything smelled of smoke, and every one was so busy wiping their eyes and blowing their noses, when the food did appear, that they hardly had time to eat.

"We get a gas stove to-day!" said Gustave, his chin set, and a very unpleasantly masculine give-me-my-coffee-damn-quick look around his mouth.

"But there isn't any gas," said Midgette, with a soft look toward him.

18

"Well, what if there isn't?" demanded Gustave, turning on her with rage. "Do you have to start the day by saying so? If I thought I had to go through this again, I couldn't paint to-day." Then he lit up a little stubby pipe, and stood shaking the match and staring at the table. "Might as well tell you girls," he remarked coldly, "that my inner man wants *food,* the real stuff, after I leave the land of dreams. That coffee—" He tried to characterize it, failed, and did a fair imitation of a seltzer bottle. Then he said: "*My God!*" and stamped out the room, slamming the door so hard after him that the whole place rocked.

"To think," said Midgette, "that I was beginning to feel that I loved him!" She, too, stared at the table, but with a different look and then she said, rather whispered: "Did you see him eat that fried egg? Done only on one side?"

Jane Hoyle, who has more sense than all of the rest of us put together, smiled, and answered, "Well, you know, Midge, men have to eat!"

Nan washed the dishes, I wiped them, the rest did the up-stairs work. Midgette was entirely herself after she had fussed around upstairs, and came down singing. She joined me on the porch, where I was sweeping away the leaves that had blown down during the night's rain.

"*Sweet* place!" she said, sitting on the railing and looking down into the water that twinkled in black and green diamond-shaped shadows below.

I caught her laziness, let my broom rest for a moment, and gazed up into the deep green of a fir tree that grew right up through one corner of the porch. It was a dear place; even after the unpleasant frights of the afternoon before, I loved it. The porch ran way out over the creek, and half of it was unroofed except for the huge trees that spread above it. These filtered the sunlight, and let splotches of it waver and dance on the gray, rough, board floor. The walls of the house were shingled, and the sloping, low roof made me think of the thatched homes of the peasant folk of France.

The whole place was a tribute to some one's understanding of the woods. It looked as if it grew there and belonged among the thick-set trees, the moist smelling fern growth, and the free-wandering creek. It was one of those long houses, built with single-room thickness, so that each room had its windows on the creek, and those on the other side looked into the woods. The next hill to this rose a little back of the wooded one, and we saw it fully only when we rounded the bend of the private lane, which took us to the main road. But—from the porch of the bungalow you could see the spot where Rudolph Loucks had lain and bled to death, in the snow of that wild, cold night.

"Look between those two little birches, April," said Midgette. "Just over those was where Rudolph Loucks lay. I wish some one could solve that mystery if, for nothing else, for his son's sake. He was an attractive boy. I—I can't imagine his speaking as Gustave did this morning!"

When she left me I sat down on the steps that led down to the boats and their landing, half of which was free of the porch and uncovered. The quiet, and the little tapping sound that the water made against the landing, turned me lazy, made my eyes half close, and my muscles sag. I sat there for perhaps ten minutes, and then I was aroused by the approach of old Nathan, who had a fishing pole in one hand and a string of fish in the other.

He came up, sat down below me, and beamed at me through thick-lensed, yellow-tinted glasses. Tobacco juice had assisted him to carry out his color scheme, and his white beard was tinted at the corners of his mouth into a perfect ochre. Altogether, Nathan Greenleaf looked like the human echo of a meerschaum pipe. I thought he would make a splendid cover for *The Country Gentlewoman*, and then and there decided I would make him pose some time when I felt in the temper for it.

I spoke to him about a stove and discovered where I could get a kerosene affair that would do very well. He told me the name of the local paper, in which we wanted to advertise our venture; and he it was who named the place for us: "The Hidden Treasure."

"Splendid!" said I, clapping my hands; for it was out of the way, out of sight, hidden by trees and hills and—we hoped to make it a jewel of a place and a real treasure. That afternoon we bought tea, our stove, some cups and saucers from the ten-cent store, advertised "The Hidden Treasure" in the Glenridge *Chronicle*, and we all felt that we were headed in the right direction.

Before Nathan Greenleaf left me I pumped him about what could have made the brick fall against our door; fall was a gentle way of putting it; it had been flung.

"I dunno," he said, "any number of things, mebbe."

"Well, what?" I questioned.

"Well, mebbe 'The Echo,' that's Beasley's boy that's not altogether." I judged he meant that he was not responsible.

"Yuh see," old Nathan went on, "he's like this; he ain't altogether. No'm, you couldn't say he's right, although he ain't dangerous. But—it's like this—"

Old Nathan's conversation was a combination of pauses, full stops, and spits. "Round these parts he's called 'The Echo,' because he up and does 'most everything he's saw. Likely he seen Hez Riggs poundin' on that there door, flingin' bricks at it, like he done when he took a notion that Rudolph Loucks, him that was murdered, had his wife, Judy Riggs, in that there house with him. Judy was settin' on the attic stringin' apples fer to dry. But Hez, he was one of them red-headed fella's that go off like one of them dollar alarm clocks, any time, and they ain't no stoppin' 'em. He'd saw Rudolph make a pretty smile at Judy, and when he finds Judy ain't around right underfoot, he notions a lot that ain't so, and he says he'd be gosh tarnationed if he wasn't goin' to up and lam Rudolph so he wouldn't fergit it fer all time. And so he brung bricks along with him, and nicked the door some. Take notice there, above the door knob?" I did. "Well, that there dent," went on Nathan, "Hez, he nicked it."

What I thought was a real idea came to settle on me. "Look here," I said. "didn't any one ever suspect this Hez Riggs?"

"No'm," Nathan replied.

"Why not—"

"Well—" he began to drawl.

"Look here," I said once again, "isn't it logical that this Hez person would harbor a grudge against Rudolph Loucks? Isn't it possible that he brooded over Rudolph Loucks's look at his wife, imagined a great deal that wasn't so about it—worked himself into a fury, began to hate Rudolph Loucks, began to plan revenge, and ended by killing him? It's logical, now, isn't it?"

Nathan considered it at length. "Yassum. I reckon it *sounds* reasonable. But yuh see, Hez Riggs, he happened to be dead hisself afore this here murder happened." Then he stood up, stretched, remarked that he must be "walkin' on," and I saw him disappear toward the woods. He left me divided between laughter and anger.

"The man's a fool!" I said at lunch, as I told the story.

"No," said Gustave, who had quite recovered temper by that time, "he's not. You were; you didn't wait for him to talk his language, which is slow. Do you know that that old fellow's photographs of wild birds, and all sorts of woods life, are shown in the best magazines?"

"They are," Gustave declared as he got up to get an extra plate. Nan had set the table, and she was already deep in the first chapter of the Great American Novel, so that there was much to be desired in the way of spoons, forks and plates.

"He has a nephew," Gustave went on, after he again settled, "who has had some education and who lives in New York. To him, old Nathan ships these plates, and he finishes them and sells them. He gets all the credit, but it is the old fellow who does the trick. He showed me some this morning. I was sketching around there and fell over the place. The old chap was splendidly hospitable. Says he'll do carpentry for us if we need it." We all at once decided we needed his services.

"I'll send him up this afternoon," said Gustave, but we refused that, since we were going to town. On the way we encountered the most amazing, horrible, and haunting smell.

Midgette turned white.

"I wonder what father will think of all this," she said, "how he will feel!" and then I understood what it was.

"You do," said Nan, holding her nose. "There is a lot in Laurence I didn't appreciate."

"Nonsense," I said sharply. "Laurence is all right, but not worth much serious consideration!"

Nan flashed an angry look at me, and I began to see what we were up against, and I knew it would make complications that would not help our affairs to run any too smoothly. I could see it, people going off and shirking work to walk together in the woods; people being annoyed when any one beside two people dared to inhabit the large living-room; stolen kisses, lovers' quarrels, excitement, happiness, and despair! For—I know Nan and I know Laurence. They are both what is called temperamental, for the lack of a better word. And I knew that all the heights would respond with bitter depths, and I could feel the quality of discontent that would follow, and force the going off of one of them. We needed all our capital.

"This is a business proposition," I said coldly. "We all agreed to ignore sex, and to keep both feet on the ground and to share work."

Then Jane started a reckoning about the stove, and how we were to share up on its expense, and peace was regained. But I was not comfortable; I foresaw complications. And they came. Heavens, how they came! Every one got on edge, every one grew cross, and the things which happened would have been hard enough to bear calmly if we had been calm at the start; and—since we weren't

—well, it was no wonder there were feuds, and that every one suspected every one else, and tried to trip him or her, instead of giving a helping hand.

But the horror did boom the tea business. My soul, how it did. Every day swarms of people would motor out, come to sit on our porch, order tea, drink it carelessly, nibble just a bit of cake or cracker, and then, looking down at the creek, ask, and almost always in a whisper, *"Where is the spot where they found the body?"*

CHAPTER IV.

THE WRAITH

A MONTH WENT by, and its passing took us into early July. For the most part that month was calm. True, Nan and Jane had a disagreement about whether Gustave or Larry worked harder; one of them, at the very moment of the scrap, hiding in the attic so he wouldn't have to carry in wood for the evening's fire, the other having gone to town to send a telegram because it was his turn to wash out the boats. But that little cloud passed quickly, and that month I can look back on with some pleasure.

People had begun to come out to have tea with us, and we were all feeling exceedingly bucked up—to be frank, not far from cocky. Nan went around with the self-satisfied expression of the individual who has made a good buy; Laurence wrote verses, many of which embodied such sentiments as "Her little heart is warm and true and wise!" I agreed about the last; however, Larry had not meant it in the slang sense, but as a compliment.

We were pretty happy during that month. No one really did much, for our afternoons were almost all taken up by tea-ing those who came to be tea-ed, and the mornings sort of went—without anyone's knowing where they had gone. The place really made you lazy. Gustave had started a picture, started it seriously, but Jane, who was posing for him, was badly attacked by wood ticks, and said she wouldn't go on unless she could wear a slicker and rubber boots. Of course that ruined the whole thing, for the picture was to be called "Sleeping Eve," and she had to be dressed like one.

She and Gustave simply screamed at each other and for two days didn't speak.

"Eve," he bawled, "in a fish skin coat! What did yuh let me start it for, if you were going lame and intended to back out! My God, these women!"

"Go and sit on a log!" she returned, in a shrill soprano. "Go and sit on a log for hours in one position, on rough bark, with things

24

eating you—not one inch of me unbitten! I shall carry the marks to my grave!"

Then he added the final straw by saying she was too skinny, anyway, and he asked Nan if she wouldn't volunteer, but she refused. "You need have no feeling," he explained. "It is all for Art—Art alone."

Gustave took to sketching backgrounds again, and Jane devoted herself to desultory dressmaking. Yes, that really was a half decent month. The oil stove made work easier, and we'd have a fair breakfast, finish drinking coffee on the porch, perhaps, dawdle through the work, and then go down to the boats and slip off down stream until something in the middle began to say: "It must be almost time for dinner." The afternoons were well filled with people who came out to boat and to have tea, and then in the evening we'd settle around the big fireplace, and discuss everything on earth, a lot that wasn't, settle nothing, and always witness or take part in at least one fight.

Nan and Laurence were wandering off together a little too often, even then; but I trusted Nan to keep Laurence good-tempered even if she did fall out with him.

In the middle of July we had four or five days of straight downpour, and those were a little trying. It was during these that Midgette found the old magazines, and, among them, that copy of the *London News* from which the note to Rudolph Loucks had been torn. How it came there, I don't know, but she unearthed it in a little side attic.

"Magazines," she said, coming down the stairs with a bundle of them under her arm. "I know the contents of the *Chronicle* by heart, and I was desperate. I think we can learn lots about the styles of 1902, and there is a paper-bound copy of 'Two Weeks.' "

A fire was blazing high, for it was cold, and we all drew near, looked at the pictures, laughed a good deal at the sleeves and hats of the period, and then Midgette held up the *News*, and commanded attention by her. "Here is the judge's writing again. I know it. He took it upon himself to write me, remonstrating against my leaving home and father."

"Well, if the smell that comes with the south breeze is any sample," said Gustave, "I'll say you were justified!"

"Father didn't mind, then," said Midgette stiffly. She did not like allusions to her home, because her father had entirely cut her allowance and had said he would have nothing whatever to do with her, or with checks made to her, until she got through with us and our enterprise.

"What's on it?" asked Nan, leaning forward.

"Me d," answered Midgette; "the rest's torn."

" 'Some day,' " said Gustave, feeling really too awfully clever, " 'I'll get you some day.' Plain as your face."

"Whose face?" asked Jane.

"Not yours," he answered in a fatuous tone—they'd made up again—and with a look that would have heated my studio in New York for the entire winter. "The note that was found said, 'I'll get you so,' didn't it? And then it was torn," Gustave continued. Midgette nodded.

"And this says 'me d' and then again it is torn," went on Gustave, "and so, I conjecture that the whole thing was that sentence. 'I'll get you some day.' Nice sort of a line to send a friend, wasn't it? You know, I'd like to solve that, and just why and how that banker—what's his name—"

"Frank Lethridge," supplied Midgette.

"—was connected with it."

"He wasn't," said Midgette. "He was ill at the time. Had pneumonia, and wasn't expected to live."

"Clever dodge," Larry said. "Probably fixed the nurses—even the doctor—"

"You're wrong there," Midgette broke in. "You see, we know our nurses in this town, and one of the oldest and most respectable had the case, with another we knew somewhat. She couldn't lie. I know her. And our doctor wouldn't have shielded any one who was guilty, for he had a pretty narrow escape himself. He was one of the suspects. He was out here attending Nathan Greenleaf that night; Nathan had an attack of pleurisy. Lots of people were sick that year. The weather was frightful, warm and cold, extremes in each. You know how sick it makes people. It was rumored that the doctor had inside information of someone's injury through Rudolph, and had been unable to stand it. He was a large-souled, kind old chap, who mothered lots of people, and took their troubles to heart quite as if they were his own."

"It was Frank Lethridge's pistol?" asked Jane.

"Yes," Midgette answered, "it was."

"Who had been in his house?" asked Nan.

"The doctor had been, of course," Midgette replied, "but so had the minister who takes the *London News,* and Judge Harkins."

"Where was Rudolph Loucks's son?" I asked.

"He was at the Opera House. 'The Red Mill,' remember it? Played here that night."

"I give up," said Gustave. "Say—how did the judge explain this writing exhibition?"

"He didn't have to very hard; he was in New York. He offered the most casual explanation," Midgette said, as she inspected the torn sheet and the age-dulled writing. "He said that it read: 'I'll get you some dry' and that it applied to champagne. Said he wanted to tell a friend so without his own wife hearing his confidence, or understanding it, if she read it. Mrs. Harkins was president of the local temperance society, but the judge drank like a fish—"

"And the judge knew wines," went on Midgette. "His selections were always safe. People knew it, and did get him to buy for them. That part sounded half reasonable."

"Smooth old guy," Laurence contributed, and he got up to go out on the porch. It was cold, and, of course, he caught one, for he had been sitting on top of the fire doing a verse about: "Vast, wide open spaces, and the wild, free wind." So—when we heard sneezes down cellar a week later we naturally blamed him, although he said he had been in the bath-tub at the time, enjoying a hot soak, and composing a poem. And the reason that we doubted that was that Nan said she had spent two hours in the tub before she knew that Laurence had.

"You liar!" he said, when she airily announced where she had spent the afternoon.

She grew red, then white, looked at him appealingly, and then tried to be casual. She laughed rather stiffly, and after it said: "Just as you say!" We were divided in opinion; some of us thinking she wanted to shield him, some of us believing she had been in the tub and that he was lying; some of us giving it up. And it happened to be the day that we all wanted to be accounted for, which was unfortunate.

That day, if I recall, was the twentieth of July, and a fair, cloudless one. It was the day that Frank Lethridge first appeared at our boards, and surprised us all by talking to Jane for a half hour. He was reputed to be a woman-hater, and if one could judge by Midgette's amazed look, his reputation was a stiff one.

It wasn't a very good day, which was strange; for, as I said, it was a gorgeous one, and at five o'clock no one was around except Jane and Frank Lethridge, who was laughing loudly at something she was telling him of her studio experiences.

Suddenly they heard noises from the kitchen, and Jane was a little upset. "Some one must have dropped something," she said, with a look over her shoulder, "but I didn't think any one was around; I wonder—"

Together they got up and went toward the kitchen, and here, on the wall was written:

F. don't do it.

R.

"What do you think—" whispered Jane, and then they heard the sneezes. Six of them, one after the other, from the direction of the cellar.

"Stay here," Frank Lethridge ordered. "I'll go down," and he disappeared. She thought she heard voices, but she was not sure, and when he reappeared, he said: "No one," and helped her wash the writing from the wall.

Then, after Nan returned, from whence Jane did not know, he left, and Nan said she had been in the tub all afternoon, and Laurence had told Gustave that he had been in the tub, had made a poem there, after which he had fallen asleep. He got it out to read, and Gustave said: "Why didn't you fall asleep first?" That remark made quite a chill in the atmosphere.

Laurence sneezed all evening, which added to the unrest. Jane swore she could recognize sneezes, and that those that had come from the cellar were his; and to that, Nan said, "I know who scribbled the message. It was Gustave. Told me he'd shoot Lethridge if he bothered around here courting you; that he had grown sort of used to having you 'round—didn't you, Gustave?"

"Didn't I what?" he asked, lowering his paper.

"Didn't you say you'd shoot Frank Lethridge if he cut in on Jane?"

"Well," he retorted, after an irritated frown, "what if I did?"

Every one remembered his saying that in the happenings of the next month, although Frank Lethridge was not shot. And Gustave, being badly frightened, went around explaining why he'd said it, which made it all the worse. Too much explaining always does that; I know, for I've done it myself!

Nan told me in confidence that she had been in town buying real food. Midgette was doing the cooking that week, and I understood. "Sneaked off," she admitted. "I knew if I didn't, Midgette would offer to go, too, and then she would be hurt if I ate. And I had to or starve. As for Laurence, I know he was in the tub, for there was a rim around it, and sand in the bottom."

"My heavens!" I gasped, after a giggle or two.

"The flat-boat stuck this morning, and he had to wade," she explained. "He said his stockings were full of sand afterward. It *was* a sandy spot!"

"You there, too!" I asked in mock amazement.

"And he doesn't lie," she went on, without noticing my joke, but I thought her reasons were rather strongly asserted. It seemed to me she was trying to convince herself as well as me. "And why should he do that?" she ended.

"I think some one is trying to have a good time," I responded. "Trying to get us all nervous by using Rudolph Loucks's initials to sign messages. Don't tell me that anything like that really does happen, for I don't believe it. If that man has reached another stage of consciousness, I don't think he'll want to come back to the place where he made so much trouble!"

"It doesn't seem as if he would," Nan responded, but her tone was doubtful.

"And as for that business on the hillside," I said, "that is rot! No one ever saw that." Nan and I had been standing on the porch on that spot from which, if you looked over silver birches, you could see where Rudolph Loucks had bled to death. Something had made us turn to look at that place as I spoke.

I don't know who saw it first, Nan or I, but I do know that suddenly we were clinging to each other, shaking and gasping, and looking with eyes that were glazed with horror, I know, toward a wavering white form against a hillside of green.

CHAPTER V.

BENEATH THE TIDE

NAN TURNED AND sank down on a wicker settee and sobbed. I sat down by her, and put my arm around her.

Then we heard Nathan's voice, and jumped as if we had been shot.

"He was carried off into them woods," he said, staring toward the spot. "The coroner, he up and done it hisself. Now, Rudolph, he don't need no help. Don't you take on so; 'tain't nothing to worry yuh. See, it's gone.

"It ain't nothin' to be skairt of," he continued in a weak, shaking voice. "He wouldn't go to hurt yuh none. Now, now—don't you care!"

But Nan would not be comforted.

"I can't stand it," she confessed, "I have always been afraid. As a child I know that I saw a ghost! It came to me when I slept alone in a big bedroom of my grandmother's house. Suppose—" Her voice failed her, but her gaze, turned in the direction of the hillside, finished what she could not say.

"He won't come pesterin' yuh none *here*—" said Nathan, his voice none too steady.

"Doesn't he—ever?" she managed to ask after she moistened her lips.

Nathan fingered his beard. "He ain't been seen more'n once or twice," he answered slowly, "and if he should, he wouldn't *hurt* yuh none—"

"I won't stay," said Nan. "I won't! I *won't!* I *hate* things like that."

I told old Nathan to go, for he wasn't helping any, although I thought he meant to. I bent over Nan and scolded her. "If you want Midgette in hysterics," I said, "and all of our plan, which *is* making money, to fail; if you want this awfully jolly crowd to break up, and poor Gustave to go back to restaurant cooking, go in and blab this; otherwise, keep quiet and stick it out. It was horrible"—I paused

30

and swallowed hard about eighteen times—"but suppose it never happened again this season, wouldn't you hate to give up, be beaten after one exhibition of a thing that, after all, couldn't hurt you?"

She sobbed again, and tried to say "Yes."

"Come on, we'll go rowing," I said. She nodded, and together we went down to the landing, my knees shaking like castanets, and poor Nan sobbing at every step.

"I wouldn't mind so much," she confided after we'd pulled off and were headed down-stream, "but as a child—" She gave up after that and began to gasp.

"I know," I said. "Forget it!"

Then she screamed, her eyes fixed behind me, and all her color fading. I dropped an oar, put a hand over my heart, and, frozen with fear, slowly managed to turn. What I saw was a large and amiable Jersey cow wading in the water at the edge of the creek. She gave us but a passing glance. I could have killed Nan.

"Do you think they can swim?" she asked, teeth chattering. "Oh, I wish I were dead. I do, I do! Let's go home; I want *Laurence!*" What was left of my ebbing patience broke.

"Shut up, you fool!" I ordered, reaching for the oar, and the boat, a mean, tippy thing, went over. We could have waded easily, but I had a hard time doing it, for Nan clutched me, clung to me, pulled on me, and yelled: "That cow, that cow! *God help us!*"

How I knew what I stepped on at that excited time, I don't know. But—I was aware that my feet touched wood that rang hollow, even under water, as I stepped on it. I had stirred things up, as I tried to sustain Nan, who was pulling off something that seemed like a cross between a hootchy-kootch and a good old mid-Victorian faint, and—during the struggle I loosened wood, which rang hollow even under water.

"What the dickens—" I thought as I dragged Nan, the boat, and oars to the cowless side of the stream, and then: "What next?" for it was several thousand too many for me!

That night Nan said she would not sleep with Midgette, because she was the jumpy sort. Jane suggested that we put up extra cots in my big room, and all sleep there. Nan warmly embraced this suggestion.

"Remember," she said as she and I sat huddled up on our cots waiting for Jane and Midgette to appear, "I said there was safety in numbers. I don't think anything would bother four of us. Oh, April! *What was that?*"

"I don't know," I answered as I slipped out of my bed and into my slippers, "but I'll go see, and—if you say 'What was that?' once more I'll go back to New York to-morrow morning!" But I knew I wouldn't, because—frankly—I hadn't enough money for the fare, and I knew that almost every one else was in the same boat.

We were making money, Laurence's books proved it, when he didn't forget to keep them; but somehow no one ever seemed to see any of it. A great deal of it went for food, boats were always having to be repaired and kerosene bought for that stove; or a load of firewood hauled in by old Nathan.

I went out in the hall. I was not frightened, for the up-stairs lantern which hangs at the head of the steps was going brightly, and the men were all up.

"What happened?" I asked.

Laurence answered me. "Gustave has been calling on Judge Harkins," he replied in the snippiest tone imaginable. "The judge is an art critic, it seems, and Gustave has evidently tried to be an alcohol critic—or lamp. He's lit, and he has the fuel with him. He is quite sure that Midgette's sweater, which hangs on the newel-post, is a flying alligator."

Nan had gathered enough courage to join me by that time, and she heard enough of the affair to sense it. "Simply disgusting!" she said as she trailed back to my room. "I think it's *very* hard on Laurence!"

"What's the matter?" asked Jane, who joined us in front of my door.

"Gustave is drunk," Nan replied.

"I don't believe it!" Jane said hotly, but after she listened from the head of the stairs for a few moments, she had to admit that he didn't seem "quite himself." "He's had a headache all day," she explained, "we mustn't blame him. I think the pain was too great for him to bear!"

Midgette didn't help by laughing at that point. But she had seen Gustave when he came up from the cellar. Jane glared at her and then went on: "You all seem to forget," she said coldly, "that Gustave is an artist, and that his nerves are as intricately balanced as a Swiss watch; he says that when he looks at some of his work he positively aches!"

"I don't wonder," said Nan, and the way she said it didn't help to smooth things.

"Well, he sells his stuff, which is more than some people in this crowd do!" retorted Jane.

"He hasn't sold any lately," responded Nan. "He even tried to borrow five dollars off me yesterday. Offered me that unfinished 'Snoring Eve' or whatever it is, as security. It's a mess."

Jane was incensed. She could hardly speak, her voice quivered, and her burning cheeks showed anger as well as nerves. She had been brushing her hair, and she waved her brush so wildly that I was sure Nan's face would suffer from it.

"A mess?" she echoed. "A mess? You don't know *tones,* you don't know *form.* Ask April. Why that—that would have been a *masterpiece*, if he had finished it. But wood ticks, just where it was difficult to retrieve them, made my going on impossible—and, Gawd, girls, that log was hard—and he—he *needed* my help! I failed him! We have all failed him, and he *needs* stimulus—"

"Well, he got it to-night," said Midgette.

Then we stopped because going on was impossible—rather, useless. The stimulated was making his way up-stairs, loudly singing "Old Black Joe" as he came. He had pitched this down at the bottom of the bass, and sobbed so that we heard him through several closed doors, because he couldn't reach the low notes.

Nan allowed her face to express the great contempt she felt. Midgette opened her eyes and looked like a sleepy kitten, and Jane allowed herself to don a pensive droop.

After some shufflings down the passage, and the slam of doors, there was quiet.

"I don't blame him," said Jane. "He has not had the understanding here that he should have had. This leads me to be frank." Again she waved the hair-brush and again at Nan: "Do you know," she went on, "that Laurence sifted ashes on him to-day?"

Again Midgette giggled. Then she tried to pretend that her giggle had been a cough, but she deceived no one. I think this noise from her irritated Jane even more, for her voice grew more shrill, and her color deepened. "I suppose it is *funny*," she said witheringly, "to see a grown man so overworked that he has to hide in the ash-bin to get away from it!"

"But it was his day to wash boats," said Nan.

"His day!" said Jane—she almost screamed it. "*His* day! And I suppose yesterday was? And the day before—"

"Well," temporized Nan, "Laurence had an inspiration—"

"And went off and left his work undone," said Jane. "Undone! And then when that simpering crowd of schoolgirls came out, their lordly escorts complained that the boats were full of mud and bait, and poor Gustave, because he was around, had to do Laurence's work. So to-day, when those old maids complained about the flat boat, and Laurence *was* around, Gustave hid.

"And then Laurence sifted ashes on him. No one ever *knew* him to sift *any* ashes before. He *knew* Gustave was crouching in that horrid, dirty place, *hounded* there by work, and did it on *purpose!*" She ended this with a whirlwind of arms, and her brush slipped from her hand, hit the mirror, and shattered it to a thousand pieces.

"Oh, damn!" said Jane.

"Seven years' bad luck," Nan vouchsafed cheerfully, after which she yawned. Jane glared at her; Midgette said it was a watery mirror, anyway, and I suggested going to bed. I thought that was a good idea, for I hoped we could escape a real blowout.

Midgette reopened it. Midgette would; not intentionally, but simply from stupidity. "Those men don't seem to like each other," she offered in a vapid tone.

"Can you blame him?" both Jane and Nan said at once, each having arrived at the point where that simple pronoun 'him' meant a certain man, and that man alone.

"I'm sick of this," I broke in. "We came out here to run this place on a business basis; not to let our personal feelings spoil the whole thing; and you girls are making it very hard for everybody! I'm *sick* of it." I have a reputation for being gentle, why, I do not know; but when I really grow angry, other people usually stop.

"All right, dear," said Nan. "We'll turn in. It's all unfair, but I'll ignore it."

"Unfair?" said Jane from her cot. "Does she think she has a monopoly on the stuff. Why, I could—"

I sat up, reached down for my slippers, muttered of going somewhere else to sleep, and there was quiet. Then Midgette blew out the candle, and we all tried to sleep; but anger kept Jane busy. I suppose she rehearsed all she might have said and didn't, as every one does; wrongs kept Nan thinking, and—the affair of that afternoon, and only Midgette slept. I heard her. She is a beautiful girl, and it's too bad, but of course there is no rose without its thorns.

CHAPTER VI.

ENTER: GLORIA

THE NIGHT WAS miserably noisy. Things banged against the landing, boats hit each other, grated and generally acted as if fifty people were shunting them this way and that. An owl hooted way off in the woods, and a dog howled. And of course that wicker furniture snapped. Everything would be as quiet as only a black, moonless night in the woods can be, and then something would *snap!* You'd jump, think: "What was that?" give it an answer, and lie back and try to unwind your tight-drawn muscles. The stairs creaked, and an andiron amused itself by falling over and clanking on the stone hearth.

"Oh, *Heavens!*" I heard Nan moan.

Jane coughed. Then she whispered: "I'm—I'm so *nervous!*" and I knew she'd been crying. Then I whispered: *"Hush!"* for some one was coming along the passage; stealthily creeping along without a light, for no crack of yellow showed beneath the door, and a sliding hand on the wall outside revealed that some one felt his or her way falteringly, and—as silently as possible.

"The flashlight!" I whispered. Of course it was lost. No one could remember where it was, or ever having seen it. I cautioned them to be quiet, and I lay back trying to listen. The pound of my heart made hearing almost impossible, and Nan's swift, sobbing breathing helped to hinder. But—I heard, whatever it was, pause before our door, and then I heard a tap.

"What is it?" I managed to gasp.

"What rimes with 'remorse'?" we heard Laurence ask.

"Dead horse!" yelled Jane hysterically.

Laurence snorted. "Have you no respect for *Art?*" he asked in a hollow, wronged, and misunderstood tone. "I have a poem here, epic poem, that will make me famous and my friends proud that they have *known* me. I give them an opportunity to help—to have themselves represented in it by a word—and—they *jeer!*"

"What time is it?" I asked, quite disregarding his remarks about Art.

He scratched a match—the doors are paper-thick, one can hear anything that happens on the other side of them—locked at his watch, and told me that it was two fifteen. It seemed as if I had been in bed nine hours.

"I can't stand this," I said, sitting up.

"Let's go down-stairs. We'll make some chocolate and poke up the fire and see if we can't feel a little better."

Every one agreed. I found matches, lit the candle, we twisted up our various hairs, put on bath-robes, kimonos, and negligees, and went tripping down. It did help. Before long we had cocoa, some crisped crackers, and macaroons on the small table which stood near the fire, and as we ate, the whole unpleasant atmosphere seemed more a joke than tragedy. Even the afternoon's happening seemed so unreal and far away that I could hardly believe it had occurred.

"What geese we were," said Nan.

"You know I like you," Jane put in quickly.

"Of course, and I do you," Nan answered. Temporary peace seemed assured.

"What frightened us so?" asked Midgette. Nan and I looked at each other and then away.

"Nerves, I suppose," said she.

"Nerves," I echoed.

"Aren't they silly things?" asked Midgette. "Thank Heaven I don't get upset easily." Every one of us knew that she would have hysterics if a fuzzy caterpillar as much as arched his back at her from across the street. "I like a calm existence, and I think that maintaining calm lies largely with the individual," she added.

Then we all grew quiet, for the leaping fire had a hypnotic spell, and we were tired.

"This is a funny business," said Jane, after some moments of silence. "Every thing is a step. I wonder where this one leads to?"

Then Midgette asked: "If you could, would you look ahead ten years?" We were divided about that. I knew that I wouldn't, for my mother's death had been sudden, and it had left me alone. I knew that the horrible want for her was bad enough to bear afterward, and if I had seen it coming—well, her going had taught me the great mercy that lies in the one-sighted life that is given to us.

"I would," said Jane, "and then, if I didn't like it, I'd suicide."

"Well, I wouldn't," I put in. "I wouldn't even look ahead a month here"—every one was amused—"for one never knows what is in store, what horror may be."

Then we heard a noise, and I got up. We weren't frightened, for the approach was too definite to be made in the spirit of harm, and the rap on the door was decided and quick. I opened it.

"Is this the Beasley house?" asked the girl who stood before me; a ravishingly pretty girl she was, if one could ignore the hard look that lay in her eyes.

"No," I answered, "that is fully two miles on."

"So I thought," she began, and then she flushed, and her voice changed. "My man's gone," she went on. "Some fool from town who didn't know the country roads. This didn't look like a farm to me, although I couldn't see much—awful night—and—he's gone!"

"Well, we can put you up," I offered. "Plenty of room here, and it's so late it will only be a matter of a few more hours, anyway."

"Good of you," she answered, stepping in. She was pretty. She would have made a perfect model, if one could have ignored her eyes. As I said, those were wrong. She was one of those dark-toned girls, whose eyelids are heavy and whose mouth always looks moist. She made me think of a tropical flower that is beautiful and gorgeous, one that you cannot help looking on, and yet—rather longing, as you look, for a simple hollyhock.

I don't express this well, but she seemed to have an odor that was heavy and stifled; and, although you wanted to touch her skin, the very silky ivory tint of it that drew you made you draw away. All of us felt it.

"I am a nurse," she said. Her voice was low and unusually sweet, and it matched her. "I was sent for because there is a shortage here, I believe. I am due at this farmhouse. The old gentleman is paralyzed, isn't he?"

"Had a stroke last Sunday," said Midgette, who always seems to know all the news about the town and countryside.

"Well," said our visitor, "I won't get there to-night. However, it won't make much difference. Pretty place you have here. Belong to one of you?"

Midgette told her we were renting it, and making it a business proposition. Her tone changed, and I felt that we all dropped several degrees in her estimation. "I'll turn in, if you please," she said briskly, "and if one of you will show me my room and give a lift to one of my bags, I'll be grateful. I have three. Thank you. Good night."

Jane was the bag-lifter, and after she and our visitor disappeared around the turn of the stairs, Midgette spoke: "What's her name?" she asked.

"She didn't tell us," answered Nan.

"A cat," said Midgette, "perfect cat. Noticed how we dropped when we were known to belong to the 'working classes'? But—wouldn't the gents fall for her?"

"Oh, no!" said Nan, and at the same time Jane, who at that moment appeared on the landing. And each again was thinking of a simple pronoun. I knew it. But I believed more in Midgette's remark than in their protest.

The next morning the lady, whose name was Gloria Vernon, warmed up, and even Gustave came out of his ham and eggs and forgot to swear about the coffee.

"Dearest place," said Miss Vernon. "I love it, and this country. Don't be surprised if I trespass on your property."

"You—you *must*," said Laurence. "We *all* want you." And my, how we all began to dislike that girl!

"Yes, indeed," Gustave added with a dark look at Laurence, "we all want you. And the boating would do you good."

"You look as if you needed some," she said softly.

"Frightful head last night," he explained. "I painted too long." Jane sniffed so that one could have heard her in town. Nan smirked, but her joy was short-lived.

"I'm going to take you up to the Beasley farm," said Laurence. "I told old Nathan to get me a team before breakfast. Now, don't thank me, it *is* a pleasure!"

"But—ought I to let him?" she appealed, looking around at us. Oh, how we hated her! But—of course we had to say "yes," and every one of us had walked to town, which was twice as far, for weeks! Laurence and Gustave got her in the rig after she had eaten a very substantial breakfast without looking as if she were eating at all, and Laurence and she drove off.

"Beautiful thing, sympathy!" said Gustave, and then: "Oh, my *gosh*, my head!"

"It's all your own fault!" said Jane. "You made yourself into a blotting-pad for poor whisky, and—"

"I want you to remember that I'm not married to you!" he said, so loudly that the rafters almost shook. "And—"

"Are not going to be," added Jane, but she didn't have the last word. He put that on, and in a mean way, I thought, although it told.

"You're dead right!" he ended simply, and then went out and sat on a sunny corner of the porch and glared ahead of him. No one worked or talked that day. We were all too busy sulking. In the evening Midgette made out a chart like a family-tree of who was angry with whom, and putting in all angers, little and big. Here it is:

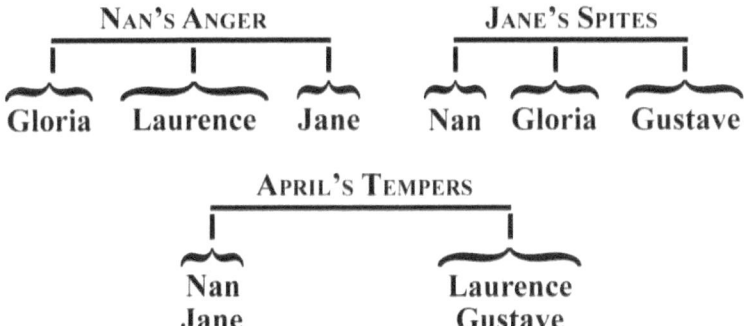

But that didn't half cover it.

I *was* angry with the crowd she had put under my spite-tree; angered with Nan and Jane for making an unpleasant atmosphere and doing their best to wreck our bark; angered with the men for making them act that way; and—angered with Midgette, who had omitted her name in all cases, for telling the tale that made Nan get us into the box and that started the whole affair.

Again I felt that miserable sensation that I had had in March when the whole thing started. I knew that something very unpleasant, if not worse, was going to happen soon. Knew it! And the thing I'd found that morning when I swept had not helped soothe me. It was a little thing, but—coming as it did, on top of that girl's arrival, and then having Jane immediately recognize it—well, everything was mixed, everything was upset. I knew that something unpleasant was going to happen—and it did!

CHAPTER VII.

THE LOCKET

THE MORNING OF the day when sulks cornered the market, I lingered over my porch sweeping. Several things made me do this; among them my wish to tell Gustave that I thought he was a pig, and that I hoped for every one's sake he would buck up, and my desire to stay outdoors. Fluffy clouds were chasing each other across the sky, and a smart, little, almost cold breeze made the trees shiver, the shadows dance, and tired leaves flutter off to go to sleep on the ground. I loved it.

"Beautiful day," I said to Gustave as I slammed aside the table and began to sweep up the relics of somebody's yesterday's tea. "Pity this affair of ours is going to fall through."

"Fall through?" he queried. "It *can't*. I haven't got a damned cent, and I haven't done a thing that would sell all summer. Expected to work up here, but *every one* prevented it. I ask you frankly, April, isn't Laurence O'Leary the poorest excuse for a man that you ever saw? Never does a stroke of work if he can get out of it."

"He sifted the ashes yesterday," I said as I bent above a table to straighten a cloth some one had forgotten to take in the night before.

At that Gustave exploded in profanity.

I swept on, now and again looking toward Gustave, who sat with his head in his hands, looking as "The Thinker" would if he were clad in a worn suit, and an indescribable, but unmistakable, morning-after flavor.

"What made you think we might go on the rocks?" Gustave questioned.

"Every one's quarreling so," I explained. "Some day some one will get really mad and pull out; some one else will sympathize, and pull with them, and then one or two some ones will find themselves with the place on their hands, a lot of work, and a lot of bills that won't appear till the end of the season. Now," I went on, after I dusted the railing with Nan's sweater, which she had forgotten to take in the night before, "if every one was pleasant, we might go through with it all right, but as it is—"

"Mean anything?" asked Gustave somewhat viciously.

"You can decide that yourself," I answered. "But—as you say you're dead broke you'd better try to Pollyanna it for a while. You see, you'd have to stick it out unless you borrowed from some one in town, and so—you'd be one of the fellows that would be left on the raft. Midgette hung up a lot of stuff in town, I know it."

"Oh, Gawd! These women!" said Gustave, after two more groans. As I went toward the end of the porch I saw the locket, a gleaming bit of gold, in the center of the floor. I picked it up. The initials on it were "F.L.," but I knew that Frank Lethridge had not dropped it in the afternoon, since some one would have picked it up. In fact, that part of the porch had been swabbed off by old Nathan at seven o'clock. A troop of children had come up after their boating and had tracked that soft, yellow river mud all over the place. The thing must have been dropped some time after seven.

I tried to pry it open, but Gustave had no knife. I went indoors.

"Look," I said, when I reached the kitchen, "what Santy left on the fire-escape!

Nan looked up from the dish-pan, and Midgette drew near. "Where did you get it?" she asked. I told her. "Let's take a look inside," she suggested. I nodded and, getting our best potato-paring knife, pried it open. When she viewed the works she said, "Oh, *Rudolph!*" which surprised me, since the picture was of a woman; a woman who had evidently been photographed some years before, for her hair was unmercifully frizzed, and one shoulder, which was half visible, showed the big stuffed sleeves that were so much worn in the eighteen nineties.

"Why did you say 'Rudolph'?" I questioned Midgette.

She flushed, and then answered. "She looks like Rudolph Loucks."

"Thought you said he was fat and bald?" Nan put in.

"I mean the son, of course," Midgette answered, shortly.

"Isn't this Mrs. Loucks?" I asked. "Don't you remember her?"

"Not well," said Midgette, "and this was taken years before I knew Mrs. Loucks—you can see that; those fringes and sleeves and the whole thing give it away, but—I believe it is!"

"Why is it in Frank Lethridge's locket?" I asked.

"Why do you think it's his?" Nan questioned. I told her. "But," she objected, "there are other people on earth whose initials are

F.L." I agreed to that, and stood wondering until Jane came in. When she saw the locket she fixed it as his.

"Don't tell me," she said, in an effort to be light—Gustave had really hurt her, I know—"that my woman-hating beau has been around here courting you!"

"His?" said I.

"Yes," she responded. "Let me see what is going on behind the curtain, will you? He wouldn't let me look at it the last time I saw him. Pretty nearly had a spasm when I got hold of it. He said, 'Don't open it, I *must* protest! I beg of you, Miss Jane, I *entreat*—' and so on. It sounded like the big scene from the heavy drama of some barn-storming company. I did want to see—thought maybe he'd gotten one of mine."

"You know, I don't trust him," said Jane. "There is something wrong with a man who doesn't try to kiss you when he has a chance; something abnormal, fishy. Now I took him down the creek, and hung up under some willows, most divine spot, and—" she faltered, "sort of quiet and—well, uninterrupted, you know—and I said something about the bough and the wilderness being there, but missing the jug. Thought maybe he'd suggest bringing some of it around, but he only asked me if I were one of those Omar enthusiasts, and then quoted Omar in the raw, I mean in direct translation, and then contrasted what he said was the poetry of Fitzgerald and not Omar. It was fierce!"

We all laughed. Jane is undeniably attractive in an elfin, mischievous, follow-me fashion that leaves very few males untouched. "I feel," she stated surely, "that he is not attracted to me, but using me in some way—for some purpose."

"Don't allow yourself to imagine a lot that isn't so," said Midgette, who had just screamed her head off because she saw a piece of wool on Nan's shoulder which she thought was a bug. "This place is sort of eery, and it makes one hysterical."

"Yes," agreed Jane, "but—when we go rowing—he's always sounding the creek bottom with his oar. Jams it down like this, and says, 'How deep do you think it is here, Miss Jane?' with a sort of would-be-sprightliness that makes me crawl. And once, when he did that, there was a whistle from the shore, and he turned absolutely white. I don't like it—"

"I don't like it," Jane repeated, and I didn't either. For—I recalled the queer way the creek bottom had felt to me that day when Nan and I had fallen in. I decided to do some creek-bottom poking on my own. But not before the next week, for the fair weather brought every one out to boat, and the tea business certainly looked up. We actually had some profits that we saw and shared, and every one began to feel better. Jane owed some bills, but she felt that her soul would be more benefited if she spent her share on a broad shade hat, which really was a bargain at fourteen dollars. She borrowed the four from Laurence, as we only pulled ten apiece.

Nan bought a wonderful bargain in old books, two tooled leather volumes of Keats; Midgette said she *had* to get a new sweater, and that there wasn't anything decent in town for less than fifteen dollars, and since we had all made her enrage her father, and Gustave had ruined her other sweater, she considered that it was up to some one to help her out. And, of course, Gustave did, being, for the most part, responsible. He said, "Damn the judge!" as he forked out the lacking bucks, and then went off toward the woods, muttering unpleasant things about women.

I kept my share because I knew I might need it to go back to New York some time, and I didn't think that there would be another dividend declared. However, there was. Things looked up wonderfully in a financial way after the horrible occurrence.

Nan, Midgette and I slaved that week. Jane was with Frank Lethridge constantly, and why, since she said he did not attract her and wasn't any more affectionate than a hunk of cold tripe, we could not see. But every day after the bank closed he came out, and they would boat, walk, or simply sit in the sun on the steps that led to the boat landing, and talk in low tones, always stopping their talk if some one crawled past them to go down to the boats. Jane acted strangely at that time; avoided us all, and wrote notes which she posted herself and would hide if any one came near. It was all very baffling.

"If you will tell me," said Nan, "why she moons around with him on an average of seven hours a day I will be grateful!"

"I can't see it," Midgette admitted.

"Said she hated him," I contributed. We were all working together getting ready for the afternoon rush, Nan cutting bread, Midgette spreading it, and I making a sandwich paste out of a piece of old omelette flavored with some tuna that was left from the night before. It was not very bad, and it *was* very cheap. We learned lots about managing those days.

"Gustave doesn't seem jealous," I said, after I had managed to get up enough courage to taste what was listed on the bill as "Anchovy paste sandwiches, .20"—Midgette said none of the natives had ever met it, so that it was safe.

"You bet he's jealous," Nan contradicted. "The other day I was hunting him and I came upon him standing at the edge of the creek, shielded by bushes; and looking through these, by his head, I saw Jane and Frank Lethridge. They were sitting together on the middle seat of the punt, if you please, talking as if they had met after fifteen years' separation. When Gustave saw me he snarled, 'Look at 'em!' and just at that moment I heard Jane say: 'Oh, Frank, you wouldn't? *Promise* me you won't!' It floated across water, as voices some-times do. We heard nothing more."

"Isn't it *queer?*" said Midgette. "Well, what did Gustave say?"

"He made his usual remark about women, showed his teeth in something that approached a snarl, and then asked why he was favored by my company. 'Kindling?' he asked. I said it was. 'And traveled over the swamp to find me!' he went on. 'Is there *no* pri-vacy?' And then—" Nan paused.

"What?" I prompted.

"Well," she went on slowly, "of course, he didn't mean it, and somehow I don't think I ought to repeat it."

"What?" Midgette and I both said at once, for that sort of a confidence is just the sort that means everything to a woman.

"He said, 'If he hurts her, I'll kill him!' "

"Nan!" we both exclaimed.

"He did!" asserted Nan, and then she stopped abruptly, bit her lips and looked rattled. The door which she faced was on a porch which is long and narrow and the steps which lead to this are not to be seen from the door. So—how long old Nathan had been on the porch none of us knew. But he was in plain sight when she looked up, his hand raised as if he were about to knock.

"Got a lot of green wood here," he said, beaming on us all. "It ain't so purty to smell, but then there's a wood pussy loose yonder, and I guess she'll kill that smell if she lets loose. Seen her last night, with her kittens. Cutest little critturs yuh ever seen, but I wasn't minded to stroke 'em none. How's business?"

"He didn't hear," Midgette whispered. Nan looked relieved. "Come in and have a sandwich?" she invited. Old Nathan entered, took off his hat after he had plenty of time to acclimate, settled on a chair, and surveyed our work. "I reckon you ain't so stuck on sandwiches no more?" he asked, in his usual slow drawl.

"If I go to hell," said Nan, "it'll be paved with 'em, and I'll have to do the paving and make the material to do it with." Nathan was pleased with this.

"The gents ain't so handy, be they?" he asked, after a shift of his cud.

"Gustave isn't," answered Nan. "That is, Mr. Gerome. Laurence is more anxious to help. When he fails it is simply because he is full of a poem and doesn't see what is to be done!"

And old Nathan actually favored me with a wink. "Well, I ain't afeared that either of 'em will get into a sweat from work," he said. "I noticed they was the settin' variety. I thank yuh kindly fer this here, and I guess I'll be gettin' on," and picking up the sandwich Nan gave him, he toddled off.

"Suppose it's silly, but I'm glad he didn't hear me say that," said Nan. "That sort of thing sounds so horrible when repeated, while, if it's said in a spurt of silly anger, it means nothing."

"I know," I answered, and then I hurried out, for I had heard a motor stop by the side steps to the porch, and then some one's footsteps. I knew it was Judge Harkins by old Nathan's greeting.

It was the first time I had seen the judge. He was dignified and imposing. To see him cowed by the crude old woodsman was strange; it made me wonder. I looked at Nathan in surprise and then at the judge, who, after a curt response, had picked up the menu. And I saw, with more surprise, that his hands shook as if he had the most severe of chills.

"Tea?" I asked.

He looked up at me, very evidently tried to pull himself together, but he answered in a wavering, uncertain, unsettled way, "E-r-r—yes," and then, "Yes, certainly, and some anchovy paste sandwiches. My, my—the last time I ate them was when I was in Naples!" Then he turned to Nathan. "Where's Lethridge?" he asked.

"Boatin'," answered Nathan. "He's sparkin' one of these-here girls. There ain't no fool as big a fool as an old bald-headed fool!" And then, spitting loquaciously, he withdrew.

"Quite a character," said the judge.

"Indeed, yes," I answered.

"Look here," said the judge, peering around apprehensively. "I want to tell you something, but no one must overhear it. Sure no one's around?" I nodded. "Then sit down," he ordered curtly.

And I did.

But the judge didn't tell me anything after all.

CHAPTER VIII

"INDIGESTION"—AND A VAMPIRE

THE JUDGE DIDN'T tell me anything; and his eyes, for some reason which I did not then fathom, had wandered to a certain spot of a rolling, peaceful looking hill, that spot seen over the tops of white birches. He moistened his lips, swallowed so hard that I saw it happen, and I knew that he saw what Nan and I had seen before. I felt sick, dizzy, and ready to faint, but I almost forgot myself in my pity for the white-haired gentleman who sat opposite me. He was gasping as if he had run up the steepest hill on earth, and in the middle of his gasps he first said, "Loucks!" and then—after a tremendous intake of breath, *"God,* Jo!"

Then—with a queer look at me, he picked up the menu and began *to read it.*

"Indigestion," he offered in a moment, "catches me that way, and I think I'm a step nearer heaven—then—vanishes, and I'm as fit as a fiddle."

I looked at him in utter bafflement.

"Beasley pasturing his cows up on that hillside you see over the birches?" he asked, after he had added to his order.

"Occasionally a Jersey," I answered. "None too friendly, either. He just sold her calf, and she mourns a good deal. Depressing to hear."

"Yes," he said, looking at the hill again and again breathing hard. "Ever—ah—bothered up here by tramps—or ah—strange noises?" he asked further.

"We're only bothered by customers," I replied, "and we expect and want that."

"To be sure, to be sure," he said, glancing back toward the hillside. I could see that he couldn't help looking in that direction, and yet—didn't want to. And I could see that for some reason he thought he was the only person who saw the fantom. I wondered why he felt that he was entitled to the exclusive right; what had made him feel that he should be haunted, would see—what others did not?

Shaking, I got up and went toward the kitchen. Here I got the judge his tea, and after I had fixed it on the tray, went back to the porch. I found old Nathan had returned and was mending a spot of the railing which I had been at him to fix for weeks. It was quite like him to fix it when we had customers.

"I came here," said the judge severely, "for—for *quiet!*" And then he mopped off his damp forehead with a large handkerchief and again began to gasp.

"Nathan," I said, going over to where he was alternately pounding and planing off a rough railing that had torn more than one good skirt, "the judge wants quiet, and—couldn't you do it to-morrow morning?" I tried to be very appealing, but he was not softened. He only changed the angle of his hat, spit over the edge of the porch, began to use the plane, and succinctly remarked, "Nope."

"*That's* all right," I said, kicking aside some shavings and wishing for a moment that I was again small enough to pin them on my hair and dream myself a fairy princess with long, golden curls. "Your planing doesn't disturb any one, but the hammering does. I don't see why you have to do that, anyway."

Nathan didn't waste words on explaining; he merely bent, and moved two palings that were ready to fall at a touch, and then he began to hammer with positive viciousness. I was annoyed and asked sharply, "Why can't you do it to-morrow morning?"

"Gotta monkey with liniment," he replied. "Good for man *or* beast. I do a lot o' that there. Beasley's woman, she wants it for her heifer."

I turned in time to see the look the judge cast toward Nathan. It was murderous. And under it, Nathan smiled!

"The judge wanted quiet," I said weakly.

"Well, it ain't what he's a goin' to *git,*" said Nathan, smartly, "unless he wants to git hisself off of these here premises. Mebbe—" Nathan paused to make his usual offering to the river—"mebbe he'd get a nice spell of quiet, if he went an' set in that there green field yonder. Think, so, jedge?" Nathan turned with this, and smiled again in the judge's direction. But his eyes, which I saw clearly, since he peered over and not through his glasses, did not smile. They seemed to hold a threat.

Judge Harkins grew red, his face seemed to swell, and his collar either grew smaller or his neck enlarged. And then—I saw the judge grip his rage, push it aside and smile, in the way a woman does who has played all afternoon for a bridge prize and seen it go to her worst enemy; he smiled too sweetly.

"Nathan's right," he said, "it won't hurt my nerves. Nothing does! —I just think so. Go right on, Nathan, don't let me disturb you!"

The judge had no opportunity to tell me his story that day. I didn't see him for a week, and then—but I must preface it by the affair which started at about that time between Gustave and this Gloria Vernon. She was a devil. I have to say it, even though affairs ended as they did the following month. She made a dead set for Gustave, played Laurence on the side, and generally raised what a woman does when she wants at least nine male stars to play opposite her lead.

She did it well. I'll hand her that. Gustave really hadn't a chance to escape, for he was not a strong man, and it would have taken genuine solid, two-yards-thick character to withstand her attack. Billy did, but then, of course, he is one in ninety-seven million; I know it now. I sent for Billy the following week, but other things preface his coming.

As I said, I'd had little opportunity to do creek-bottom-poking, and when I did, I saw some of the more intimate display of Gloria's art. I am pretty used to the free expression of anything that wants to be expressed, but even I was jarred. It was a Sunday afternoon; most of the natives thought boating devilish on Sunday, and so we were almost alone.

"Going up the creek," said Gustave, as he passed Jane and me, who were playing double Canfield on one of the porch tables.

"Alone?" asked Jane, and with a pathetic hint in her tone.

"Yes, I am," he replied, in a very solid way, and it left no doubt that Gustave intended to go alone, even if he had to use force to do it.

"Give my love to the mosquitoes," I put in, merely to relieve an awkward pause. He knocked the contents of his pipe out against the railing, and without reply went on. I began to talk about the new silhouette that I'd seen in a Moneymaker ad, and I was surprised on looking up to see that Jane was crying. She smiled mistily as she met my eyes, and then said: "I don't care who knows it; I do and he doesn't," she went on, as she wiped away her tears. "He did—but something's changed him. He doesn't now."

"He's a fool!" I said sharply. She didn't reply, and I saw that her lips were unsteady. She dealt the cards too swiftly, nervousness making her hands shake, and her rows anything but even. "Probably only a little jealousy," I said. "You know, Frank Lethridge's coming here bothered him, probably does now, and he's taking this way of showing it."

"He said he didn't care," Jane answered. "I asked him. Said I'd never speak to Frank again, if he didn't want me to."

I saw that she was pretty far gone, and—that she'd done the most foolish thing any woman can do. "But he did care for you," I assured her, and my statement came from wonder as much as anything.

"Yes. He did, he told me so. But—" Jane waved her hands, sighed deeply, and then got up. "Haven't you noticed that Vernon woman? She came here until he was interested, then she stopped."

"Why, I thought Laurence was the one," I said.

"He was her bait," said Jane. But at that time she did not convince me. I thought she imagined that the perfect "He" was chased, sought after, and pursued. Billy has been, a lot, although he will never admit it, but it is utterly idiotic to think that any one except a girl who was frankly bored sick with the country would chase either Laurence or Gustave. She did come to care for Gustave, but I know she wasn't really stirred at first.

After Jane stood up, she stretched with elaborate carelessness, said that I mustn't take her little upset too seriously, that she was going driving with Frank Lethridge at two and so she supposed she'd have to change her clothes. She left me, and I, alone for the first time that week, thought of my search plans. I took one of the canoes, because I swim well, and like the way they glide through the water. I thought I could manage the sounding without tipping the thing and didn't care very much if I did go in. It was a hot, heavy day.

When I reached the spot where I wanted to poke, I saw a man whom I'd never seen around there before, sitting at the creek's edge. He was smoking and staring rather absently across the water, and he seemed startled when he saw me. Naturally, I couldn't stop and poke then.

Then I butted into the first act of Gloria's vamping. She and Gustave were in a flat-boat which they had moored below willows, and she was sitting in the bottom of the boat by his feet, sprawled all over the place, and yet close held in his arms; and—as I drew near, I heard her say, "Suppose she does care—are two lives to be ruined? You know how I feel, and you—" she drew off, looked at him, and the inquiry she put in her eyes was wonderful.

"*God!*" I heard Gustave whisper, "you know! You know—*Gloria*—"

Then I did a cat trick! I deliberately slid closer, and then—when I was within ten feet of them, began to whistle. I'll say for Gustave's nerve that he didn't jump, but she did. And when she looked at me, I knew I had gained a real hater, and not for my team, either. "Your day to bring in the wood," I sang out to Gustave.

"You go to hell!" he answered. Now we're used to saying that sort of thing down where I live in New York. We make it a point not to differ in what we say to women or men. But this was different. If I had been able, I would have licked Gustave for that. I had not started out to spy on them, and it was not my fault that I came upon them as I did. I didn't reply, but I saw Gloria veil her eyes, and smile as if the enjoyment were all her own. I turned and paddled off up stream.

The man whom I'd passed had gone, and so I stopped and poked, but there wasn't a thing but sand to be felt. I tipped over, and after that, stayed out, dragged the canoe, and investigated thoroughly. I could not understand it, until, suddenly—I stepped off the edge into a deeper hole; the drop was four feet.

Now I understood; whatever had been there had been removed, and it was into the spot where the box had been that I had fallen—

Then I saw another thing. At the side of the creek where the man had been sitting was a clearing and a sloping beach over which anything could be dragged with ease. Some one had built a fire on a bank the night before, I imagined, and the ashes, which lay over everything, quite covered any tracks that the drag of a water-soaked box would have made. It would have left tracks, because the river was mud-edged at the spot, and not with sand and pebbles as it was in some other places. Every year it ate into the meadows as the rains made it high, and each year its course varied, sometimes by feet, and again only by inches. These changes kept the banks always in the process of making, and few of them were the matured, wa-ter-seasoned, pebble-trimmed edges that the firm, true river grows.

I went over to look at the ashes. I poked around them, but could find nothing. Then I went over to a pile of dead wood from which the fire had been made, and here I again found Frank Lethridge's locket. I looked at it in some surprise. Then I tied it in a corner of my handkerchief, put that in the front of my blouse, pulled my canoe as near shore as I could, and managed to get into it. Jane had returned that locket to Frank Lethridge, who accepted it without explanations. Evidently he had dropped it; probably he had made the fire. But why—should he cover the tracks of the box? And why, if he had dragged it out, didn't he know where it was without going all over the creek?

After paddling for perhaps fifteen minutes, I came on old Nathan fishing. "Them big ones," he said, "is careless about bitin' because they knows it's Sunday." He unhooked a huge fish as he spoke, flung it in a basket where it flopped until all my pity was present and crying for rest. "That there'll make a swell fry," he announced. I nodded, and then I told him about the fire and warned him about watching for trespassers. He spit, scratched his head, then readjusted his hat and cast again. "Might as well try agin, though I s'pose you've spiled the fishin'," he said. "I built that there fire. I was a-frawgin' last night."

"Were you alone?" I asked, thinking of the locket. Old Nathan bent a sharp, quick look at me. It said, as plainly as if he had spoken, "How much do you know?"

"Ain't I generally alone?" he asked, after the interval that almost invariably preceded his remarks.

"I don't know," I replied. "We really know very little about you."

After I left him I encountered Gustave. He was alone, and he pulled his punt up by me and spoke. "I suppose you think I'm a cad?" he asked, through set teeth.

I looked at him and didn't reply. He knew what I must think, so words were futile.

"Well, if you understood—" he said uncertainly, and then, "but—I don't myself. I'm suffering more than Jane is!"

"But you're making hers, she's not making yours," I reminded.

"Oh, I know all that," he answered wearily. "I know every side of the problem, and—no answer. I tell you, *I can't help it.* I asked Jane to marry me, and I'll stick to that, but—but—*I can't help this!*"

"That is the chant of a good many weak men and women," I replied scornfully, "and I think Jane is well rid of you. Do you know," I demanded, "that I saw Laurence coming down the lane with Miss Vernon last week, acting a good deal as you did, and without any protest from the kissed?"

He grew white. Then he said, "She told me."

"When you loved Jane, you said you'd kill any one who hurt her. Doesn't it teach you anything?" I asked.

"Oh, I know—" he answered. "I tell you, I know all of it. But—I *can't help it.* My God, the *call* of her, April!"

"You *cad!*" I flung out, and I left him, paddling as fast as I could to get out of earshot of him.

He called after me. "I'd kill any one who hurt Jane to-day," and he almost sobbed on that. Then he positively shouted: "I love her—but—April, wait—" However, I didn't; I went back to the bungalow, so angry that I could hardly see. In the first place both he and Jane had cheated, for we had all of us sworn that we would not complicate the summer by any affairs; that, even if we did find that we cared, we would be quiet; that no engagements, promises, or anything else were to be made; and this—was the result of that solemn vow.

On reaching the house I learned that Jane and Frank Lethridge had gone off together. Judge Harkins had been there, asked for me, and then had gone wandering off up the creek. I'd missed him because I had gone down. But I wasn't sorry; I wasn't ready to receive guests. I sang as I slipped out of my wet things and hunted dry duds.

It was the last time I sang for a long time.

Nathan, who had turned toward his home, when I paddled off toward mine, had heard Gustave say he'd kill any one who harmed Jane. It was the second time he heard Gustave say that, for we were mistaken and he had heard our talk from the back porch that day; it all came out that following week. But Judge Harkins had been up the creek that afternoon, old Nathan said, and also, he had heard him say to Frank Lethridge, "Keep your hands off of it!" which the judge did not deny.

Almost every one was involved. No one could be convicted, yet no one entirely escaped suspicion. Jane and Gustave, perhaps, caught most of it, although my wet clothes were put up against me. I sent for Billy when Gloria Vernon told the detective that she had seen me that afternoon, and that I had evidently been out late since Nathan had seen me later. Certainly she gave me a mighty unpleasant day or two. I knew, for an absolute certainty, that none of our crowd did it. How—I don't know; but I was sure of this—absolutely sure.

Then—Frank Lethridge's body was found the next evening, floating around in some weeds that grow in shallow water opposite the bungalow.

CHAPTER IX.

INVESTIGATION

IT WAS FOUND by Jane, who asked: "What's washing up over there? I saw it when the Lily started out." The Lily is our motor-boat.

"Don't know," Laurence answered. Gustave walked down to the end of the porch and stood staring down at the boats. I think he was trying to get up courage to go off to hunt Gloria.

Then Jane screwed a little frown between her eyes, leaped far over the balcony, and said: "I think—we ought to go to see, I think—*it's a man!*"

"You are a cheerful cuss," growled Gustave, with the first words he had given her for days.

"But," she said, growing white, "I think it is. Don't you see the head? There, under the big lily pad? And an arm—"

"I'll certainly faint if I do," said Laurence. "Death affects me *profoundly*. I don't think—"

But Gustave cut him short. "Try to be a man for once in your life, O'Leary," he said brutally. "We'll need one around. You girls get in the house. There *is* some one over there, drowned."

They started over, but we didn't go in the house.

"I wish," said Midgette, "I'd stayed with father. He needed me. He really did—and suppose we are blamed? Who can it be? I know I am going to faint. Do let us be calm! This morning when I was eating breakfast I knew something horrible was going to happen—it *is* a man; they're pulling him up—*oh!*"

We all joined that, for we saw Laurence sit down precipitately, and Gustave turn to say something to him; then we saw him get to his feet and, with Gustave, drag the body into the boat. They came to us the color of chalk.

"Better go in," advised Gustave. "You—you'd better." His teeth were chattering so that he could hardly speak. Laurence was beyond speech; his eyes were fixed on the most horrible thing about that body, the stub of a wrist, torn and raw—all that was left of Frank Lethridge's left hand.

Midgette fainted. That was what we expected. But we did not expect to see Gustave faint, which was what happened after he and Laurence had laid the water-soaked corpse out on the landing. Yet Gustave is not the fainting sort.

After we had all quieted a little, some one whispered: "We'd better telephone the police department" Some one else whispered: "Yes," and then some one else went to do it. Jane and I sat on the bottom step of the stair that led to the landing. "I suppose," she said, with a shudder, "that some one ought to stay."

I nodded. Then she slipped her hand in mine, and I shook from the frightful cold of it. I will never forget the look of that landing, that scene. The sun was beginning to sink, and the high hills which surrounded us always made our twilights deeper and earlier than those of the levels. A heavy mist was rising on the creek, and somewhere a frog began to boom. I felt Jane shake and then cover her eyes; and I knew that she, with me, could not help looking at the awful human wreck that lay before us, and that with every look she grew nauseatingly, horribly sick.

His skin was peculiarly grey, and his eyes, wide-open, looked as if they would burst from the sockets. There was an agonized, stranded look in them that turned one dizzy to view. And the hand—the horror of that, all that it hinted—left one gasping and close to a swoon.

"The—the hand—" Jane whispered.

I swallowed hard, moistened my lips and managed to get out: "Yes."

"What?" she asked. I could only shake my head. She began to cry.

"Where—where's Gustave?" she asked.

"Telephoning town," I responded.

"Laurence?" she questioned further.

I said I didn't know, and in the queer way one's mind acts on such occasions, I thought that probably he was writing a verse on "Death." It amused me, even in the middle of that horror, and I heard myself voicing my thought.

"Probably," answered Jane, without a smile. Then she said: "*It moved!*" But it was only the slap of the water against the landing that had made a board shake.

"Nathan will have to put in some nails—that board's loose," I whispered, my eyes fixed on the figure; I had gotten so that I couldn't look away.

"Yes," she replied. "It was that. But—April, *it did move—*"

"You go—" I whispered. "I'll stay—" And she did, after a little more urging. It was really hardest on her, for she had known Frank Lethridge better than we had. After I had sat there either ten minutes or five hours—I don't know which—Gustave joined me. He sat down by me, and whispered, as Jane had. "They'll be out in a little while," he said. I nodded.

"Want to go?" he asked, and I thought it was decent of him, for I knew he wanted some one to stay; being there alone wasn't pleasant.

"Oh, no," I answered, and as easily as I possibly could. "I'll stick it out."

"You're all right, April—" he said, and I felt his hand close over mine. I let it stay there; there is something wonderfully comforting in any human touch when the murky black and cold of death confronts you. Gustave's hand was warm, and the contact strengthened me. I found myself clinging to it

"Jane said his Jap telephoned this morning, asking if he'd been seen. Said he often didn't come home, but always went to the bank. They'd telephoned from there."

"Is that so?" I heard myself say.

"Yes. She said she left him at the main road yesterday at a little after five. For some reason she didn't let him motor her down. She didn't say why."

"Did you ask her?"

"Yes. She only said: 'I don't know.' Seemed upset. Think she"—Gustave stopped and coughed—"cared for him?"

"Probably," I responded.

"That's the *devil* of a note," he said resentfully. "Last thing I knew she, cared for *me*. Never trust a woman!" And again, right in the middle of all that horror, I wanted to smile. Gustave had actually spoken aloud. I think his anger at Jane had, for the moment, pushed his sick fear aside. Then again he remembered.

"That hand—" he whispered. I nodded. "What happened to it?" he went on. I said I didn't know. "What I mean is," he continued, "what *could* have torn it off that way?"

I managed to gasp: "Don't!" and then I had to lay my head down somewhere, and the nearest somewhere was Gustave's shoulder. So—when the police found us, as they did just then, they immediately decided that I was Gustave's sweetheart, and I know that my position at that moment discounted what I had to say about where I had seen Gustave.

"Well," said one of the men who had come down on the landing, "this is the second affair of this sort that's happened around here. And we intend to find out who did it, this time!"

"Yes," said another one slowly. "And—perhaps it'll reflect some light on the other—" and then they looked at us and grew silent.

"Better go, April," said Gustave, and I was very glad to stagger off. I found Midgette at the height of her folly when I gained our living-room. She was actually working the ouija board, stopping now and again to mop away her tears and blow her nose. "It—it says it doesn't know," she moaned. "I—I wish I were *dead!*"

I went to the kitchen and put on some water for coffee. Nan joined me, and at my direction, began to cut bread. She seemed calm, but she tried to cut it with a tea-strainer, so I realized she wasn't.

"We haven't eaten, and we'll have to," I said.

"Yes," she answered. Then she began to bite her thumb-nail and to stare at me with miserable, horror-filled eyes. "*That hand—*" she whispered.

"Forget it," I said, and I tried to say it briskly. Then I set every one to work, made people eat, and for a small while we felt a little better. But—when the dark came! Well, of course it had to be one of those low, moaning-nights; the sort when every breeze holds a sob. The boats banged against the landing with a dull, slow thud. From outside came the boom of frogs, the swish of boughs moving in the wind; then once and again the smart snap of willow, and we would gasp, some one would say: "*What was that?*" and some one else would answer: "The willow rocker," and again we would become quiet, listening—listening—for what, we knew not.

I had telegraphed Billy soon after the affair. I did it by telephone, with an especial emphasis on the "Rush," and in the telegram I asked him to come. I was glad to think that, if he had any message in time, he could get a sleeper at nine and be with us the next morning. The idea of his coming cheered me; I almost prayed that he would make that train.

At ten we made sleeping arrangements, for we girls decided to bunk together again.

"Take my room," said Gustave. "It's bigger, and not too close to the—the—"

"Landing," I finished for him.

"Yes," he answered; "and I'll sleep in yours. We'll switch until we all feel better." I thanked him, and felt a new respect for him. He was the man of that party. Laurence was doing a large imitation of a soggy, cold wet sponge. He actually cried half the time and made verses the rest—which was worse—these entitled: "Death, what lies beyond your cold, gray arms?" and: "From the River's Depths!"

We did change rooms, and I cleared out my clothes in a hurry, too big a hurry; it led me to do an awful thing! Then we put up two cots in Gustave's room, and turned in. Of course we didn't sleep. In the first place Laurence kept pacing the halls and moaning, and then the wind had risen and the trees began to slap the sides of the house.

"Do you suppose they could blame Laurence?" asked Nan, her hands working nervously and her lips trembling.

Jane answered this with truth, if not politeness. "For Heaven's sake, no!" she said. "Any one who sees him now would know that he couldn't kill a rabbit without sniveling. Wonderful oak you've picked out to vine yourself over!"

"He is so sensitive!" said Nan happily, and then her face changed, grew white, as did ours, I suppose; for we heard noises on the porch, heavy footsteps, and then a banging on the door. It was then nearing two, and any one's coming was strange. Gustave went down, with Laurence clinging to his bathrobe and sobbing at every step.

It was a telegram from Billy. It read:

> Charmed to come.   Arrive to-morrow.
> Why didn't you write?   BILL.

"Damn Bill!" said Gustave, after I explained.

"I just told him to come—not why. He didn't know that this would come in the middle of the night, or, if it did, that it would upset us."

"I want to go b—back to New York," babbled Laurence, who still clung to Gustave's bathrobe. It was too much for Gustave, who frankly lifted his left foot, with intent, and kicked back of him at Laurence. It landed plumb on Laurence's shin.

"Go write a verse on pain, you damn-fool!" he snarled, when Laurence had let go of his bathrobe and was clutching his shin with both hands. "Go do anything! Only—let go of me—or I'll—" Then Gustave stopped; no one was mentioning murder that night. No one ever tells funny stories about drunks when they have one of the real story-makers in their own family; then it ceases to be humorous. We no longer mentioned death and murder.

I thanked Gustave once more, apologized to every one for frightening them, and again lay down. We left a lamp burning, and the light from it helped—but what soothed me was a little yellow slip of paper with "Western Union Telegram" written on it. I kept my hand on this a good deal of the night, and the words, in which Billy said that he was coming, sang through me even in those fleeting moments of sleep. I wanted him to come, most awfully.

Early the next morning we had a detective and several policemen call on us. They made a pretty thorough overhauling of the house, and even investigated old Nathan's cabin. I never thought of that locket, which was the silliest folly I ever committed, until one of the men came downstairs—carrying it.

"You say you know nothing of Mr. Lethridge's disappearance, Mr. Gerome, but if that is true, why is this locket, which he carried on his watch chain, hidden in the room in which I am told you sleep? I found it under a loose board. Will you be kind enough to explain?"

I began to speak, but I was silenced.

The officer smiled at me, and in his smile I saw a little bit of yesterday which he had hung in his memory, and that bit was my head on Gustave's shoulder. How I hated and scorned myself for my stupidity, and how I despaired about righting it. It seemed impossible.

"I never saw it before!" said Gustave.

"He didn't!" said I.

"I changed rooms with her," he went on—simply to tell the truth, I am sure, and not to blame me—"and probably some one—some one else put it there, some one who can explain—"

"Blame this little yellow-haired person for that?" asked the officer. "Why, all she needs is wings, and she'd be one. Come on, be a man; tell us the truth—the whole truth!"

"It is the truth!" I said, breathing fast; and I told them about finding it, but I felt that no one believed me.

"My dear," said the man who questioned us, "he isn't worth it. He really isn't!" And the eyes that he turned on me were kind, although he would not believe my truth.

"This man loves *that* girl," I went on, pointing to Jane, "and she does him—don't you, Jane?" Jane looked at him, and forgot all wisdom through the hurt that he had given her.

"Love him?" she echoed. Then she laughed, and her laughter held a sneer. "Well, *hardly!*"

"You fool!" I said sharply.

"Too bad!" said one of the men. "Too bad!"

"I'll prove it!" I said.

"Go ahead," I heard. And then I stopped. How could I, what could I do, and what was to come to Gustave through my folly? I heard myself say, "Oh, I wish that Billy would come!" and at that very moment he tapped lightly at the door.

I kissed him when he came in, and he looked very much surprised.

"Pretty good," said one of the men.

"Clever touch, but he didn't take his cue. This young lady ever kiss you before, stranger?"

"No," said Billy, "but, thank Heaven, she's begun!"

"You fool!" I said again, and this time half crying, and again I explained; but no one outside our party believed me; and clearing up the affair—showing the real truth—seemed hopeless.

CHAPTER X.

THE SEVERED HAND

BREAKFAST DID NOT seem good to me the morning after that terrible affair. The coffee smelled and tasted as it does after you've been bilious for a week, and Midgette opened a boiled egg that was almost ready to fly.

Very loftily Laurence told her to be calm, and at that Gustave sneered. Then one of the officers who was sitting on the side lines asked if he might have a cup of coffee. I gave it to him, and after he drank it, he said it was enough to make any one irresponsible. Nan, who had got breakfast, was really hurt, and Laurence said he'd thrash the cad after he finished a verse on "Courage"; but he didn't. Nan said he had forgotten, but I wasn't so sure of that.

At about ten o'clock, the sun, which had been making feeble efforts to shine, broke through the haze of fog, and every one felt better.

"Never want to see another creek or river in my life—" said Jane, with a shudder. I was with her on that. She looked across the water and half whispered "What do you suppose?"

I only shook my head. We were silent for a space, because we were both seeing that horrible, rigid figure as it lay dripping on the dock. "Why did he come out to see you?" I asked, after several minutes had gone by.

"He was shadowing old Nathan," she answered, in a sort of shamed, silly way. "It sounds perfectly idiotic, but he almost persuaded me. I watched Nathan for him, too. Frank—" she paused a second after the name, "said Nathan was connected with the murder of Rudolph Loucks, and was up to something worse now. Frank had been getting letters, anonymous ones, warning him against stirring up inquiries about the old affair—that was after he came here that first day—and telling him to keep off the ground."

"Why didn't he consult the police?" I asked.

"Well, you know what they are here. He said if there was enough cleverness in the guilty ones, or one, to evade the search for all these years, there would be more than enough to dodge the local sleuths. And—he had a feeling about working it out himself.

"He said no one would dare attack him in broad daylight, since a shot would be heard by the farms near by, and that too many people would be astir to make it safe.

"He never came out at night except the time he followed Gloria Vernon—he knew something about her he didn't tell me. Not that she is in the least implicated. He thought Nathan—"

"I can't think old Nathan would do it—even be connected with it," said I.

She shook her head. "It always sounded crazy to me," she answered, "but—Frank was convincing. He assured me that more than murder would be unearthed. I wrote him almost every day. He asked me to happen into Nathan's cabin once and again, to look around pretty thoroughly if possible, and to report what I saw. I did. One time he was cleaning fish and another time fussing with the spark plug of the Beasleys' flivver. He's quite a mechanic, you know. But—as for anything suspicious—well, there simply wasn't a thing of that sort!"

At that very moment old Nathan appeared. He had a way of doing that quickly and of being almost upon you before you realized it. Woods life had made him silent-footed.

"I found something," he announced. And—he held out a corkscrew.

"Where?" asked Jane, with no great interest.

"Up-stream a ways," he replied, and with a good deal of triumph in his tone. "Blood on it," he announced next, "and the ground tramped considerable where I picked it up at."

We looked at it with a little more interest.

"The jedge happen around here yesterday?" he asked next. I nodded. "He went walking up the path by the creek," said Jane, "after he found that April was out."

"So I reckoned," said Nathan.

"How?" I asked.

"Well," he drawled, after a marvelous display of the spitting art, "it's like this: when a woman, she up and pins a white ribbon over her waist, real prominent placed, you can *reely* safe on it that somethin' made her think of that particular branch of *ree*form. Usually it's a husband who likes his little jug. And—I ask yuh, is there any likelier citizen in this here town *to* carry a corkscrew than the jedge of this here district?"

We smiled. It was true; the judge was redolent of alcohol, never drunk, and in the opinion of some, never really sober. He was one of those home drinkers, who do it alone—in the cellar—and who only show what they have done by a flush, a smell, and a heavy, sleepy look around the eyes.

"Did you find it where the fire had been built?" I asked sharply. Nathan nodded.

"I found Frank Lethridge's locket there," I went on. "And it had a picture of *Rudolph Loucks's wife in it.*"

"Yassem," replied Nathan. "I ain't surprised."

"Why?" I asked.

"Well, they was sweet on each other. She up and married Rudolph in a huff. Frank Lethridge and her had had a tiff. Right up here they had it. I was settin' in one of than willers, waiting fer a oriole to come hang on her nest; wanted photeegraphs for a article on mother birds. Well, I'd set there two days pretty regular, and I wasn't going to holler just as I almost had that there oriole enough tamed to be sociable like and set fer her picture. So I heard it. Wasn't no bungalow here then, and they was walkin'. They set on a log." He stopped, and surveyed the corkscrew.

"Go on," said Jane.

"Well, they set. They set quite a while arguin'. It was her mother who wanted to live with 'em, and she was a cantankerous old kangaroo, always gettin' her feelin's hurt and leaving the church and such like. She wanted to live with 'em. Well, Frank, bein' a level-headed one, he wasn't so anxious for that, so he offered her a nice sum of money, to be hers every month, understand, and offered that she could have a house he owned at the south side of the town.

"Then this here girl, who loved her maw, up and repeats some of the things maw had jawed out about Frank. Well, it went on that way mebbe an hour, then she gets up like a man o' war, and begins to edge off. He says, hoarse, 'Then this is the end?' And she says, 'Since you will it so—' Well, he kinda sobbed like, and says, 'No—*my darling!*' Right romantic it was, but she up and got, and I guess that was all.

"It wasn't so long afta that that she took Rudolph, on a spite like. Rudolph, he wasn't no lady, but he had some things on his side, too." His tone changed. "I know," he went on. "My wife, she up and run off with a man who had money and owned factories and sich. *That* was thirty-two year ago, but—I ain't got over it yit, and some day—" Old Nathan stopped speaking, his threat unfinished; but his eyes held it clearly.

Both Jane and I pitied him. He was a good old fellow, and his outdoor life had given him a charm so great that one could overlook the tobacco juice, the dirty hands, and broken nails. He was, as I have said before, a piece of the woods. And if, as a young man, he had the same gentle manner, his wife was a fool.

"It ain't no joke," he mattered, "havin' yer wife pretty up fer some one else. It ain't no joke to set and see it crawlin' on yuh—that there ache that never finishes, and that there hate that never stops. So—I say Rudolph was to be pitied, too. It ain't no joke!"

"You'd better go in and tell that part to the police who have been insulting Nan about this," said Jane, "and I'll tell him about Mr. Lethridge's suspicions—" I shook my head violently. I couldn't see her get old Nathan tangled in it.

"I only mean his suspicions about some one's doing something they shouldn't around here," she explained.

"All right," I answered, and she disappeared. Old Nathan went with her, and Billy came out.

"You send for me, April," he said, "and then treat me like a *dog.*"

"You're such a fool!" I answered irritably.

"Why should you want to protect Gustave?" he asked, his chin sticking out an inch farther than it does in times of peace. I explained why, and how my stupidity had misrepresented him.

"Swapping rooms!" he said after I had finished my narrative. "It is disgusting. Can't you *see* how impossible this whole thing *is?* Can't you see that decent people won't have anything to do with you? Can't you see that you can't ignore conventions like this, and—" But he stopped, for I had moved away.

"I sent for you to comfort me," I said over my shoulder. "You *are* indeed a great help."

"Oh, *April!*" he appealed, and I knew he was miserable, but I thought he ought to be. I hurried off the porch and almost ran toward a path that twists up through the woods on to the top of the hill. But Billy ran faster than I did. And when he caught up to me he almost shook me.

"You're bad-tempered," he said, "spoiled, and cruel!"

"Then I think you're very silly to run after me," I responded.

"So do I!" he groaned. Then we puffed on. It is an awfully steep path.

"Sit down," Billy ordered, and I did. Not because he ordered me to, but because I was tired. He had selected a log for my roost, and he settled by me and began to pull grass out of its root sheaves. It was tall, rank and strong, and the labor this pursuit involved seemed to completely engross him. I maintained silence until he began to divert his attention to poison ivy. Then I spoke.

"That's poison ivy," I said.

"I don't care!" he replied, which I considered childish.

"I want you to know," he said, after he laid down a bunch of carefully plucked grass and had mopped off his forehead, "that I am going to stay up here with you until you go back to New York. If Aunt Myra ever hears of it, it will kill her, but you are not to be trusted alone."

"You needn't inconvenience yourself, or your Aunt Myra," I said. "I don't want you around."

"My *gosh,* you're cruel!"

I did not reply.

"But so lovely—so lovely—" he went on, and then he buried his head in his hands. I began to feel a lot better. Billy always manages to cheer me up. And his whole attitude was so much more sensible that I decided that I'd be a little kinder.

"Billy, dear," I said, moving a little closer.

"Darling?"

"I have to stay, I can't pull out now; I promised I'd see it through. And do you think it would be decent to cut and run when everything is so frightfully upset? The rest can't; we're all dead broke."

"I suppose it wouldn't be fair!"

"Oh, it wouldn't!" I said.

He put his arm around me: "You're such a square little person," he said, "in spite of being so wonderfully round. You're the *dearest thing!*" He drew a long breath after this. I loosened his arm, but let him keep my hand.

"I love you," he asserted, "so much that some day you've *got* to love me—*got* to!"

Then he stopped speaking, and we both listened, for some one was coming up the path. "I have it—I have it—I have it—" the some one was saying, and I knew that it was that poor deficient son of Jason Beasley, the paralyzed man who was being nursed by Gloria Vernon.

"What's up?" asked Billy. I explained. Then he passed us. A lank boy of uncertain years, he was. Nathan said he was not a boy, but that he looked so because worries hadn't settled on his spirit. He had that clear, unlined look that is often seen in those half-awake. He was pathetic.

I always hated meeting him; the sight of him touched something inside of me that I would rather keep subdued, and that is the feeling about whether there is a going on—whether, in another consciousness, he would have all of his, why he should have been, and—other little wonders. I can't look at stars for long, and lack of reason, death, and great spaces have always depressed me.

"What's he dragging?" asked Billy, as he took out his cigarette-case and hunted a match.

"Don't know," I answered, "but we'll see soon." And we did. He had the end of a rope in his hand, and to this was attached something reasonably heavy, for the rope jerked as he pulled it, letting one see that the something that was being dragged caught on the roots that ridged the path. We waited with a mild interest. When the end of the rope appeared we first saw a steel trap, that heavy type which is, I think, used for bears. I leaned forward and felt my heart stop, miss a beat, then double on the next. My mouth grew dry.

"What the dickens?" said Billy weakly, and then I sagged against him and saw only black for—I don't know how long. When I came back I was held in Billy's arms, and he was almost shouting.

"You sha'n't be frightened like this! I *will* take you off!" I shook my head.

"Where has he gone?" I asked weakly.

"I don't know—I don't care!"

"But perhaps it held a clue," I said.

Billy picked me up. "I'd rather walk," I protested, but to no effect; I did not walk until we were in sight of the bungalow, when Billy set me down, but kept a firm hold on my arm. I did sway a little, and it was no wonder that I did.

To see—first that vacant-faced boy chanting words he'd heard some one say somewhere—to wonder idly what he was dragging, to lean forward to see, and then to see—it was far worse than horrible—to see a hand, pallid, almost green from water, torn, with one of the bones gone from the back of it; and then to see it slipping along before you—catching the dust of dried, trampled leaves, seeming to twitch with every jerk of the rope—it was no wonder I fainted; even Billy was gray.

When we gained the porch he spoke.

"This is rotten," he said. "I am going to stay. This has *got* to be cleared up. Are you strong enough to go in alone, dear? I'm going to get that boy—"

I nodded, and he dashed off.

CHAPTER XI.

THE MAN-TRAP

THE DEVELOPMENTS OF the next week preluded a calm, perhaps I should say, an outer calm; for inside, things stung, hurt, perplexed and irritated all of us. Wonderings and worries did not cease as the suspicion of the town's folk quieted.

That morning after the tragedy and after I had been up the hill with Billy, I saw the judge. I found him waiting for me. Billy had run to catch the individual whom all the countryside call "The Echo" or "Beasley's boy," and I went in the bungalow alone. The living-room was empty except for the judge, who was stirring around by the fireplace and, when I entered, was just about to open a cupboard at the side of this which was once used for wines. His attitude was suspicious, and it made me wonder. And I was even more perplexed when I saw old Nathan peering in one of the windows with the most indescribable look of cunning on his face. I coughed, and the judge jumped.

"Used to know this bungalow well," he said, after greeting me with some constraint. "Found it, ah—natural to—ah, move around, look things over. Hope, ah—you don't mind. Seemed like home."

"Indeed?" I said, and then I sat down on the edge of a chair, and the judge settled near me and began to "ah" and "ahem." He wanted to say *something* to me, and didn't quite dare. I had the queerest feeling of hidden depths that ever was. It was quite as if one looked at an unrippled pond, and yet knew that currents were raging beneath the surface, and that quicksand edged the placid place.

We talked about the murder, accident, suicide, or whatever it was, for perhaps ten or fifteen minutes. Then from outside I heard old Nathan's planing, and it helped me to gain steadiness and to hurry the judge on with his errand; it was a soothing sound, that slip of the plane.

"You wanted to see me, I believe?" I prompted.

"Ah, yes," he said; "ah, yes. Difficult to explain, but you have that, ah—look of innocence—"

I stiffened. I have had men say that to me before, and twice, when they had most uninnocent proposals to make. "Have you," went on the judge, "ever been to Florence?" I nodded.

"Fra Angelico painted you in one of the cells," he said.

"San Marco is a charming place," I replied stiffly, and then: "What was it that you wished to see me about?"

"I don't want you to be hurt!" he said, leaning forward. "The rest—the rest are hardened, world-wise young fools who can take care of themselves; you—young lady, *I must tell you that*—"

And then suddenly old Nathan's hammer began; the judge grew white, and stopped speaking. "Indigestion," he gasped. "*Water*—"

I got it, but I found he had recovered when I returned. He sat, looking quite his usual bloated, puffed self, tapping his finger-tips together and staring at a sketch of Gustave's, a bit of the down-stream creek, with a bridge, cows, and a punt in it. He had done it in crayons, and it was a fairly good color bit.

"Um—good," said the judge; "but that young man has been taught to see too much gray and purple."

I agreed with him, but I was enraged. He had excited me, half announced what I knew to be a large missing link in our mystery, and then—without explanation, started a light patter about painting. "Um—" he continued. "His sight isn't the best. Careless about measurement?"

I broke out with: "I don't want to discuss painting. What were you going to say?"

He moved uneasily, turned, and I looked back of him, where his eyes were now focused. Old Nathan was taking off the screen door which, for two weeks, had not quite closed.

"I guess I won't disturb yuh, jedge?" inquired Nathan.

"Oh, no!" said the judge. "Oh, no!" Then he laughed in a silly, half-hearted way. I grew more angry.

"Leave that door alone, Nathan," I ordered. "You can do it at another time, or not at all. The judge wants to speak to me privately."

"Same to me," said Nathan. "I ain't in no sweat to work at this here. Miss Severance, she decreed that I fix her up, that's all. I'll go monkey with liniment, or fix them shingles on my cabin ruff. It's the same to me!"

And he departed. I heard him fixing the shingles on his roof, and the judge had another attack of indigestion. "Getting old," he said, when he could speak, "getting old. Some day I'll slip off, and then

—perhaps there'll be real *rest.*" I felt sorry for him—a horrible want for peace showed in his voice.

But—the mystery remained, and it was at that point a menace. I probed. "You know your corkscrew was found up the creek?" I said.

"Where?" he asked; and then he changed color, said he never carried one, and grew not a little pompous in his haughtiness. I smiled at him meaningly, which is the crudest and most powerful thing any woman can do. Again he began to breathe hard, and for a moment the short sound of his breath and old Nathan's pounding were the only things to be heard.

"I lost it, Sunday," he admitted.

"So I thought," I replied.

"I—I wanted to find Lethridge; to warn him—" Again he stopped speaking and began to breathe bard.

"Mr. Lethridge had been warned," I said, "by anonymous letters. Some one, in these, told him that the truth about the murder of Rudolph Loucks would come out, if he bothered around here. What is the mystery about this place? Is some one trying to protect us? Was he a dangerous character? Was he implicated—connected with the first affair? I feel that there is a link—"

Then Nathan spoke from the door-way:

"I heard yuh tell Frank Lethridge, Sunday," he announced, "to keep his hands off. Offa what, jedge? I jest sorta *wondered*—"

"It was—it was a matter of investments," he explained, fumblingly. "We bought some copper stock together, which did not—did not do as well as we hoped. Lethridge wanted to sell, and I believe in holding when the rest unload. My principle in speculation has been that the public is, if you will pardon the somewhat crude expression, a sucker, and when they bite, I do not; when they do not, I do. I have never lost, and I have played the market for over thirty-two years."

That made me doubt his word. I didn't believe it was possible.

"Kind of you to warn him," said Nathan, with undue smoothness.

"We were friends," said the judge, sitting more straight, and growing red.

"I reckon," said Nathan, "you took his pistol, too, didn't you? That there time he was so broke up by Rudolph Loucks's wife's sufferings that he was a meditatin' suicide."

"I—" began the judge after a gasp.

"Yessir," went on Nathan with unusual haste, "I overheered it. I was settin' in a tree up the crick a ways, settin' and waitin' fer a owl to come out. And I heered you comin', walkin' down with Frank Lethridge. You says: 'Frank, give it to me. No man does it. Fight it out, stay here. This is your fight! You won't help her by doing this!' Real nice and manly it *did* sound. He says: 'But—I made her do it! I—and to think what she is sufferin'!' But he forked over his pistol, now didn't he, jedge?"

The judge did not reply.

"Now the wonder of it is," went on old Nathan, "what'll happen if the truth about this here comes out? Don't yuh think mebbe the two crimes was connected? Don't yuh think mebbe if one is found out, t'other will foller? Well, that's the way it looks to me. I'll take this here down to my cabin and plane her there, and you folks can jaw along real sociable, all alone!" And then he lifted off the screen door and carried it away.

For several moments the judge looked a great deal like a frog that is endeavoring to swallow a fly seven times too large for his swallower. He sat before me, gasping and attempting to engulf something, which was, I surmised, his nervous shock.

"My heart's weak," he said, when he could speak; "always was. Old Nathan's got a valvular defect in his. Did you know that?" I said I had not. "Well, he has," the judge asserted; "bad one. Doctors have said for years that he might slip off any day. Don't be surprised"—the judge stopped and wiped his forehead with a heavy linen handkerchief—"if you don't hear him around some morning, and find him dead. They've all predicted that would happen. He'll just slip off some day as I will. Quietly, and naturally. They all said he would—why, ten years ago a doctor from Quincy said: 'That man'll live two years, no more!' And look at him. But—I shouldn't be surprised if he would go some day—"

Something horrible flashed over me. I stood up, shaking, and growing sick, and I saw in that saturnine old face before me all the cunning and cruelty of a fiend—a fiend planning another murder.

"You were going to warn me against Nathan, weren't you?"

He bit his lips.

"*Weren't* you?" I repeated, bending toward him.

He whispered a feeble "Yes," after a backward look. "A coward, too," I thought. It proved it for me.

"You needn't worry," I said. "I'll take care of myself *and* Nathan."

He stood up. "So long as you understand," he said, as he reached for his hat. His hands shook almost uncontrollably, and again I pitied, even as I scorned him.

"I think I am beginning to understand," I said with some emphasis. "I think I am beginning to get a light."

"Then," he said, with a frightful smile, "*be careful*. Walk carefully, or else you'll be hurt. Avoid the—the pit. *Do* you understand?"

"I think so," I said, playing at cross-purposes with him, and honestly loving the game. He reached toward me, clutched my wrist, and whispered: "Don't—" and then he had to stop, for the crowd who, I found afterward, had to go to town with the police force, returned. They came in, but hardly noticed the judge or his departure.

I hurried to Nathan's cabin. I found him working on a sort of light that he said he used in the woods to catch moths. Then he showed me some he had caught, told me something of the sort peculiar to the country and various woods, and then he talked:

"Wouldn't 'a' said what I did to the jedge," he confided, "fer I ain't one to go nosin' trouble, but I hadda be sassy fer this here reason: Twict now I heard that there artist gent you got with yuh say as how he'll kill any one who so much as teches his gal. Well, Frank Lethridge and her was gettin' thick, and I ain't fer seein' any of your crowd hung. I wouldn't shield no guilty man without I had princeeple back of me, and here I hev. Fer—I know what it is to get notioned on one woman and then hev her take up with somebody else."

"But Gustave didn't!" I said, growing white. I felt the blood leave my face and heart.

"No," agreed Nathan, "we'll say he didn't, fer there air sins and sins, and them that is thought the worst sins is sometimes only *truth*."

I sank down on a bench by old Nathan's work table. "Nathan," I whispered, "I know he didn't! No one else heard him say that."

"I dunno. I reckon not, but I'll fix it."

I clasped my hands tightly together, and stared at the floor, a heavy board one, the cracks of which were full of the dirt of ages. I heard Nathan move around, but I was honestly too ill to lift my head.

After I heard Nathan go up a ladder to his loft and then return, I looked up. He held a trap of the sort "The Echo" had pulled up the path on the hill that same morning.

"This here," he announced, "is a bear trap. Now you know there *is* bears up in the mountains not so fur from here, and once and agin in the big spring rains one of these here has washed down. Now we'll say this got tangled like in a rut in the rick, and that Frank

Lethridge told his Jane gal he'd up and git her some water lilies, since she was partial to 'em.

"And so he moseyed up the crick. And he leaned over in the real deep water, and he seen somethin' aside lilies. Mebbe he'd fell in and didn't mind wettin' his clothes, so he dives down to see, and when he gets this here thing he feels—"

I nodded. Thai I managed to speak.

"Did you see the body?" I asked. Nathan had not. I told him about the hand, and then I told him about the trap. His jaw dropped about eight inches and he began to gasp.

"I'll be goll-darned," he said, "if that *ain't* it! Why, he was always rootin' around this here crick bottom, huntin' Gawd knows *what,* and I suppose—he thought this here was whatever he *was* a huntin'—" Nathan stopped, looked down at the bear trap, and so did I. "I'll be *goll*-darned!" he repeated.

And I echoed that. Then I began to cry, for I had been fearfully afraid, and worried almost into madness by the fear that I had hurt Gustave by my carelessness.

"I thought the judge—" I began, and then I stopped. "How," I asked with new energy in my voice, "did the person who did have that pistol get it?"

"Easy enough," answered Nathan. "Afore this here murder, nobody locked their doors; we was a peaceable, Gawd-fearin' little village then—nothin' ever happened. As I says, I was just puttin' in to be sassy and to shet him up. I do remember Frank Lethridge and the jedge discussin' suicide, and he did take the pistol, but that ain't saying nothin'—"

"No," I responded, "there doesn't seem to be much proof of anything, but if we can only avert suspicion from Gustave—that is all I ask."

Nathan nodded. Then he looked up and out of his door, although I, of city-untrained ears, had heard nothing. Gloria Vernon passed, and old Nathan vouchsafed a comment. "I ain't a trustin' that there female," he said, eyes narrowing. "I'm afeered—" And then he, like a good many others, ceased speaking without finishing his sentence.

I got up and went up to the bungalow. Gloria was there, and she was honestly upset.

"Suspicion pointed to *you!*" she almost screamed at Gustave, who nodded. Her face grew as hard as I have ever seen a face. Then she laughed shortly. "Why, you were with me!" she said shrilly.

"That's not worth while," I put in. "Nathan and the judge both know he wasn't; that he left you before this happened."

"Do you want him hung?" she asked, turning to me.

"No, I don't. That's the reason I want the truth, not lies," I answered. Then I saw that she did care, for she went up to him, put her arms around his neck—and we were all in the living-room together—and I heard her whisper: "Do you think I'd *let* them—*let* you be hurt?"

It was almost savage, her attitude; something primal, revolting, and yet beautiful, shone through it. I heard Jane gasp. I saw Gustave look at Jane with agonized, *trapped*, pleading eyes, stand stiff for a minute under Gloria's touch, and then melt and almost forget us all.

"Oh, God, Gloria!" he stammered, "what does it matter? *What* does it matter!" and he kissed her. I got up and left, Jane went to the kitchen to sink down beside a table and hide her head in her arms —she was past tears—and the rest faded in different directions.

Billy followed me through the kitchen, and we wandered toward the road to town.

"Like to soak him!" he said. "That poor kid!" He was speaking of Jane.

"Yes," I agreed. "I'm so tired of it all! I hope I'll never see another representative of or dabbler in any of the arts, after I shake this crowd. I'd like a peaceful apple-pie, sock-darning existence where Russian music is unknown and Futurist paintings undreamed of."

"Marry me," said Billy. "I'll guarantee to supply the sock hunger. Oh, April, if you only would—"

I felt a sudden wish for it and a great rising of love for Billy—but I knew that my softening wasn't to be trusted to last; and that my feelings of that hectic, horrible time might not be mine even to-morrow, and most certainly not a month from then.

"Not now," I said. "I can't tell what I want. I can't be bothered about deciding. We'll talk of that later, Billy."

He looked crestfallen, but had to accept it. "After this simmers down?" he questioned.

"Yes," I agreed. "Then I *will* decide."

"Then it's got to quiet—"

"It will," I responded, and I told him something of what old Nathan supposed. But—I added that there had been mysteries right along, since the start of things. So we sat down on a fence that surrounded the field where Rudolph Loucks was shot, and I told him these things.

CHAPTER XII.

BILLY SUMS UP

HE WROTE THEM down carefully as I related the various happenings. This is the way the line-up appeared in his note-book:

Blood on walls and banister (first afternoon).
Dog jumped through window of cellar, finger prints in blood on door. Dog unhurt. Brick hurled against door that evening.
"F. Don't do it, R." written on kitchen wall, first day that Frank Lethridge called.

"Anybody but Laurence ever see that dog?" queried Billy. When I told him "No," he drew a line through the dog item. I had to admit that it didn't amount to much.

The data I supplied made this page in his note-book:

Laurence has cold. Sneezes heard in cellar. Frank Lethridge, going down, said no one was there. Both Laurence and Nan say they spent afternoon in bath-tub.

Billy stopped after I'd dictated this item and sharpened his pencil. "Can't you see how *disgusting* the whole affair is?" he asked.

"If you're going to act that way—" I began, threatening to slip from the railing, but I didn't, for Billy's hand closed around my arm. "You'll stay right here," he announced, "until I finish this thing."

I pretended to sulk, but I enjoyed his ruling. Every woman does like some male to boss the job, and especially those flat-heeled females who constitutionally look like Boston on a rainy day and seem to wear cast-iron wills. They wilt at a touch. I've seen it. I'm not one of them, but I have enough of a will to enjoy the new sensation that comes with losing it.

After Billy had finished, sharpening his pencil he went on, and he wrote something that I hated to see on record. Billy scoffed at me, saying that no one would ever see it, and that after he'd struck a trial balance he'd dispose of the evidence. It was:

Gustave says he'll shoot any one who hurts Jane.

"How many times did he say that?" Billy asked.

"I don't remember exactly—perhaps three or four," I answered.

"Enough," said Billy, writing "four times" after his item about Gustave. "What did the darned fool do it for?" he asked further. I couldn't say.

I began to get down again, and again something restrained me. This time it was around my waist. "Oh, honey," said Billy, "don't be a grouch! You know I love you. What else did you see?" I said only a cow, that day, and tried to pry off Billy's arm, but without much success. So I gave it up, held the note-book on his knee and he held me and the pencil. The next entry on the pad was:

Frank Lethridge's locket is found on porch. Must have been dropped after Nathan swept at seven. Gloria Vernon arrives same night. Jane says F. L. followed Gloria. Why? Picture of Rudolph Loucks's wife in locket belonging to F. L.

"Don't go into that," I said, "it will take too long. He was much mashed on Rudolph Loucks's wife, you know."

"Yes, you told me about that. Did Frank Lethridge come here for any particular reason?"

"He poked the creek. I think he was hunting what I found one day by accident and then never could find again." And I went on to tell Billy about the box I'd stepped on, and the hole it had left that I had stepped in, and then about the spot where it had been dragged to shore, and how a fire had been built to cover its tracks. "Old Nathan said he was frogging," I explained.

"Um—" grunted Billy, looking down at the pad. Then he asked me if I knew I was the sweetest thing on earth, and when I said "Yes, of course I do!" shook me a little, but very gently. "Gosh, I want to get this cleared up," he said. "You know what you promised," I nodded.

"Such funny things were heard," I went on.

"What?"

"Well, Nan heard Jane say: 'Oh, Frank, you wouldn't? *Promise me you won't!*' She heard that one day when she was hunting Gustave, who, as usual, had crawled across nine swamps and walked fifteen miles to avoid his share of the work. He, Gustave, was peeking at Jane and Frank, and he was—awfully jealous at that time."

"Um—"

"It *is* baffling. After Gustave heard Jane say that, he turned to Nan and said: 'If he hurts her I'll kill him!' Nathan heard Nan repeat that later; we didn't know he was on the porch." Then I went on, and Billy wrote:

Judge Harkins comes up to find Lethridge. Starts to warn April—but sees Rudolph Loucks's shade on hillside and devotes himself to tea instead of telling the thrilling tale.

"The judge is afraid of Nathan," I told him.

"When the judge appears, Nathan always uses his hammer just to let him know he's around, and the judge always has what he calls indigestion, and what I think is something close to apoplexy, induced by fright. The judge and Frank Lethridge were tangled in some way. Nathan heard the judge tell him to keep, his 'hands off.' "

"Why do you exonerate Gustave?" asked Billy, after a cautious look around.

"Because of Gloria," I replied. "He's simply mad about her. She's an obsession, and Jane—simply *isn't* any more."

"Oh, stuff," said Billy; then he explained what made him say that. He felt that Gustave hated Gloria for what she'd done to him, even while he reveled in what she gave him; he believed that Gustave had undergone a great deal of suffering, and felt much remorse because of Jane; and was sure that if any one really hurt Jane, or tried to, that he would shake off Gloria, if only for a few hours, to repay the doer of the wrong.

"Can't you see," Billy said, "that the very fact that he has been a brute might make him half savage in a wish to make it up to Jane somehow? Gustave knows what that Vernon woman is like—he's not a baby—and he knows what Jane's like; he knows she's a good, true little pal, and that he's acted like a devil. He knows that this Gloria has got hold of his worst side and is making that live so strongly that there is no chance for the other."

"I can't possibly believe it," I said doubtfully.

"Not a pretty story this," said Billy, "but it illustrates what I mean, and so I'll tell it. Comfortable, dear? Well," he went on, "when I was up at New Haven there was a chap in my class named

I. Gillman Parker, a Southerner, and about the worst rotter I ever met. But—sort of attractive in spite of his really vicious ways of living. He was engaged to a mighty pretty girl, if she looked *anything* like her tin-type. He wrote this girl pretty regularly, and seemed in love with her; but even then she didn't hold him, and it was a wonder that he was not expelled. But he was a smooth one, and had friends. It did not surprise me, therefore, to hear, about three years after his marriage, that he was absolutely neglecting his wife and was paying devoted court to a lady who had once graced the Follies, and for whom he had set up and maintained an establishment in Baltimore.

"I think he went home about once in every four or five months, and when there, frankly ignored his wife—or worse. But when the negroes on the place got drunk, and she was alone; and a new servant burst in the door and chased her to the roof, and she chose the jump to the ground and death—instead of the horror that was back of her—well, then I. Gillman Parker came back to her.

" 'She was good!' he shouted. 'Good! I know her. She was *too* good to hold me.' And then he put in some frightful qualifications about his lady who lived in Baltimore, after which—he hunted the servant.

"He found him hiding in a cabin way up in a pine woods, and—there wasn't enough left of him to use for hash. Parker slashed him up as he lived, and how he did it no one ever knew, for the negro was a big, husky boy who had been a groom. But—they knew that he had suffered for the rest of the gang, and all of them began chanting their prayers. After it was finished, I. Gillman Parker came out of the cabin, dripping with blood and laughing, and then he went to a madhouse."

"Oh, *Heavens!*" I said.

"Was I a brute to tell you that?" Billy asked anxiously, bending closer to me and tightening his arm.

I shook my head.

"I only wanted to explain," he continued, "why a man might avenge a wrong done a woman he *chooses to ignore*; why he might suffer all the more from it because of his own deficiencies—deficiencies which make him cruel to her, but also make him reverence her and turn a fiend at thought of her suffering."

"I don't believe Gustave did it," I said.

"That is from feeling, not reason," Billy replied.

I admitted it.

"We've got to see all sides," he asserted; "suspect every one, and then—perhaps we'll find the truth."

"It would be interesting if the other affair were cleared up, too. Most of us feel that perhaps they are linked."

"Perhaps," said Billy. Then he wrote down those clues; which were Frank Lethridge's pistol which had been in Judge Harkins's possession—the judge being in New York that night—and the judge's threats made on a paper to which a local divine was the one subscriber. Then he asked what companies Rudolph Loucks had been most interested in. These were an independent oil concern, the gas company, and the water company. I didn't see that Billy was getting anywhere, but I supplied facts for him, and let him jot them down.

"Then there's the corkscrew that Nathan found where that box was dragged in," I went on, "and I found Frank Lethridge's locket there that day, too. Was that only yesterday? It seems years ago! And old Nathan thinks it really was a bear-trap. He says they're sometimes washed down in the spring, and that one of Gus Dirks's cows got tangled in one last spring and broke her leg. He followed me up to say that."

Then Billy explained how he had Jane up to the farmhouse and found Mrs. Beasley out looking for Miss Vernon, and the boy sitting down on the steps, but no trace of the trap. She hadn't seen it; he told her it was only a trap he was looking for, and there was no getting anything out of him. The boy repeated: "Trap—trap," after Billy. "Maddening and horrible," he concluded and I agreed.

I laid my cheek against his shoulder.

"Oh, you *dear!*" he whispered, and then we heard some one coming, and sat apart. It was Laurence, sniffing and breathing so fast that he seemed to sob.

"They want *you*," he said, his eyes fixed on me. "That Vernon woman—I'm sure I think she is *most* unladylike—says *you* did it. Says you had his locket—that she saw you boating—that your clothes were wet—"

"*I?*" I said, with about as much expression as the Beasley boy would employ.

Billy helped me get down to the ground. "Don't be frightened, April," he said; "this is the utmost folly, and it will be cleared up in no time. Come, dear—"

"So upsetting," said Laurence. "Suspicion's breath, like chill north winds—a *pencil!* Some one give me a pencil, *quick!*"

Billy gave him something, and then put his arm around me.
"Don't be frightened, dear," he whispered, "it's absolutely crazy,
and we'll clear it up in no time," and then we walked up to the
bungalow. Nan was watching for us from a side window.

I felt dizzy, and horribly afraid. When we entered the living-room of the bungalow there was absolute quiet for a moment,
and then Gloria Vernon spoke.

She had been crying, in the nice neat way a woman does, when
she cries for effect and not for relief. She had not damaged her looks
by it; in fact her tear-wet lashes even made her more beautiful than
ever.

Gustave stood by the fireplace, frankly giving himself up to
gazing at her. Nan had left the window when we entered, and sat by
a small table, nervously fingering a little box that was supposed to
hold stamps and never did. Midgette stood, Jane and Laurence were
seated on the wood-box, and three strange men, the one who had
asked for a cup of coffee being one of them, were there, also seated.
They all looked at me, every one in that room, and the silence
throbbed with their suspicions and fears. Gloria Vernon broke it
with: "This *kills* me to do, but I saw her, and I feel that the truth
must be known. She was wet, her clothes were half torn off, her hair
was coming down, and—*she had that locket!*"

I felt Billy's hand tremble—it was on my arm—and then I saw
Laurence's mouth move. I suppose he was planning one that he
hoped would put "the female of the species" out of business. I spoke
calmly, which was strange, for I was not calm inside.

"I did have the locket," I said. "You know I said I had found it.
But I didn't even see Frank Lethridge until he was laid on the
dock—after it happened. He was a strong man; how could I do that?
And why would I want to?"

"That's what we're trying to find out," said one of the men—the
one who had drunk the coffee. He had been very unpleasant since,
and I could not blame him!

"Nobody *knows* a thing," he went on, "but Frank Lethridge was
coming here regular, and was with this here little party a good deal
of the time, now wasn't he?"

"No," answered Gustave, "he was with that girl," and he pointed
toward Jane.

"I saw April Barry with Frank Lethridge the afternoon before he
was murdered," said Gloria.

I felt my knees shake.

CHAPTER XIII.

"FAR CROW Y PEEK THEM."

"WHERE?" ASKED ONE of the men, taking out a pencil.

"They were sitting in a boat," she said. "Miss Barry was at his feet and his arms were around her. I was surprised to see it, for I knew that Mr. Lethridge had been paying attention to Miss Hoyle, but—knowing these artistic people—" She lifted her shoulders after that. "Little rules of conventional society are not always observed; and I thought there had been a change of heart I was not greatly surprised, because"—she paused—"one expects anything of people who live together as this crowd have done this summer.

I saw Gustave grow white at that.

Jane's lips curled, and Billy was growing so angry that I was afraid he would put another murder on the books.

"Who had the punt on Sunday afternoon?" I asked.

She changed color, but she brazened it out.

"I can't say," she replied.

"I can," said Laurence. "Gustave had it. I know, for I wanted to go out myself—"

"It was your day to swab our boats," said Gustave. "Of course you wanted to go."

Some one said "That will do," and I went on with: "I had the Laurel, the tippiest canoe on the place. Send for Nathan. He'll tell you what I was in." And Nathan was sent for.

He backed up my statement, and I had the satisfaction of telling Miss Vernon to go try the position she described with so much real feeling and understanding, in the boat I paddled that day.

"Gustave," I said, "you know I was alone."

Gustave did not answer, for Gloria had moved over to him, laid her hand on his arm, and made him look into her eyes.

"Was she?" asked our breakfast guest.

"I don't know," said Gustave.

"Did you see her? Now think."

"Yes," he answered hesitatingly; and then sharply: "Yes, I did."

79

"Where?"

"At the bend in the creek, the bend where the cows come down to drink."

"Was she alone then? You must know."

"She was alone," said Gustave, after a deep breath.

"Yes, she was alone then," broke in Gloria. "I saw her before I met Mr. Gerome. I stood watching from behind those sumac bushes that grow along Gus Dirks's pasture land; and I saw them together. She let him out, and he said 'Five o'clock?' and she said 'Yes, five.' Then she paddled off. I suppose she fooled around on the stream until then."

I was never so astounded. It sounded so real as she told it.

"She came home," said Nan. "I know, because I told her that Judge Harkins had called on her; she was home by four, I know."

"Frank Lethridge left me at six," said Jane. "We were driving in his car, and I didn't let him take me down here."

"Why not?" asked one of our questioners sharply.

Jane changed color. Then she looked at Nathan appealingly.

"Why," she stammered, "I wanted to walk down the hill alone; it was pleasant, and, unkind as it sounds now, I was a little tired of Frank Lethridge. You see, we had been together all afternoon."

"Where is his car?" one of the men, who wore plain clothes and a star, asked.

"I don't know," several people replied.

"What make was it?"

"Callidac," answered Gustave. "1917."

"You were alone with him?"

She nodded.

"About what did you talk?"

"Why, I don't know," she said evasively. "Everything—nothing important—the weather, pictures, town gossip, reconstruction in France. I can't remember it all; there was nothing I should re-member particularly."

"There wasn't?" asked one of the men who questioned. "Are you sure there wasn't?"

"Yes," she answered, her cheeks beginning to burn.

"Why did he kiss you good-by?" asked one of the men who had hitherto been silent. '

Gustave moved quickly and looked outraged.

Jane turned the color of a fair-to-morrow sunset, and every one was surprised. One could not imagine it, and Jane, usually frank to the point of brutality and ashamed of nothing she did, had said he was as stiff as a poker and had never even held her hand.

"Perhaps he wanted to," she responded pertly. "I hope that isn't inconceivable."

"This is outrageous!" said Gustave, glaring in her direction. "And disgusting!"

If the time hadn't been so solemn I would have smiled!

"You should know just how disgusting it is," she responded, looking at him for a fleeting second. That stopped further comment from his direction.

"I heerd the jedge warn him to keep his hands off o' something," said Nathan. "I was settin' up the crick a ways, a talkin' to Miss Barry. She set there with me after she let Mr. Lethridge off into Gus Dirks's pasture. Then Miss Barry she came over and squatted on a log with me. I was settin' there a fish—*meditatin'* " he corrected hurriedly, with an anxious look toward the law—"and she comes over and squats like I says.

"Then she paddles off to the bungalow like Miss Nan says, fetching there at something to three, I reckon, if the sun was right, and it don't usually fail to tell the truth about the time of day.

"Now I"—old Nathan leaned over and picked up a trap—"I know Miss Aprile Barry didn't do it. And I know more. You can take it or leave it, but here's what I know, and it's truth." And he told his story of the affair, which included a theory about Frank Lethridge's wits, and a steel trap that had been washed down from the hillside.

"He, Frank Lethridge," said Nathan, "wasn't hisself. Don't his sparkin' that gal prove it?" Every one smiled a little—that is, every one but Jane, who looked indignant.

"Him, that set out to be a woman-hater from time on," went on Nathan—"him a gettin' gay, when it was high time for him to consider embalmin' fluids and undertakers? He wasn't no chicken. Why, him and me we went to the same school, and I'm kicking close to seventy if I calculate correct.

"It's this way: he notioned there was somethin' in the bottom of the crick, and he figured it would look odd if he poked alone, and so he up and asked this maid to go with him. Ain't that possible?"

We admitted it.

"He got bit with that air bug. Mebbe there *was* somethin' at the bottom of the crick. Mebbe the *jedge* knows what it is. Mebbe it gets shipped here in coffins, and mebbe it would look funny fer to haul it to the jedge's in daylight; and so mebbe our undertaker, Mr.

Hatch C. Grim, hauls it out here in the dead o' night. Mebbe he sinks it in a box—I ain't sayin' he *is,* understand; I jest say *mebbe.*

"Mebbe the jedge he comes out the road past Dirks's place—you might happen to ask Gus about that—and mebbe he fools around the river bank; and mebbe him and that there feller that chawfers fer him, mebbe they haul in a box and take it off to town underneath a pile of vegetables, which they allows they comes out past Gus Dirks's place to buy. Now, why do they up and pass Gus's? He sells good vegetables. Gus he asks me that many a time. I says 'Don't ask me; but mebbe—' "

"That'll do," shouts one of the men; and then: "*My God, Terry! I believe we're getting it.*"

"But the murder," said the man who had been addressed as Terry. "Why do you think this has a great deal to do with that?"

"It's like this," said Nathan. "That there Frank Lethridge, he notioned I done the whisky hidin', and he was all fer trappin' me. Wasn't that true?"

Jane nodded, amazement in her face.

"He explains to this here girl that that whisky is doin' harm in town, and that he's going to catch the moonshiner who's makin' or shippin' it in here. Ain't that true?"

Jane nodded.

"So he appeals to her adventure and romance like, and she goes a pokin' with him. And now's the funny part: The jedge he gets wind of it and gets nervous. We all know the jedge and his little habits. He begins to warn Frank Lethridge. Likely he says: 'These here are dangerous characters you're handlin', Frank. Better let 'em lay!' I heerd him say 'Keep your hands off!' But Frank, he won't.

"A trap is washed down from the hills by the spring rains; it drifts till it ketches. Frank Lethridge, spyin' this, or feelin' this with his paddle, leans over, can't reach it, can't wait fer a pole—thinkin' it's the hasp of a box or a handle—and dives. He's caught—you seen his hands. Gents, that there's the story. You can take 'er or leave 'er, but that's the truth!"

"Teny, I believe it," said one of the men in a low voice.

It was a peach of a tale—but I did not believe it.

Gloria looked stunned for a moment, and then recovered. And I realized when she did it that if she deliberately made war, one would have a hard adversary to face. She caught her breath on a sob, moved toward me, and held out her hands.

"Can you," she whispered, "forgive me? I had to speak—you see, I thought—" Her hands dropped to her sides with a dramatic but really beautiful gesture, and her head sunk forward.

"It's turned out all right," I answered. "So we won't worry."

"You are so good, so generous," she said; "but I know you haven't forgiven me, and I cannot blame you." And then she turned away.

"Nothing to forgive," said one of the men from town. "All evidence is requested." He turned a look toward me that was none too kind.

I saw that Gloria had done her trick, and done it well. The sympathy of the outsiders, at least, was with her. She had done a soft-pedaled appeal, to which I had responded in the key of common sense. And common sense does not usually get applause from the world gallery. If I had bleated "You are forgiven!" after a fifteen-pound-pressure sob, and held out my arms—if I had done that, I would have gotten a soft look from the town detective; but I failed. She was a great actress; I am not.

Just after that dramatic moment Gus Dirks appeared. He stood in the doorway twirling his hat and blinking, quite as if he faced a strong sunlight, instead of backing it. Before he spoke I placed him. He had, quite evidently, been a carrot in some previous existence; for his hair was sandy, his skin that red-yellow tint that so often goes with the strawberry-blond make-up; and freckles of a brown-red tone added to his relationship with a part of the vegetable kingdom.

"Well, what is it?" asked one of the town officers, at the same moment that Nathan said "Howdy, Gus!"

"It's this way," he announced, positively whirling his hat—"it's this way: I ain't had a thing to do with that there murder. My wife, she kin testeefy that I was sleepin' in the orchard all Sunday afternoon; but Frank Lethridge's automobile, it's a settin' by the spring house. It's a settin' there, and—"

"All right," broke in the man called Terry. "It's settin'— What else?"

"Well, this here was found in it. My wife, she found it. She had jest took a pail of skim milk down to the hawgs, and she come on this here automobile sudden. Well, she—"

"What did she find?" prompted some one.

"This here," said Gus Dirks, blinking more rapidly than ever, and holding out a small slip of paper.

One of the men read it and frowned.

"What is it?" asked Gustave.

"I'll ask you all to write;" said the man called Terry. "Pencils and paper, if you please."

Then we all gathered around the table, and, at Terry's dictation, wrote, three times—first, as he said the words, then slowly, then fast. What he made us write was:

Far crow y peek them.

It sounded idiotic.

After we had done this, the men moved around, looked at our papers, and went off to stand by a window with these and the note that Gus, who was still twirling his hat, had brought.

"Not here," said one.

"No," admitted another grudgingly, and as if he were disappointed. He held my paper.

"I'm inclined to believe—" we heard; and then the voices thinned to whispers, but we judged that Nathan's story was accredited, for they went off after that with a warning to Gus.

"Keep what you have read and seen to yourself," said one of the men as he picked up his hat.

His words were not what kept Gus silent. But his look was.

"Yes, sir," answered Gus. "I ain't a aimin' to say nothin'! I ain't. I kin keep a secret. I ain't one to talk. Now, my wife, she—" And he went on at length, disclosing several confidences made to him by several indiscreet folk. Them, after another assurance, that he would be as silent as the tomb, he disappeared.

Old Nathan stayed with us a few moments, and before he left the fat gentleman named Terry returned.

"Nathan," he said, "have you any writing of the judge's?"

"I hev a check," answered Nathan. "Did a little work on his ruff, barn ruff, last week. He gimme the pay this way, on his check. I ain't so much fer 'em, but he said 'twas the same as money, and I knowed he wasn't aimin' to do me. Here 'tis."

He pulled it out. I saw it. Judge Harkins's name was printed on the affair. It was made out to Nathan, and it was for seven dollars and eighty-nine cents, which sounded like Nathan's reckoning, and did not surprise me; his bills were always amazing in their little exactnesses. But when I saw the writing I was surprised. The writing was not the writing that was on the *London News;* it was not the writing that Midgette said she knew belonged to the judge; and yet—it was on his check.

I wondered whether the check was false, and if so, how Nathan had gotten it. I knew that he had worked for the judge the week before, for he had told me he was starting out to the judge's one morning when we met as I went for the milk. If that was the judge's writing, why was Midgette lying? What was her game? Who was shielding whom? And if Frank Lethridge had met his death through a hunt for an illicit whisky dealer, and a bear-trap, why was the falsifying going on? The whole affair was confusing and—more confusion was arising constantly.

After Terry left, Nathan pocketed his check and went toward his woods. Then Gloria and Gustave disappeared, and Jane, Nan, Laurence, Billy, and I settled down to speculate and wonder.

"What do you think was in that note Gus Dirks found?" I asked.

"I'll tell you what I think," said Billy. He picked up a pencil and wrote a sentence below that which had made our copy. We looked.

"I believe you're right," said Nan.

CHAPTER XIV.

THE DEATH CARD

"F. KEEP AWAY from the creek," Billy had scrawled. "Same letters that are in 'Far crow y peek them," he explained; "and it backs Nathan's theory. For—if they'd wanted to murder him, whoever did it would have invited him to be present at a little informal murder—say, from three to four, or Sunday, at the creek."

"Oh, don't!" begged Laurence, as he put out a hand toward Nan and looked back of him nervously.

"That's all right," I said, "but isn't it possible that some one else knew of some one's intentions, and was warning him?"

"Well," admitted Billy, with an almost rheumatically creaking change of view-point, "that *might* be so. I hadn't thought of that."

I saw that he was irritated because he had to reconstruct his ideas and make room for a new one.

"Oh," I went on, "Nathan's story sounded well, but I don't—know—I think there is a good deal more to this than we imagine, and I am sure that this affair and the murder of Loucks are related."

"Why are you sure?" asked Billy.

I couldn't explain, because it was—that sureness of mine —almost all a feeling, backed by flimsy little bits of evidence; I felt that Nathan had something on the old judge and that this something was more than a small indiscretion that might hurt him socially; I felt that it was large, and that Nathan took an almost fiendish pleasure in following the judge around and in pounding when he *was* around, so that the judge should be aware of him.

In Nathan I sensed the reserve that comes from being, for long years, the vase that holds the ashes of a tragedy—close guards and protects these from the eyes of the mob. It seemed to me that his slow speech came from more than a quieting existence in the woods; I thought it had grown from caution. When I explained my suspicions I was laughed into silence.

"You attribute too much intelligence to him," said Jane. "Why, the old fellow can hardly write. He always gets some one or other to address the plates he sends his nephew in New York. They tease him down at the post-office about his changing script. I was down there getting an immediate off one day when he parcel-posted some, and I heard them. They told him his hand showed that he was maturing."

"No," Billy added, "his silences aren't the fruit of thought. They're the fruit of its lack. People always suppose that the silent are the thoughtful. It isn't always so."

I was downed, but I did not agree with them. "All right," I had to content myself with saying, "but—you wait!"

"We will!" said Jane, and then I got up and went off to hunt Nathan, first frankly telling Billy that I did not need an escort.

I found Nathan puttering about the dock, nailing down boards that had been loose for weeks.

"What made you say I was with Frank Lethridge?" I asked, without preface. "You know I wasn't."

"She had it fixed you *was*," replied Nathan, after he had taken at least nine pounds of nails from his mouth. "There wasn't no combatin' *that* and makin' it sound reasonable. I figured it would set her back some if I j'ined her lie and went her one better. And—it done the trick."

"I see," I said, and again I thought that our crowd was making a big mistake about Nathan's intelligence—or lack of it, as they thought.

"No'm," he went on, after he had pounded in a few nails and planed down a board he had put over a crack that was dangerously wide—"no'm; she had it fixed that you *was* with Frank Lethridge. If I had o' come out with it that you was with me, why, one of them towners, he'd 'a' thought, 'She's been nice to that old bumpkin; guess he don't like to see her hung.' So I done a pretty lie. It sounded better—I tell yuh, there ain't nothing that hasn't a use in this world. Gawd, He up and put lies in, so you and me could use 'em when it's right and proper and moral to up and do it."

And after this he again relapsed into his customary silence, and I couldn't get another thing but "yassem" and "no'm" out of him.

I went back to the crowd, who were all talking loudly. Gustave had returned, and for two days he spent a good deal of time with us, tried to be decently polite, considerate, and human. But—he snapped now and again, and I knew what made it. He was trying at that point to cut loose from Gloria, and no man who is giving up whisky, smoking, or a woman is an angel. Disgusting as the whole affair was, I did pity him and tried to be nice to him, which greatly disgusted Billy.

But—he was to be pitied. He was simply insane about Gloria Vernon. When she was near—when even her name was spoken —his face changed and grew none too pleasant to look on. It was as if some one had pulled the curtain away from his worst desires and left them bared. I don't see, looking back, why I say "as if," for Gloria had done just that. When you saw them together you looked away. I know that he tried to cut loose at that point, but she took to visiting us often, although Nan and I left the room when she came, and—with her touch, poor Gustave was lost.

So, after a few days in which he was pretty regularly at home, he took to wandering again, to haunting the Beasley farm, to sullen acknowledgments of our greetings.

Laurence, of course, made poems about it; Nan sharpened his pencils, and said they were wonderful.

In those hectic days, I do not think it was remarkable that Billy and I forgot the notes that we made the morning before I was summoned, to be accused of murder by Gloria Vernon. It was Laurence who brought the whole affair back. He wanted some lines he had written on a note-book Billy had given him at the same time he supplied a pencil.

"I did give you that, didn't I?" asked Billy, beginning to look gray, and I am sure I did, too; for I remembered what he had so carefully written out about Gustave and his threats to avenge any one who hurt Jane.

"Yes," agreed Laurence irritably, "and I started a verse in it. And—it's gone! Where is it? I am weary of mysteries. It was a red-covered book, wasn't it, Watts?"

"Where did you put it?" I asked.

"On the window-sill," Laurence answered. "I suppose those officers took it. No, they didn't. I didn't put it there until they left. But some one *did* "—his tone grew triumphant—"for the screen is broken at that corner! Some one saw me writing it, and means to steal it!"

"That Beasley boy is the only one around here who would do that," said Gustave, with the first attempt at humor he'd made for weeks. "Better chase him up, unless it's driven him to suicide."

Laurence successfully damned this little attempt at levity. He responded: "I am not the one in this party who visits the Beasley farm at all hours." And then he found a new slip of paper and began to write.

I went over to the window and found that the screen had been tampered with.

"Now we've done it!" I said to Billy, who had slunk up behind me.

"I was a fool!" he acknowledged.

"Who do you suppose—"

But I couldn't supply the answer to that any more than I could to a hundred other questions that kept continually buzzing within our heads.

"Yes," I agreed, "you were." And of course he was mad; many men call themselves fools, but no man accepts that appellation from any one else without protest.

"Maybe," he said, "but who started listing things, anyway? Didn't you suggest getting things down so that we could remember 'em without counting on our fingers? I tell you, April, I may have been unwise, but you—"

"You'd make a lovely husband!"

"I really do regret losing it," said Laurence. "I am so afraid—"

"Oh, hell!" said Billy, and he went out, slamming the door after him.

I sat down and tried to play canfield. This didn't go well, and Midgette demanded attention.

"Tell my fortune, April," she whimpered. "It'll—it 'll divert me. How can you be so calm after these happenings—Oh, a red ace means love, doesn't it? Followed by a jack—what?"

"You will fall in love with a light-haired gentleman who is ten years your senior. And—" But then I stopped. "Wait a minute," I said, and I redealt.

Now, as I said before, I am a grounded person. I do *not* float around on clouds, and however I came to be an artist I do not know; for I pay my bills, believe in marriage, families, the fact that love can last, and I adore an honest, roomy, two-story home with a real kitchen stove on which you can cook something more nourishing than fudge. I do not believe in ouija boards, nor omens; but—when I turned up the ace of spades, which I read as death, and this was followed by a dark-haired man and a low club, the number of which means a weapon used against some one, and when I saw a murder to come, I was a little rattled. One was quite enough, I thought; we had plenty of suspects, and no clues with any of them.

"I feel so much better," said Midgette after I'd finished the greatest lot of stupid drivel about light-haired men, letters, jealousy, money, and a happy marriage. "You really cheered me up, April, and I think it's cheered you, too."

I smiled and said it had, but—in spite of all my reason, and in spite of the fact that I knew I was acting like a hysterical school-girl—I saw the card that meant death, followed by a card that meant a weapon, and a third that meant murder.

"Midgette," I said, "work your ouija for me. Ask 'What weapon?' "

Probably because we all *felt* the creek continually, and because the horror that had come through it was impressed so deeply in our minds, the little affair on wheels spelled "Water."

"Water!" said Midgette. "How silly!"

"Yes," I answered, with relief, "isn't it?"

But—it wasn't.

CHAPTER XV.

"PUT IT HERE, BOYS."

IF THE EVIDENCE had been less generally spread, one of us would certainly have been hung. But as it was, there were black marks against us all, including the judge, and the chorus of suspects saved the day. A week after the horrible affair things at the bungalow were running about as usual—at least on the surface—and none of us regarded as guilty. Old Nathan's theory was accepted, and the coroner's verdict was "Death caused by accident." But not one of our group really believed this.

A bit of evidence which made Nathan's surmise stronger and generally believed by the town people was the finding of a big case of whisky among low-water growth, well up-stream. What made this evidence weak to me was—finding the Echo puddling around there and trying to sink a bunch of sticks, which he had tied together with a rope, saying as he tried to do this: "Put it here, boys; it'll seem more likely."

I sat in my canoe, watching the affair, and reasoning about it. I decided that in the queer, mirror slant his malady had taken, he echoed not only that which he had heard recently, but also, perhaps, long before; the "long before" brought to the surface of his poor, clouded mind by association of scene. I knew that he always insisted in sitting on the one same chair of our bungalow porch, because he sat in that one chair the first time he came. First action evidently made his pattern, and the scenes which backed it kept it fresh for him.

I was, therefore, absolutely sure that he had seen some one sinking that box, which was well filled with bottles of three star; and I was certain that the words he said had been said by one of the sinkers.

"Hello, Hiram!" I called to him that day.

He looked up at me dully, and stopped speaking aloud, but I saw that his lips still formed the words which were a part of his game.

91

And, after a fleeting regard of me, he again began to try to sink his sticks.

I turned my canoe, headed it toward home, and went to hunt up Billy. I found him on the back porch reading a letter from his aunt, who had heard that he was with us and that there was no chaperon. She had evidently been upset by it and had done her best to pass some of her upset on to her nephew.

"It *is* disgusting," he admitted, looking at the letter he held. I realized that he was probably quoting, and I did not feel any especial warming toward the quoted.

I sat down on the steps before I replied: "You needn't stay." This of course enraged him, since it was the truth and undeniable.

"To leave you here at the mercy of this crowd?" he spluttered. "Why—"

I interrupted with: "You're not responsible." And this proved to be another truth that did not please him.

"You promised you'd consider me seriously after this was cleared up," he said sulkily, as he poked holes in the dirt path at his feet with a short stick; he sat on the lowest step.

"It's not cleared up."

"Why not?"

"I don't know why not. But—you don't believe Nathan's story any more than I do. You know it."

"It might be true. I don't know why I do doubt it."

"I don't know why I doubt it, either," I agreed, "but I do. In fact, I know that isn't the truth!" And after that I told Billy about Beasley's boy. He was interested.

"Let's go back up there," be suggested.

I nodded and stood up, but just at that moment Jane appeared in the doorway, the new Jane, who was a quiet soul with less vivacity and a dull, weary look in her eyes.

"The judge is here," she announced, "asking especially for you, April. He is always babbling about your being a Fra Angelico angel come to life and dressed on Fifth Avenue."

I looked down at my rags and laughed. Jane did too, but Billy did not.

"You always look stunning," he said, with a cool glance toward Jane.

"You do put them on well," Jane offered, in semiapology, and after that we went in. Nan was at the sink—it was her potato-paring week—and she was slashing viciously.

"I don't know why I'm doing this," she remarked, "for there isn't any fire, and won't be. It is Gustave's wood-carrying week, and Laurence has done it every day—"

"Not yesterday or the day before," said Billy, and I let Nan know how I felt about that with a direct glance. Billy is frightfully overworked and imposed upon, and I resented it.

"Well, almost every day," she amended, "and I told him he shouldn't to-day. If Gustave doesn't come home, we'll simply eat raw meat, that's all. I've made a beef loaf, and it will take the large oven. When Gustave appears, perhaps he'll be sorry."

But he wasn't, because he stayed out for dinner. We were the sorry ones!

We found the judge in the living-room, listening to one of Laurence's poems. He looked nervous and ill at ease, and he kept studying the many sheets that Laurence held, with visible apprehension.

"Ah, Miss April," said the judge pompously, as he arose. "And how did you leave the cloisters to-day?"

"Cells," I corrected.

"Old *fool!*" said Billy. I was frightfully afraid he would be heard, so I talked as fast as I could, and was unusually pleasant to the judge. I asked about his wife, and he said she was attending a temperance convention in New York State. Then he began to do some hinting, and he did it well. In recalling it afterward Billy and I could not anchor one thing he had said against Nathan, but—we knew—in some way—all he felt against him.

It made Billy furious. "That old rustic?" asked Billy. "That old rustic, a deep-dyed villain? Oh, nonsense, judge!"

The judge spluttered. "I—I can't explain," he wheezed, "but I—" and then he covered his eyes with his hands and breathed heavily. Billy looked at me and shook his head. I sneered at that doubled-up old man and thought of what whisky, taken as he took it, had done to him, and I pitied his wife; but I hadn't seen her at that time.

After a little time the judge stood up. "Going to stay here?" he asked of Billy. Billy said he was afraid so. "Well," said the judge, "you—you take care of Miss Barry."

"You needn't prompt me to do that," Billy responded.

"If things happen," the judge went on, "I mean any excitement —Nathan getting sick—he has a valvular heart defect, he's going off some day, might go off any day—" he stopped speaking, looked back of him, and then his eyes, which I thought looked crafty, became anxious. "If he gets sick and calls for her, go along. Don't let any one else be suspected."

"I don't think any one else in *this* crowd will be," responded Billy, with unpleasant emphasis. "I hear that suspicion is centering in a different place." The judge turned white, and then, as Nathan's hammering began, sank to a chair. "Water!" he gasped, and Jane hurried off to get it. When he could speak he said, "Don't—don't let her—" and then stopped, his glazed, protruding eyes fixed on me. At that moment Nathan, in his silent way, appeared, seemingly from nowhere.

"Seen yer automobile, jedge," he announced from the doorway, "and thought I'd step around. That there ruff you spoke to me about a while back, I'll come in Monday or Tuesday an' fix her. It's them seams that is leakin'."

"I know you're a busy man, Nathan," said the judge.

"Jest wanted you to know I wasn't goin' to *fergit* yuh," said Nathan, peering over his glasses.

"I—I didn't think you would—" stammered the judge.

"I'll say I'll be in Monday morning," said Nathan, as he withdrew.

The judge stood up, and began to make his ponderous, mid-Victorian adieux. Jane and I followed him to the porch, for we were worried about his attack of gasps, and the unsteady way he moved gave us further anxiety.

We found Nathan had lingered outside, having suddenly decided to mend a rocking chair that had been broken for a month. This he had turned upside down, and he had already driven some tacks in the wavering rung. I was glad to find he had not gone; Nathan always cheered me. There is something wholesome and cleanly constructive about carpentry. I love the smell of wood, especially when, shaved by the plane, it grows yellow, and widely scatters its grained, streaked and freshly odorous curls.

"That cheered me," I said to the judge, "when things were at their worst. Nathan never seemed upset, and his tapping hammer told me that work and people must go on sanely working, whatever happens."

"Quite so," said the judge. "And poor Frank has no one to blame but himself"—Nathan righted the chair with a bang—"he shouldn't have gone poking. I—I warned him. People of that sort are dangerous to deal with—" He drew a long breath, and then suddenly said, "but dangerous people are always discovered, and punished. That is—eventually—"

"Yes," put in Nathan, "they air. That's what I says, jedge. I says, 'Who ever done it—if it wasn't that there bear trap—he'll get his come-uppance.' I says, 'Likely t'other murderer will be fixed, too. Likely the whole thing'll come out!' I says, 'There is some things around here that ain't right,'—I've been a-feelin' that fer these many years—and time *and* agin I says, 'The Lord'll see to it in *His* time, and all will be righted.' "

The judge nodded, and with the assistance of his chauffeur, got into his car. As he disappeared Nathan's hammer tapped vigorously, almost belligerently, certainly with triumphant energy.

I stopped to speak to him, but had to leave him quickly for a pasty-faced young man with two girls drove up in a chummy roadster, and they wanted their tea.

I got the tea, and then reminded Jane with some frigidity that it was her afternoon to serve. I decided I would take my pencil and pad to a spot on the hill, from which one can see a valley, a bit of creek, the bungalow and rolling fields. I thought that sketching would settle me. Of course, Billy tagged along.

The day was divine, and the woods were spicy and cool. Pine trees made the green above us almost black in its deepest shades, and their needles made the path a perilous but fascinating thing to travel. The soft feel under foot—the slip, and the absolute silence that they gave to walking was delightful.

A chipmunk ran across our path, chattering his disapproval of us; deep in the undergrowth a bird sang, and then, afterward, came quiet, all the more glorious from contrast. The smells, the fresh earth and growing-green tang in the breeze, the silence, had its effect on me. I felt let-down, and as if some tight-wound spring within my soul had loosened with a snap.

"Here we are," I said, as we, stepped into a little clearing and began to make our way toward a high rock which was shaded by pine trees. "You can see for miles from that place. I meant to visit it a lot, because my perspective is faulty, and I knew drawing from it would help me, but—I haven't. None of us have done what we expected to here."

"Wish this was a desert island," said Billy. I smiled at him. I have never yet had a man even faintly in love with me who didn't want to be shipwrecked with me, alone, on some uninhabited island. And, I have had other girls tell me that that wish is as much a part of man as his Adam's apple. It always amuses me, because I never met one man, no matter how adoring, who didn't want to go off with the boys occasionally, and sometimes more often.

"You'd have to do the cooking," I said. "I'm tired of it."

"No sandwiches," said Billy, as I settled. I agreed, hard!

"Look here, April—" said Billy, after I had taken two sights and had put in a fence and a barn roof. "Gustave or the judge did it."

"Gustave?" I echoed, as I let my pencil drop and turned to him.

"Yes, Gustave—Gustave has been my bet right along. Nathan heard him say to Jane, 'Don't think that fellow will marry you. Why, in this jay burg they think a model's the perfect synonym for wickedness. He may try to make some other arrangement, but not that.' "

"Pretty crude," I said.

"Yes, but some sense to it, too. You know when people hear that a girl parades around in her birthday suit—"

"Never mind about that," I broke in irritably, "I know how you and the rest of your stodgy set feel, but what makes you think he wasn't just warning her in a friendly way?"

"Well," said Billy, as he lit a cigarette, "he was engaged to her, and that was before Gloria made her entrance. He may have turned to Gloria at first, out of jealousy."

"Hum, I don't know—" I answered doubtfully.

"I only say he *may* have. Then he threatened, you know how many times, to kill any one who hurt her. He must have been worried."

"He was perplexed; we all were. We knew Frank Lethridge was a woman-hater, and that Jane evidently wasn't much attracted, and yet—she would go off with him by the day."

"Do you believe he told her that about hunting the suds?"

"Yes," I answered.

"She can't lie. At least, you know it when she does. Her eyes won't stay on the level. They waver. There is something more I want to talk to you about. If you could ignore paint and remember me, I might tell you," said Billy.

His eyes teased me, and I wanted to be aloof, but—I couldn't. For curiosity and skirts have been mine since the beginning of things. I put up my pencil, laid aside my tablet and moved closer to Billy. He sat, absolutely coolly forgetful of me—or so it seemed then—staring off across the hills.

"Go on Billy," I said, putting my hand on his arm. He turned quickly.

"In the first place, I love you," he said, "and then—"

CHAPTER XVI.

THE GHOST AGAIN

"THEN," HE SAID, his face changing, "I want to protect you. That old beast—trying to flirt by calling you a Fra Angelico angel—saying things that make me want to kill him—"

"*Don't!*" I begged. "Don't ever say that."

"But I will! I *would* if he—if he ever—"

"This whole affair has gotten on your nerves," I said. "You're simply absurd, Billy."

I patted his arm a little, thinking it might calm him, but it didn't. He turned, put his arms around me, drew me close, and so that my head, lying against his shoulder, was just below him. Then he deliberately bent to kiss me, again and again, in spite of my struggles and protests. "I love you," he whispered, his voice roughened, and unsteady. "I love you. I *love* you! And—you love me, April. You do—oh, my *darling!*"

"I hate you," I said loudly, but I might as well have spoken of the weather, for Billy only muttered, "*Sweet*heart!" I was angry, but not only with Billy; I was angry with myself because I found that I really enjoyed having Billy—act that way. And—I had always planned to be a famous artist. Unfortunately, I can not do two things at one time, and so I thought Billy would not be done—at least by me. Before that afternoon I had always been able to decide coldly that Billy P. Watts could not be in my scheme of things; but—with that afternoon, my suffering began. I still realized that it would be Art or Billy, and I still betted on Art, but—it hurt to bet. Billy had made it hurt by acting—that way.

"I hope you are satisfied," I managed to say with some degree of hauteur, as I sat erect and free of his arm.

"Oh, not *half!*" he answered, after a deep, catchily drawn breath.

Then I told him what I thought of him, growing more angry as I heard what I did think of him. It was terrible. "I shall never trust you again," I said, toward the close.

97

"But April," said Billy, in a very subdued, hurt way. "You know, dear, you must know, that you don't hate me. You—you sorta returned the compliment while I was kissing you—once or twice. You sorta—"

I stood up. It was true, but I didn't think Billy would mention my kissing him, even to me. I explained that I was awfully absent-minded, and that if I did I probably hadn't meant to, and—but I got no further, for Billy, who was standing, too, tilted my chin, and laughed down at me.

"Leather goods and William P. Watts don't fit in with your schemes for life, do they?" he asked. I said decidedly not. "And so—" he went on, "you are fighting something that belongs to you quite as much as does your adorable, little turned-up nose, and your little rose-bud mouth—" He stopped speaking and his eyes grew serious. "Dearest, I wish you'd be absent-minded again," he whispered. "Oh, *April—*"

But I began to feel the ache that was to trouble me so much after that, and so I was cruel.

"Really, Billy," I said, "this whole thing bores me. I came up here to sketch, you promised to tell me of your suspicions, and instead—" I shrugged my shoulders. "First," I continued, "you insult a perfectly well-meaning old man, and then—"

"Well-meaning old man?" he shouted. "Well-meaning? If you weren't so absolute sweet and innocent you'd see that whisky-soaked old devil's attitude. I—" Billy's voice failed, he was growing apoplectic. "If he were younger—" he finished, "I'd—I don't know what I *wouldn't* do! As it is—if he fools around here much more I'll fill him up with bird-shot! I'll fix anybody who bothers you. You may not know it, but you *do* belong to me, *understand?*"

With these words he took hold of my shoulders and turned me, until I faced him. For various reasons I avoided his eyes, and —looking past him, into the woods, I saw a face—fairly close to us, this face, and peering through low-grown bushes. For some reason I did not then sense, and do not understand now, I did not cry out or tell Billy what I saw.

Again I said, "You bore me!" and this time sharply and nervously. And then, Billy's hands falling away, I gathered up my pencils and pad and I whispered, "If you say another word about this now, I'll never forgive you!" But—that did not work.

"Don't tell me you champion that old idiot!" shouted Billy. "Don't tell me you don't see through him! I'll tell you, April, Nathan has something on him. I know it!"

"Hush!" I entreated.

"I won't!" Billy sung out. "If he's made an impression on you, enlisted your sympathies, you might as well know that Nathan has the goods on him—"

But he stopped then, for I ran down the path and Billy followed. "The judge is connected with this," he said when he caught up to me, "and he's trying to avert suspicion. He's planting it here, that's why he warns *you* about being caught in the clues. Old Nathan—"

I turned to him, and spoke sharply.

"Billy P. Watts, you are the biggest *fool* that ever lived. When I do marry, I will choose a man with some discretion, and one whom I can respect. Some one heard every word we said—some one I've seen before—I can't think where—"

"What do you mean?" asked Billy.

I told him.

"Back of us up there?" be asked, stupidly.

I nodded.

"Suppose he heard it all?"

"How could he help it?" I replied.

"You shouted, for one thing, that you'd love to fill the judge with bird-shot, and that you longed to decrease the population. You howled threats!"

"Oh, dammit!" said Billy.

I slipped, and he put his hand under my arm.

"Suppose they think you're guilty?" I asked, my heart almost stopping with the thought.

"I wasn't here," answered Billy.

"But suppose," I said, and I don't know what made me, "something *else* happens?"

"Something else? My Heavens, April, aren't you satisfied?"

"Absolutely—" I answered, "but—" and then, very quickly I said: "I know where I saw him."

"Where?"

"Up the creek, the day of the murder or suicide—I passed him. He was sitting just where I wanted to poke—you see, I'd felt the box—and I didn't dare. I had to go on. I went on, you know, saw Gloria and Gustave, and then came back and he had gone."

"Would you know him again?"

"I think so."

"You *know* this was the man?"

I answered very certainly, for I was certain, entirely certain. "Yes," I replied, "it was he."

"Well, I'll be damned!" said Billy.

"If," I said, after some moments that were full of uncomfortable reflection, "Old Nathan is interrupting the judge to keep him quiet, isn't old Nathan probably the guilty one?"

"Just why would a man of the judge's standing bother to shield an old woodsman?" Billy asked. "Be intimidated by him, and—if he were aware of a crime he committed, keep quiet about it? No, Nathan has something on the judge. For reasons best known to himself, probably because of cleverly put threats of the judge's, he is not revealing what he knows; but, when the judge troubles you, and Nathan hears the judge hint against him, why then he takes what he knows up for defense, and reminds the judge that he is there. Isn't that the best solution?"

I nodded.

"Nathan likes and means to protect you. He knows the judge and men like him; for the judge, most intimate friend of this notorious Rudolph Loucks, was, perhaps, in his day, another one—he concealed his little affairs more cleverly, no doubt; but there were probably enough to hang him if they had been unearthed. Nathan was Rudolph Loucks's caretaker. Perhaps he has one of the judge's indiscretions stored up from that time. Perhaps"—Billy paused as he threw down a cigarette and stamped out the fire—"he has a later and more serious offense of the judge's in mind. The judge was here the day that Frank Lethridge was killed or—committed suicide. The judge was warning him 'about investments.' Well, I've investigated. They hadn't one made together. From various reasons I am sure of this."

"Perhaps they were in one name?" I suggested.

"No, I think not," Billy replied. "Frank Lethridge played safe. He had seen too many losses to do otherwise. The judge is a plunger. They say he's lost two sizeable fortunes through reckless buying"—I recalled my doubt at the time he boasted of his successful investments—"just now he's fooling with silver and an oil project—Texas oil. The thing hasn't even been drilled yet.

"Don't tell me that men of those opposite beliefs would go together on anything. I've been sitting in the club a lot in town, listening and pumping. Those two chaps were direct opposites. No one seems to have thought it queer that they would do business together, but—I do, and I don't believe it. And tell me, if you please, why would a customer of the First National Bank go to the Conewango Valley Bank cashier with investments? It seems the judge had a row with Frank Lethridge's bank ten years ago, and walked out with his account, swearing never to return. Likely, isn't it, that he and Frank Lethridge would join forces?

"I asked about Lethridge's affairs. His money was in farm mortgages, water stock, street railways, municipal bonds, good safe and sane little banks; he owned an ice company in Oklahoma, a hotel in Southern Kansas. All of them paid well, but not spectacularly. Now the judge always expects to make heavily, and plays to do so. That means risk. Why, their playing together is rot!"

"Nathan said the judge warned him against whisky," I put in, "because he wanted his hiding-place undisturbed; that that was really it."

"Another lie. It is shipped in here in Hatch Grim's caskets, but it comes out of those and goes into the judge's cellar direct. Hatch Grim owns a piece of wood land out past the Beasley farm. He's cutting it for firewood. This is stored in his cellars down-town. The judge goes in and says: 'Might send us up, some of your pine knots, Grim. My wife likes the open fire.'

"Well, Grim sends it up—in baskets. Pine knots go in 'em, and underneath—something else—well, the judge's chauffeur unloads it. I met him dead drunk the other night. He burbled about firewood. I asked where it was sold, went into Hatch Grim's, slipped him twenty-five, asked him for firewood, said I wanted to *look* at it, and I was shown the cellar. In that romantic spot, backed by coffins of every description, one drinks. I met two worthy gentlemen down there who were so far gone that they couldn't stand. One of them was snoring loudly, lying on what is known in the undertaking world as a 'cooling board,' and the other was gracing a side-opening casket and sobbing about 'death being among us on every hand.'

"The undertaker's assistant mixes the drinks—rather shoves you a bottle—you go sit on a coffin and sling it in. And it was the rottenest stuff! Combination of hair tonic and liquid fire. I fanned my tongue all the way home. But—to get down to the tacks, it *isn't* hauled out of town; it comes right from the undertaker's cellar to the judge's cellar. Maybe Frank Lethridge *thought* there was some buried out here, but why did the judge warn him? And—about what?"

I said I gave it up. It was too baffling.

"The judge comes out past Gus Dirks's farm," went on Billy. "He rides, out there regularly—to get vegetables. Perhaps he does, but why does he pass Gus's place? Gus has the best and cheapest vegetables in this part of the country. Why are the tracks of his motor around the river so often? Why did I find a pole there one morning near that car's wheels? Why do I hear Nathan say: 'Ain't you a worryin' around here a *little mite too often,* jedge?' And then hear the judge reply: '*I intend to fish in this creek!*' Use his best oratorical voice in that simple response, and then—*see* him go white and quail, mutter about getting into town, turn, and *slink* off? Why did Nathan go off chuckling?"

"I give up!" I said.

"I wish you'd come off with me," said Billy, his voice growing tender. "I'm worried; I'll admit I am. *I don't like you to be here!*"

"It is not fair to leave them now," I answered. "Nan is completely engrossed with Laurence, Gustave is half insane, Jane is alone and morbid, Midgette hysterical. I think I should stay and do what little I can; I promised to. We all did, Billy; we made a solemn vow."

"But I wish you could see it differently," Billy added.

We came out of the hill woods and stepped on the level. Jane came running toward us crying. "The ghost on the hillside—" she gasped. "I saw it, and so d-did others. I wish I were dead, I do, I *do!*"

Billy ran ahead to the spot where you could see the far hillside, and here I joined him, after giving a little comfort to Jane—or trying to. "Some one is playing a joke," said Billy; but his color had changed, rather faded. I did not answer, because in times like those my mouth grows dry and speech grows difficult. Together we watched the figure slip into the woods. It slid over the ground, slowly slid over the ground, and then—disappeared into the black of the woods which backed that rolling, peaceful-looking field.

"We mustn't tell Midgette," gasped Jane. "She'd have a fit, and I think she will stick it out if nothing new disturbs her—but this—"

I nodded.

"And she'd take all the furniture with her," went on Jane, after a breath so deep that it was almost a sob: "I know her. And then where would we be? I haven't enough to go back to New York, and besides—I don't want to go—beaten. We told everyone, you know."

I kept my eyes on the field as she talked. And, although there was nothing to see there at that time, it was hard to look away.

"I'm going up there, dear," said Billy, and was off.

"You forgot our vows," said Jane piously after Billy hurried off.

"I wouldn't say much about that," I replied before I reflected. Jane didn't answer. "And," I continued, in a hurry, " 'dear' means nothing when Billy says it. He calls every one that."

"I know," agreed Jane. "I heard him call the girl who brings the milk, dear, the other morning. I was only joking."

I felt myself grow red and then white; I have never been so enraged! And I knew then for a certainty that Billy didn't matter, but I meant to pay him back, and make him just as uncomfortable as I possibly could for that piece of wicked treachery. But, even though his presence and safety were nothing to me, I was glad, a half-hour later, to see him come up the steps of the bungalow porch and to hear his voice.

He told Midgette that there was a caterpillar sitting on her lap; did this just for fun, so I judged that nothing was greatly amiss. Later in the evening he approached me and I conquered my loathing long enough to ask him what he'd found.

"First," he said, "will you please tell me what I've done? Is this great coolness just the natural reaction from that mass of garbage which masqueraded as a dinner, or have I put my good number eleven in it again?"

"I'm sure I don't know what you mean," I replied.

"You know very well," said Billy, "that you're peeved. I don't know what I've done, but it's easy enough to see that I've *done* it."

"Oh, you're mistaken," I answered, as women do when they are really put out. "I'm not a bit annoyed. Perhaps I'm a little tired and would like to be alone."

"You're a spiteful little cat!" said Billy. And then I asked what he'd found on the hillside.

"Was it red paint?" I asked, quoting from the notes that had been stolen.

"No," said Billy, "it was not." His face changed, and he frowned. "Damn it all, April," he went on quickly, "it was blood, and it was warm!"

I nodded. For I supposed that was what he would find. His acknowledging it made me a little sick; made me feel crawly and cold; but, I'd half expected it, even from the material, money-grubbing Billy. I started toward the lights from the living-room window.

"April," called Billy.

"What?" I asked, not turning my head.

"Don't go in—there's going to be a ripping moon."

"She'll have to rip without me," I answered.

"There is something the matter."

Again I said: "I don't know what you mean," and then I went inside. Midgette and Jane were playing slap-jack. They scratched each other's fingers doing it, acted like children, and pretended to be much amused by their idiotic pursuit. They were really giggling at Laurence, who was reading aloud a half-blown poem to Nan. She sat on the edge of a chair, hands clasped, and her face in the grip of a tenth-ward expression, burbling: "Perfect!" or "Too *lovely*. Oh, *Laurence! Divine!*"

I wasn't feeling particularly good-humored, but even I smiled. Then I forgot Laurence and Nan, and asked a perfectly natural question. I wondered why I had never seen the girl who delivered the milk—when they didn't forget to deliver it—and I asked what she looked like.

"Curly hair," said Midgette.

"And the most adorable laugh," put in Jane.

"Cunning little feet," added Midgette.

"And a lisp," Jane said. I got up from the chair in which I'd flung myself and said I thought I'd go to bed. I hate girls who lisp. The idea of this one lisping enraged me.

"Better get up and see her," said Midgette. "She's worth it!"

"Nothing's worth getting up for," I answered. "I've never seen a morning-glory, and never intend to. Even a sunrise never tempted me. As for milkmaids—" I stopped expressively, and then I went upstairs. As I mounted the last steps I heard laughter from below. I suppose they thought I was jealous. Well, of course I wasn't, that was absurd; but I suppose the afternoon and seeing that horrible thing had upset me, for I did wish I was dead!

I reflected a good deal about my funeral as I slipped out of my clothes, and about just how I would look, and I grew so sorry for myself that I almost cried. But after I staged Billy against my death I felt better. I had him turn with utter loathing from his infatuation for the country maid; I saw him kiss my pallid lips; I really heard him say: "*Too late!*" After which I imagined him covering his eyes with his hands. I did get up early the next morning, because I hadn't slept well, and for no other reason.

CHAPTER XVII.

IN THE FOG

"MY HEAVENS!" SAID Billy, pretending to faint as I came down the stairs. I ignored him, because I felt frightfully groggy, irritable, and abused.

"The milk hasn't come," said Jane with a smile. Midgette giggled. I ignored this also. Billy followed me to the living-room, and deliberately opened himself to a rebuff by saying: "Why, I had to get my affections all tangled around the human icehouse!"

"You might as well untangle them," I answered.

He said: "I wish I could!"

And then Nan called us to breakfast. It was a frightful meal, and to see Gustave accept it without a murmur was really sad. The only thing he said was: "Is this coffee or tea?" And when Nan told him, quite sharply, he murmured: "Thank you, I hope I didn't offend; I only wondered." Then I heard a noise at the kitchen door, and decided I wanted a drink, so I followed Billy, who had immediately jumped up to admit the milk. And he did kiss her, and she did lisp; I think she was six or seven.

"Crazy about that youngster," he said, as I passed. "She is a cunning kiddy. April, don't you—" But I didn't hear the rest, for I had slipped out of the door and had hurried down to the landing. Here I got into the Jean-Marie and paddled off into the fog. Tears of mortification and—something else—smarted beneath my eyelids. I hated Jane and Midgette for stringing me as they had, and Billy for making me miserable—for being able to make me miserable.

The fog got into my throat and made me cough, and the great white sheet frightened and awed me. But I could not go back and face that jeering mob, and Billy's jubilant tenderness, for I knew that Jane and Midgette would tell the tale. I suppose I would have enjoyed it if it had happened to any one else; but, as it was, the relief I had felt terrified me and made me want solitude.

I went a little way up-stream and then rested my paddle, and in the middle of the creek, on that cold, white-shrouded morning, I thought of the things a girl does think of, who balances a career and marriage. The two can go together for few people, I am convinced of that. The people who embrace both—the women, I mean—have to be very strong, splendid, and altogether super-women, or they neglect a husband or a career.

And I had wanted to paint; to grow as famous as Forman Stockwell, or Montgomery Post; to have my things on the best covers, and associated with covering the best I had dreamed of a real studio in Paris—not the sort I had had there, in a fifth-rate pension, with a dingy proprietress ever banging at my door to re-mind me of the unpaid rent! I'd wanted a two-storied hall in which I could hang rare tapestries, and the finest bits of color—something like Iris Stocky's place. Oh, I'd dreamed it—every inch—and I was to make it for myself and then stand before it.

But, against that curtain of fog, I saw Billy and life in his town, which is fifty-some miles from New York. I saw the buttons that I would be morally responsible for; the orders to the grocer, which would embrace carrots, fly-paper, onions, and potatoes, and other things, with which one does not associate art. But, somehow, Billy and that small girl overshadowed the other, and I suddenly found myself crying—crying hard, as women who don't cry easily do when things that matter happen.

But suddenly I forgot Billy; I forgot the thing that had troubled and then made me most divinely happy, for through the fog I heard voices, and one of these was Gloria Vernon's.

Perhaps they were not as close as they seemed; I could not tell, for the fog took strange liberties with sounds, carrying them boldly and far in its white folds, or dimming them. Any one who has fished on a river in the early morning will know what I mean; how you may, for a minute, hear the creak of an oar-lock which seems about ten feet away, and then have it fade, and when it again reappears, hear it as it is, fifty or sixty feet up or down-stream. I raised my head and sat tensely held as I heard a mutter in a man's low-pitched voice. Then I heard the swirl of water, and Gloria Vernon's voice.

"If," she said shrilly, "yuh think you'll plant it on *him*, you're left!"

He muttered something which I took to be a warning from her response which was: "My God, *they* aren't up. Come down to brass ones, Zip. I tell you not to fix it on him. Understand?"

"Why not?" This voice was heavy and it carried a sneer.

"Because I say not. And I'm working with yuh. *See?*"

"No," the heavy voice replied. "I *don't*, my girl."

"Well, by God, you'd better!" said Gloria of the erstwhile liquid voice. "Look here, Harry—" Her voice sank; I couldn't get what she said. His had sunk, too, and I could only catch tones. I longed to move closer to them, and didn't dare. And I loved the fog that I had, up to the moment of their voices, feared. "Nathan—" I heard her say shrilly, and then, after a moment; "but he won't be livin' so much more anyway, so why not? I tell you he's about ready to kick off."

I wanted them to remain unaware that some one had been sitting almost on top of them that morning of the heavy mist; that some one had heard not all, but enough to matter greatly. I wanted to get them alive and on the job; this man, whoever he was, and Gloria, or, as he called her, Vera.

"But Sing Sing—" said the man after what I judged to be a protest.

"Why not let it rest?" said the voice I knew to be Gloria Vernon's. "No one's going to kick. Five, six months, and then—"

"Suppose," I heard after moments of muttering, "they find one—"

"It was a trap"—her voice responded—"they can't say—"

Again there were mutters, and then the man forgot caution. "By God, Vera," he said, "*if I thought you was*—"

"You shut up, you—" But I can't go on with her characterization. I am used to free speech; to the careless "God," and the matter of course "damn"; but this was simply vile, that's all. I wondered how in the world she could store all that filth up without its running over and into her every-day talk. It almost made me sick.

After she finished that, and he made some muttered apologies, they whispered some more and only forgot caution once or twice. The sun was rising, and I began to be hysterically afraid that I would be discovered, and that all I had heard would amount to nothing. I knew I ran grave danger, and that, if they found me, getting away would not be easy; but that was not what worried me—my canoe was swift, and I can paddle; I judged that they were in Nathan's punt—what worried me was letting them get wind of being watched.

"Where'd yuh plant 'em?" I heard next. Gloria's voice.

"Up"—voice faded for several words—"until Wednesday. Then"—again a fade of meaning, and only the blurred tone—"and by God, if he don't keep it still he'll land in hell!"

Gloria laughed.

"You say he did last Tuesday?" she asked.

His voice faded. It rose on: "The writing was a woman's, and you see—"

"Don't I?" she responded. "I know that old—my God, he'll jump for it. Can you see"—a lull in which I could not hear —"and after he opens it—" Then they both laughed. After that came her voice again. She almost shouted: "They all deserve it! We'll teach-'em! We who suffer—we—" It slipped into a mumble.

"I warn yuh, Vera," said the man's voice, and then—I heard a sound across the water. My heart absolutely stopped as some one's paddle dipped, and rose to dip again. Someone was coming toward me in a rowboat, for I heard the creak of oarlocks that needed oil.

CHAPTER XVIII.

HANGED IN EFFIGY

NEVER IN MY life have I said a prayer so intensely as I did at that moment; said it in unformed words; said it with a feeling that resolved itself into "please—*please*—" and then I heard another sound. I heard the man mutter: "*Sit tight*—" and another slip of something into water. I had been right; it was a punt, and it was going swiftly.

Soon I heard a whistle, and knew it for Billy's. He came on me as the sun began to make itself felt, and the fog thinned.

"Sweetheart," he whispered, putting his hand on the edge of my canoe, "I've been hunting you everywhere—"

"Billy," I whispered, "I've found something new."

"Yes?"

"Yes. I heard it here in the fog. Gloria Vernon and some man—"

"She's in New York."

"She can't be," I protested; "I heard her, not five minutes ago, Billy, right here—"

"Must have been some one else," he answered. "Must have been April. Old Nathan drove her down and saw her off. Gustave saw her off, too. Went down, happened in at the station, accidentally, I suppose, for Nan, who was there looking for a box of books, saw the send-off."

"She must have come back," I said. "I heard her, Billy—not five minutes ago."

"Did you see them?"

"Certainly not," I answered, and then I told the tale. "He called her Vera," I said as I ended, "but I know it was Gloria Vernon. There are not two voices like hers around; it was coarsened, as if she had forgotten to smooth it, or didn't want to; but it was hers."

Billy frowned intently. "Let's paddle up the creek and see if we can see anything. They won't suspect if we look a little sentimental."

I parked my boat and got into his. "Better?" asked Billy, after I'd settled by him.

"A little," I answered.

"I love you," he announced, "even before breakfast."

"Don't—now—" I begged. I didn't want it to be spoiled, and I was upset—not ready for it. I knew when I really began it would take me a long time, and I also knew that we must follow the clue, which was still warm.

Silently we rowed up-stream. Now, I do not like morning, except when viewed from the bosom of a wide, soft bed; but I will admit that, as a morning, this one was a success. The mystery was weighing upon us both and making us wonder. We grew silent. Then we heard a noise from the side of the creek, a sort of a sawing, creaking noise. Billy took out an oar and began to paddle. He didn't make any more noise than he had before. Whatever it was did not silence as we drew near.

"It's that poor Beasley boy!" I said, with a disappointed half laugh as we drew near.

"Oh, drat it!" said Billy, as he put down his oar and began to row again. "Now isn't that anti-climax?" he asked disgustedly. I agreed that it was.

"What's he doing?" asked Billy idly.

"Don't know," I answered, as I looked in the direction of that pathetic, lank creature. But as I looked I grew rigid, and I felt Billy stiffen, too. The noise we heard came from a rope that was swung over a fork in a heavy tree. The rope, crossing the bark, had rasped the tune that we heard, and it continued as we drew near. And on the end of the rope was that trap, and in it, what was left of the hand that had once belonged to Frank Lethridge.

I felt sick, and I saw Billy moisten his lips. "What the dickens made him do that?" he asked, as he looked at the hand swinging up, up and up, and then dropping down to earth again.

"Don't know," I answered, "but they call him the Echo—"

"Lethridge was *drowned.*"

"Yes, but what makes this? What has started the Echo doing this?"

Billy signified utter bewilderment by a shake of his head, and then he called a greeting to Hiram Beasley. Hiram looked up, and then, as he sometimes did, ran off, full tear, into the densest woods, and out of sight. And as he ran he clutched a rotting piece of human flesh, from which bones were beginning to protrude; close clutched this, and held it pressed tight to his shabby brown coat, the rope trailing behind him. After what might have been minutes or seconds, I don't know which, the last swirling bit of this chapped over a high clump of ferns, and all trace of it was gone.

"Hideous!" I whispered.

"Um—" grunted Billy. Again he moistened his lips, and then he turned the boat and we rowed downstream toward the bungalow. Nathan was out fishing as we returned. I was surprised to see him; I didn't know he ever dallied, for he considered fishing such at that hour.

"Hello!" I called.

"Mornin', Miss *Aprile*," he responded, and then after a curt "Howdy" to Billy, he answered my question.

"Yassem, she's went to New York," he responded. "I druv her down myself, bein' as Beasley's flivver seems to want to set. Ain't hatchin' nothin' that *I* can see; but there she sets!"

"I wanted her to come down to lunch," I heard myself say. "But—I'll ask her another time. Thank you, Nathan; you saved me a trip—"

"Yassem, yer welcome," he responded, and then with a whir, cast off.

"What the dickens?" asked Billy after we were out of sight of Nathan. He knows my Gloria sentiments, and the idea of my asking her to lunch must have seemed queer.

"Well, if Nathan knows anything," I answered, "I don't want him to know I know, although I know he doesn't!"

"Wait till I digest that," said Billy, and then—"I guess you're right. Silence is best, even if the other fellow is O.K., and you know it. You and I will go in partnership, will we? With no one else admitted?"

I nodded.

"Men shake hands on a thing like that," he said; "but my soul, that's the dickens of a way to fix it! All right if you went in business with an insurgent old maid with flat-heeled shoes; but if you didn't—"

"This has been a horrible morning," I said, "and I don't see any use of spoiling its flavor, so go to it, Billy."

And he did.

Nathan interrupted it. He swung alongside of us without as much as a whistle. "Jest thought I'd tell yuh that Gus Dirks is a waterin' his cows," he announced. "He's settin' over there on the fence."

"Oh, *darn* Gus Dirks!" said Billy, after an awful glare toward something that I had thought was a stump. Then, without a word to

Nathan, he rowed on. "Say you love me!" he whispered as we neared the bungalow.

"You know—" I began, and then Gustave stepped out on the landing and howled, and at that moment my sympathy for him dried up.

"Your day to swab boats!" he yelled cheerfully. "Come in and get busy. And your day to wash dishes, April. Where have you been? We've been hunting you everywhere."

"I suppose you have walked miles to find us," I said witheringly. "Some people would simply go anywhere to avoid work!"

"So I notice. Where's the 'Jean-Marie'?"

"Up-stream," I replied, a little foolishly.

"Well," said Gustave, "I'll go get that. Good luck to your swab-bing, Bill. So-long!"

"I'll come in and wipe them, April," said Billy, as he helped me out. And after he'd wiped out one boat and thrown the sponge in the next one he meant to make tidy, he did; and it took us two hours and thirty-nine minutes to wash and wipe the dishes that morning; there seemed to be so many interruptions!

CHAPTER XIX.

ENTER: RICHARD CODMAN

GLORIA VERNON *WAS* away. I wandered up to the Beasley farm late that afternoon, and found Mrs. Beasley sitting on her kitchen steps shelling lima beans. I was surprised at her occupation, as I thought that they were started without wrappers. Hiram helped her.

"He helps me real nice," she said, as I spoke to him. And then, in answer to my question: "Yessum, she went yesterday morning. She's comin' back Friday, I guess. The doctor said we had to have one of them there trained nurses, but it ain't so nice. I'm used to doin' fer him."

I nodded as I sat down beside her on the step—I understood. She had her rut, and Gloria had pushed her from it. Sickness, "doctor's orders," which were holy and unbreakable things to Mrs. Beasley's order of humanity, had made a new soil and a transplanting for a woman who was too old to start new roots. I felt a great deal of sympathy for her.

"I suppose you miss waiting on him," I said, as I picked up a pod and awkwardly tried to unload it. I was surprised, on looking up, at the light I saw in her eyes; it held resentment, and sullen anger.

"Thirty-nine years," she said dully, "I been doin' fer him—doin' all fer him—till now."

"But you have more time to rest, haven't you?" I said, trying to do something to change her feeling.

"Rest?" she said. "I dunno how. I ain't much fer restin'." Stupidly she looked around the barn-yard, and I did, too. Shining milk-pails hung over the pickets of a whitewashed fence — whitewashed by a woman at the order of a man, I'll wager. "Linda, you whitewash that there fence while I'm down in the north field!" I imagine it that way.

Chickens ran to and fro—chickens that had to be fed, cared for, and decently housed; from the direction of the barn I heard thumpings and grunts, and in a field below us the cows grazed — cows that Beasley's woman milked. And their milk Beasley's woman strained, skimmed, churned to butter, got ready for town, carried to the pigs, every day—every day.

I could see it; her patient plodding in one groove until the groove had so worn her to its shape that she could not use another. All the endlessly dull things she had done daily, I saw in her; flat-chested, stooped, her knuckles large and her hands red—the skin of them had that stretched, sodden look that much washing of heavy clothes gives.

She wore a faded brown calico wrapper, which slunk around her heels behind and rose dizzily in front to show worn shoes and thickened ankles. Her hair was knotted up in a tiny tight wad. I had heard that the man who now lay stricken with paralysis had not always been good to her, and that the countryside thought a beating had made the Echo what he was; but—I could understand her wanting to care for him. He was a habit. Like her son, she could move with a pattern before her, but without it—I did not think she could or would go on—at that time I entirely doubted her initiative.

"Any news up this way?" I asked.

"No'm, I guess not. I don't hear so much. I ain't one to stand and jaw. I never had no time to, and now—I reckon it don't come natural."

"Whom did Miss Vernon go to see?"

"Her mother. Her mother was took real sick, and Miss Vernon hadda go quick. She had a telegram."

"I see," I said, but I did not. She had told Laurence that she was an orphan; told him that the morning he drove her up to the Beasley's farm. It had left him maudlinly tender, and only when Gustave frankly eclipsed all his chances did he remember that she was not the only orphan on the map. Nan and I are motherless and fatherless, too.

After a moment more Mrs. Beasley stood up, muttered of going up to "see about him," and told me that she would return. I begged her not to hurry, and not to come down at all if it wasn't convenient. She nodded and disappeared. I heard the stairs' door slap smartly after her, and then the Echo got up and began to poke around among some currant bushes that lined a fence. I watched him carelessly, since I was still struggling with the lima-beans, which were exceedingly loth to leave their nests. Only when Mrs. Beasley returned did I see what he had found.

"It's Jep," she said, going to the spot where Hiram stood, looking down at a dead collie. "It's Jep. Sometimes he roams—I thought he was a doin' it now. He's been gone two, three days."

I got up and went over to stand beside her.

"Was he a good watch-dog?" I asked.

"None better," she answered, in her dull, lifeless way.

"Who's been here lately?" I asked.

"No one but Jedge Harkins; he come up to see my husband Tuesday."

"Was Judge Harkins a friend of your husband's?"

"No'm," she responded. "He says as how he come in to give sympathy. Him and her talked."

"Who?"

"Miss Vernon."

"Were you in the room?" I asked.

"No'm. Miss Vernon she don't 'low me in none to mention. She says I excite him. I don't"—again something akin to hate flared in her eyes—"I done fer him these thirty odd years. I don't guess I hurt him none jest by *lookin'* at him."

"Was he a good husband?" I dared to ask.

"Good husband?" she repeated. I nodded. Then she plaited a bit of her skirt. "He was my man," she answered dully. I got it, and I saw in it a picture of something that will never fade, no matter who prattles of sex equality, or no matter how loudly. I saw in it the great riddle of human endurance, and one which will never be answered and therefore has come to stay. There are millions of women like Beasley's woman—women who belong to and are worked by their men like cattle, and yet—dumbly accept all injustice and hurts and, if they do not give love to their men, give something curiously like it.

I saw lots of it that summer. It stuck out in those farmers, who were of the older type, and their women, who frankly followed at their heels like watch-dogs. That attitude made the supposition of Nathan about the next affair half possible.

"What killed him?" I asked, looking down at Jep.

"Pizen," answered Mrs. Beasley.

"Really?" I asked incredulously.

"I reckon, ma'm. It looks it." She went on after that to assert her reasons, and I believe it. At that moment the Echo came around the side of the house, where he had disappeared a moment before, carrying a pan of water. This he set by the dog, and then bent above him, crooning queer, unpleasantly, unintelligible little sounds.

"They was friends," said Mrs. Beasley.

"Who could have poisoned him?" I asked.

"I dunno," she answered.

"Could he have gotten into some some one left out for rats?"

"It ain't likely. Every one hereabouts keeps chickens, and they don't dast to use pizen thataway. They mostly uses traps." As she spoke she picked up a spade and began to dig a hole near the house. "Hiram," she said; "Hiram, dig—" An idiotic smile lit his face and he began to scrape at the ground with his fingers.

"No," said his mother, "this way—" and she gave him the spade. He put to, and in no time had dug a good grave for poor Jep.

"I didn't know he understood," I said.

"He helps me real nice," she answered proudly, and then—something snapped in her, and her old dull reticence faded. Just for a few moments this faded, but long enough to give me more clues, and more avenues for wonderings.

"He talks," she said. "Leastways," she continued, "I heered two men talking that day the jedge called. I crawled up real careful and put my ear to the keyhole. I heered two men a talkin', but when I go in, he won't talk. He jest lays there, like dead, a tryin' to say somethin' with his eyes. I see it. I see it!

"T'other night I heered a man's voice. I got up, and I crep' up to the door. *She* had it locked. I pounded with my hands till they was sore. She opened up and she was white. 'My man,' I says, 'I heered him.' 'You must a been dreamin', Mrs. Beasley,' she says, real sweet and soft, like she does; 'he was a sleepin' nice till you pounded like this'; but—I pushed by her and went in. And he was layin' there, and he was makin' funny noises and tryin' to speak. He wants fer to tell me somethin' but he can't. *She's put a spell on him.*"

"My dear Mrs. Beasley," I said, as I put my arm around her poor, misshapen shoulders, "that can't be true."

"This here's more of her work," she went on, with a look toward the stiff dog.

"Why don't you get rid of her?" I asked. '

Mrs. Beasley put a rough, red hand over her twitching lips, and then she looked around. "No'm," she said, half hysterically. "No'm. I can't do that. I'm *afeered!*"

"She couldn't hurt you," I said.

"Have yuh saw the pasture lot where Loucks was stabbed?" she asked. I knew what she meant, and I nodded. "He comes here," she went on in a whisper, "*she* ain't afeered of him. He come here in the dead o' night, draped in white. She leaned outa the winder. *They whispered.*"

"When was this?" I asked.

"Two nights ago," she answered, "when the moon was under and the clouds was low."

I leaned forward, gripped her shoulders, and almost shook her. "Go on!" I said sharply. "Go on!"

"It was a sickenin' night, you remember? Low clouds blowed across a dull sky. I had my wash out, fer it was market day, and what with washin' and fixin' the vegetables, I hadn't had no time to do my work afore. The wind it billowed them sheets and made 'em ghostly. Hiram he got one of his spells and set an' moaned like he does. I put that moan on him, some thinks; one time when he was five months growed, I—"

She stopped, looked up to where a man lay half alive, half dead, and then she was silent. I understood, I saw it; a woman heavy and misshapen with a coming life, being driven too far by work—giving up to tears and hysterical truths, then a heavy hand, a punishment, and silence that was broken by her moans.

"Go on," I said again, but this time not sharply.

"Them sheets billowed," she continued. "Jep howled—it was the night afore he left—the air was heavy and sickish like—and Hiram he set a moanin'. Then the real dark come, and it was heavy. I went upstairs carryin' my candle, and she was real nice. She says: 'Come in and see him, Mrs. Beasley.' I done it. He lay there tryin' to say somethin'. I says, 'Can't yuh tell me?' and he shook his head. Moved it mebbe half an inch.

" 'Tell yuh what, Mrs. Beasley?' she asked. I says: 'I dunno, but it's somethin'; then she says: 'Nonsense!' real sharp, and says he was a going to sleep. 'Time to sleep,' she says, lookin' toward the winder. And she told me to go. I set by my winder an hour. I was tired, but somethin', I dunno what, kept me from sleepin'. After a spell I put out the candle, and then after another spell I seen it. It come sliding in, wavin' its arms. Jep didn't bark none after he let out a few. He sniffed and slunk away. I seen it come closer. I wanted to move away, but couldn't—and then—*she* leaned out, and they whispered. I heard 'em once."

"What did you hear?" I asked.

"He said it," she responded. "He says, real loud: 'To die, that men may live!' "

We talked quite a few minutes after that. I tried to cheer her, tried to persuade her to ask the doctor to get her another nurse, and accomplished nothing. All she would say was: "No'm, I'm afeered!" and cover her trembling, yellowed lips with her work-scarred hand. After a few more minutes I stood up, asked her to sell me a few eggs, and with these, started home. I was miserably nervous, and somehow the tears started.

Linda Beasley's tale had made me miserable. I was frightfully un-happy as I reviewed our situation, and pretty tear-stained when I went in the house. I found a strange man there, a friend of Billy's. His name was Richard Codman, a name which meant nothing to me then, inasmuch as I didn't know much about detectives.

"Hello, Miss Barry," he said, as I came in. "I have seen about forty thousand pictures of you in Bill's boudoir, and so I recognize you. I have come out here to board. Hear the scenery is guaranteed to wash, and that you are running a nine-reel thriller. Came out here after quiet, didn't you? Now isn't that a joke?"

I agreed that it was, as I shook hands with the man who very soon came to be Dick with all of us. He was short, fat, comforta-ble-looking, and with eyes that disclaimed all inner, rather, alone thought. What he felt, or imagined, you were sure you knew.

I never met such complete guilelessness. It was cheering. His suit, which was a trifle too assertive in check for good form, added to his every-day, business-man appearance, and I could hardly be-lieve that his was one of those ferreting brains that are able to put nine and seven together and make them total thirteen with absolute logic, if necessary.

"I've been telling Mr. Codman that we're absolute Bohemians," said Midgette, with her most entrancing expression; "but that if he can stand free verse and cold meals, we'll *love* having him." I added my hospitality to hers, and with a little relief. Midgette's resources were something we counted on, and she was beginning to get res-tive. In this new adjunct I saw a piece of human and much-checked flypaper that would hold her, and I was right.

"Now this little lady's been crying," said Richard Codman loudly, "and I want to know why? You don't look like the sort who does it easily—tell me about it!"

I found myself doing it. We all found ourselves confiding. I think his great success lay right here: so much himself, confided so genially, he compelled you to tell him all you knew. I sat down and began. He listened without the surprise that would have made me wonder what I was saying. When he went up-stairs I was pumped dry, and Midgette was angry.

"Why didn't you tell *us* these things?" she asked.

"Why," I responded, "I promised not to tell any one but Billy," and then—only then, I realized what I had done.

CHAPTER XX.

THE TERROR BY NIGHT

AN HOUR AFTER that I came Upon Gustave, who was sitting in a punt.

As I drew near in the Jean-Marie, which is swift, and makes no noise, I saw first a big Jersey, who raised her head to look at me, and then Gustave. His head was in his arms. Something about the angle of it and the sag of his shoulders made your throat ache. A man is a pretty sad thing when everybody disapproves of him; the hard bravado he puts on is the coat he wears to cover shames; but when he openly despises himself, and doesn't bother to hide it—well, that, I think, is the limit. I tried to kick up a little disturbance with the paddle, but I couldn't wake him to my presence. After a moment I called: "Hi, Gustave!"

He raised his head slowly and blinked. I saw that something had been happening inside of him that had not left him happy.

"We have a new boarder," I announced, simply to make talk.

"Who?" he asked. I told him, and I was extremely surprised to see his expression change, and his color fade and then come back in double force.

"He seems nice," I said quickly. "I feel sure you'll like him."

The eyes Gustave turned on me were almost belligerent. "He'd better let me alone," he said sullenly.

"Why, Gustave!" I said.

He looked a little ashamed, and then again anger soared, and he spoke hotly: "Don't think I don't realize I'm shadowed—" he said, a sneer creeping in his voice. "I know I am. I'm not such a damned fool that I can't hear—"

"You're crazy!" I asserted. "What makes you say anything so absolutely mad?"

"What makes you lie? You don't usually—why, only a week ago I saw Jane's dress through the trees, that pink-checked one she wore so much when we first came here; I saw that, and I chased it and—I got a piece. Jane evidently tangled in the underbrush!" He laughed

119

after this, unpleasantly, coldly; looking at me with a "Well-what-can-you-say-to-that?" expression.

"That dress was lost in the wash four weeks ago," I stated. "I know, because Jane had had it only two months and was put out about it. Mrs. Beasley was doing Jane's wash. Jane hadn't the heart to ask her to make good, and so it was a dead loss. Perhaps," I ventured boldly, "your ladylove wore it for a joke?"

Gustave glared at me. "Wrong again," he answered. "She was with me. That's when I'm shadowed." His sneer faded, and he flared. "By God, a man's free!" he said, his voice rough and close to breaking. "I may be—I know I'm a beast, but I'm free! Free—understand?"

"Most certainly you are," I replied, longing with all my soul to paste him an awfully good one.

"Well," he went on, after several, quick-drawn breaths, "then can't—can't you let us alone? It's—it's scaring her. She has some nervous dread of being seen with me. Suppose she thinks Jane might try to even up in some way. She—almost had hysterics the other day when we were together and she heard some one coming. It was Hiram Beasley, I don't know what she thought, but she knows about Jane, and I suppose—"

"Tell her to make herself easy," I said as I made little ripples on the water by flicking the paddle across it, "Jane doesn't want you." And I indulged in something that approached a sneer.

"I suppose not," answered Gustave.

"No one in our crowd is following you," I stated surely. "I know this, Gustave. We are almost invariably together in the evenings, which is the time you are almost always out—"

He looked at me doubtfully.

"Really!" I said. "That is really the truth."

"Then who," he asked; "who is bothering us? I meet Gloria, I can't tell you where, for I promised her I wouldn't, but there's a cabin near here—" He stopped speaking suddenly, as if he regretted having told me anything. "I can't go to see her at the Beasley place," he went on; "you girls make the bungalow impossible, and so—"

"And you feel that you've been shadowed?" I interrupted, to save myself the nausea of listening to anything that concerned the affair.

"*Know* it," he answered. "Why, I've heard it a million times, more times than she has; a stealthy footfall, then a step that snaps a twig; hideous silence until we speak again, then the creeping close and closer—"

"Why don't you face it—him or her?" I asked.

"I can't—it fades. It's too quick for me."

"It frightens Miss Vernon?"

"Almost to death. I—" Gustave's voice faded, and then, after a moment, went on: "Like a drug," he said in a low, shaken voice. "*God,* she's got me!" He met my eyes, tried to answer my gaze squarely, and failed.

I pushed off from his punt, righted my paddle, and spoke of getting on. After I took one stroke, I paused and asked a question. "Since she is in New York, why are you out every evening now?" I asked.

He looked at me and seemed to appeal for mercy. "I can't tell you," he replied, "but it's all right. There's nothing wrong about it. April"—I paddled back to his punt, and he reached out to hold my canoe —"April," he said, his voice strained and anxious, "promise me you won't try to find out. Promise me you won't follow me!"

"Follow you?" I repeated, some scorn in my tone.

"Of course you wouldn't. But—don't tell of this. Please! I beg of you. It means more than life to me—right now."

"I don't know whether I'll promise or not," I answered.

Gustave looked at me, and then suddenly reaching out, clasped my wrist. I felt it begin to sting, then ache frightfully. His face wavered before me, and I heard him say: *"Promise!* God, April, you've got to—got to—promise, or I'll—"

I set my teeth on my lips, and I think I shook my head. I meant to, but he hurt me so frightfully that I don't know quite what I did. Then he dropped my wrist and covered his face with his hands. I sat still. I couldn't have gone on then. He had sprained my wrist a little; Gustave is very strong.

"Let's see it," he whispered after a little time. I held out my hand, and he did just what an emotionally imbalanced man would do after he had hurt a woman and acted the brute; he kissed it.

"Please stop that," I said, "and we'll call it straight," and then I became aware of some one's gaze, and saw Billy; he sat in a canoe not twenty feet away from us.

"Sorry to interrupt," he said coldly and, turning, made off.

"April!" said Gustave, sensing the thing. "What have I done?"

"Never mind," I answered, "I don't want a husband who asks me what I said to the iceman, and why the agent for the vacuum cleaner stayed so long. I don't want a jealous husband." But I knew I lied, for I did seem to want Billy for a husband, and he would be a frightfully jealous one.

Then we talked a little longer, and because of Gustave's almost hysterical contrition, I promised not to mention his going off or the mystery I found it involved.

I did not see Billy until late that night. I think it was a quarter of twelve when he came in. Gustave was out, and the rest of us sat around the fire talking. Billy flung himself into a chair without looking my way, and he replied to Dick Codman's questions with scant courtesy.

Yes, he had been out. Wonderfully clever, Dick's noticing it. No, he hadn't noticed the moon. Where had he been? To a tea dance, and then he had dropped into one of Mrs. Beasley's little studio suppers. Well, where did we suppose he had been? Walking, of course. Wasn't much else to do, and he was sick of doing it. But walking was better than boating. Sometimes things he saw while boating made him sick, absolutely *sick*—this with a look toward me, the only one he gave me that evening—thought he was going back to New York in the morning. Had to, business.

I knew he lied, and I also knew that in some way Dick Codman was aware that my eyes were dangerously full of tears. No one else saw them, I am sure. Dick Codman saw my wrist, too.

"How'd that happen?" he asked in an aside as we bent over a book of phonograph records, hunting one of the Browne Brothers' affairs to fox to; Billy had rented a Pictrola, and we enjoyed it.

"Sprained it a little, I guess," I said, trying to wiggle it. It didn't wiggle easily.

"U-m—" grunted Dick, and then he said: "How'd you do all that?"

I told him I had caught it between the heavy punt and the pier. I tried to do it carelessly, and I think any one else would have been persuaded, but I felt that he was not. He asked whether I'd been out alone, and I said yes, and when, perhaps ten minutes later, he smoothly directed talk into the boating achievements of the crowd, and they described the one and only occasion when I had poled a boat, and had gone out of it with the pole, instead of releasing the affair I knew that I was caught. I felt myself color, and I avoided looking at him for the rest of that evening.

Just before I went up-stairs, I humbled myself, and asked Billy to dance with me. It was hard to do, and the way he turned me down made me hate myself for being humble.

"Don't feel like dancing," he said, and then—danced with Midgette. And at that something grew hard inside of me, and I made up my mind that I was through with him and would stay so. But I didn't! The thing that so closely followed that evening was so big, so terrible, that there was no room left for little spites.

That night, nervous affair that it was, was really awfully funny, funny in spite of Midgette's hysterics and Laurence's tears. And it was the last time that the ridiculous touched us in that bungalow. Thereafter the tragic close-grazed us all, too successfully sobering us. That night, too, revealed the worst attack of "What-was-that's"; even Dick Codman had them.

In the first place Hiram Beasley elected to climb a huge oak-tree that stands back of the bungalow, and here, where no one could reach him, he began to moan; moaning triumphantly, loudly, gruesomely until one's hair stood on end and little chills one-stepped up and down one's spine.

"What was that?" asked Dick Codman after the first moan penetrated our bungalow. I told him. He said: "Judas Priest!" with a great deal of emphasis. I judged the noise did not appeal to him.

When Midgette was half undressed her lamp burned out, and at that moment one of the chairs on the veranda was knocked over. She screamed, and then shrieked: "What was that!" after which she fell to sobbing as Gustave, who had encountered the chair in the dark, came plugging up the stairs. He was airing some first-rate profanity as he came, the chair having greeted him in the shins, and Laurence took occasion to air his ideas about "cursing." As a reward of virtue he drew some choice bits upon himself. Gustave slammed his door until the walls shook, and locked it.

"Happy family, you have here," said Dick Codman, who was standing at the head of the little stairs that led to the room I occupied when we first arrived.

"Oh, charming!" I agreed, and then hurried on to Midgette, who tearfully entreated that I stay with her. "Can't they *stop* that boy?" she asked. "He—he drives me *insane!*"

I said I didn't know how one could, that Billy had been out trying to scare him off the rocks, but that he had only climbed higher.

"He might get in here and kill us all!" she went on cheerfully. "You know he can climb anywhere, and sometimes he—he goes killing things. Es-especially after he sees his mother kill chickens. He killed one of Gus Dirks's prize cows last year, after he'd seen his mother butcher."

"We'll lock the windows," I said.

"I have nails driven in the sashes," she said, "they haven't been opened since the first excitement began. I will probably have tuberculosis, but I'd rather die of that than be murdered!"

"All right," I said. "Crawl in." She did.

"Why don't you leave the lamp going?" asked Jane. She had said she wasn't a bit nervous.

"Make you frightfully head-achy tomorrow," said Nan, who at that moment appeared in the door, lugging her cot after her.

"I'd rather have a headache than sleep in the dark," said Jane. I was on her side, although as it turned out, it wouldn't have been sleeping, but staying awake in the dark.

"Refuse to sleep alone," said Nan, "and when April leaves that end of the house I get nervous. I hope you won't snore tonight, Midgette. If you lie on your side don't you think—"

"Never snored in my life!" broke in Midgette hotly, and after a little disagreement, woman retrenchments and soft smoothings, came good nights, and we settled. Midgette was soon sleeping audibly, Nan's eyelids drooped, and she slept. I heard Jane cry a little, and then her sniffs ceased, and I judged she was slipping off. Then I heard the clock in the living-room boom one.

I thought of the afternoon, of Gustave, and then of Billy, and I reviewed, as one does, the whole affair: what I shouldn't have done, what I should have done, how disappointed I was in Billy and—how I cared. Then I heard the clock down-stairs strike two. The Beasley boy's moans were now intermittent, and they were softened by a night wind that had sprung up from somewhere to say that rain was coming.

I looked at the lamp and let the wavering flame hypnotize me, and I felt myself slipping softly into the dream half of life; slipping, slipping; I was on the river, Billy rowed up in a punt that was painted in green and blue stripes. He held up Frank Lethridge's hand and began to slash it with a long, sharp knife; I saw the blood spurt, and I awoke, horror-filled, shaking, wet with nervous sweat, as you do after a nightmare. Billy's terrible grin was still with me, and I shook myself, trying to wake fully and to relegate that dream to the bin of absurdities.

But—somehow, I could not get my balance. I thought that something more than that dream had startled me from sleep. I was aware, with that queer subconscious knowing which follows certain people even into sleep, that some strange noise had been that should not have been.

I found myself straining every nerve to listen; lying tense, with heavy, sleep-dimmed eyes so firmly fixed on the door that they saw, lurking in the shadows, things that weren't.

Then I became aware that the lamp was dimming and going low. I sat up, breathing fast, and hunted for matches. I found them, safety-matches, and no box to strike them on. Then I remembered that Midgette had taken the box out to the hall to light up the lantern that hung there. I supposed she'd left them on the sill of a high window. Shaking, I put a foot out of bed. It seemed imperative that I reach the hall, call the men, and get lights—everywhere!

Suddenly the light went out, and I really heard the noise, a scratching and a queer wailing—from outside the first burst of rain, and again the loud moans of the Beasley boy, who was still perched high, and evidently vocally renewed. The noise was in the hall, coming closer to our room, that scratching noise. Midgette awoke to scream—scream loudly and get out her "What *was* that! Oh, girls, what *was* that?"

I heard Jane's quick breathing, a door down the passage open, then the rattle of a tin candlestick dropped from some one's hand; a noise like a thunder-clap from Laurence's room, then a moment's deadly silence, after which came his moans.

Gustave's voice rose. I caught "What the h—" then I heard Dick Codman's reassuringly calm voice saying: "Put out the lamp," and then—it broke loose: it, whatever it was, tore up and down the passage, howling, hissing, wailing; I never heard so much noise. The pitch black of the night, the beating of the swishing rain, and the moans of the Beasley boy helped to terrify us. Midgette began her mixture of sobs and laughter, and then Nan screamed for Laurence—which, even through terror, fanned my sense of the ridiculous. Then there was a lull, and some one stepped in our door.

"Want a light?" asked Dick Codman.

I laughed hysterically; Jane said: "Oh, *please, please!*" and Midgette went on crying. He struck a match, lit a candle, and went out, avoiding any glance in our several directions.

We got up, bundled up in our kimonos, or at least in what we thought were they at the time; it turned out that I had draped myself in a bath-towel, Midgette had put on a garden hat—it did look silly, topping her costume, which consisted of pink pajamas and bare feet—Nan, who is a perfect young telegraph-pole, had slid into my negligee, which about reached her knees, and Jane alone had donned the proper belongings properly.

Thus clad, we hurried down-stairs. Dick Codman was bending over the biggest cat I had ever seen, what had apparently been having a fit. It had frothed at the mouth, and Laurence, who had not recovered from his shakes, suggested that it had been drinking.

"Some one has fed the poor animal beer!" he said. "See it on the whiskers? No doubt Gustave left some out. Perfectly, logical; the way it tore around proves that it was drunk. I am *entirely* unnerved! I must say, I think it was *very* careless of you, Gustave!"

"What was that frightful thump?" asked Jane.

Laurence answered with dignity, and was enraged when every one laughed. "It was I," he explained. "I woke suddenly, hearing this horrible noise, and tried to leap from bed. Unfortunately, I had got mixed and leaped into the wall, instead of on the floor. The shock was *frightful!*"

Dick Codman joined our howls. The walls are sealed in that end of the house, and it was no wonder that it had made the noise it did. Nan, of course, glared at us all and began to mutter little pities over a huge bump on Laurence's forehead. After that Dick said he sympathized, and grew unnaturally solemn, until he caught a glimpse of Midgette, and then again he frankly gave way.

"Wouldn't have missed it for a fortune!" he admitted. "You people are never bored, anyway, are you?" Then he bent above the dead cat and said: "Well, what do you suppose—" and I told him what I knew of the Beasley boy, and at that very moment we heard him outside.

Gustave let him in. He was making unintelligible noises, and laughing; laughing as an idiot would, aimlessly. He fastened his hands on Dick's arms, shaking him to and fro, pounding him, and then—he stood back, only to lean over and kiss his hand.

And then—"The Echo" spoke, and what he said made Gustave turn white, Jane's lips tremble, and the rest of us wonder. What he said was "*Gloria!*"

CHAPTER XXI.

THE FACE IN THE WATER

NO ONE WENT to bed that night, or the following night. Just as we were halfway calm, and after some one had persuaded the Beasley boy out of the tree, and started him off, with a repetition of "Home—home—" and a shove down the road, something else occurred.

"Now," he said, "we can all turn in and get some rest—no cause to be alarmed, you know."

We all agreed that there wasn't, but—all of us had a tendency to look behind us into the shadows, and—to want the lights high. Gustave, who always rose to situations, lit our candles for us, even joked a little, and Laurence said that he hadn't really been upset at all. Then he told Nan that he would protect and care for her, and she bleated out a "Laurence, *you're so cheering!*" and then—it came. A noise of something dropping on the third floor.

Dick went up, five or six steps at a time; Billy and Gustave following. Laurence stayed down with us, and joined our cowering chorus. What they found was a wall torn open, and cupboard heretofore unknown, disclosed. A window that was almost in a pine-tree was open, and into this they thought the intruder had jumped.

There was plenty of stirring around after that.

Gustave, unarmed and alone, went off to find Nathan, whose presence it was thought would prove a help. But he did not come over, for he was in the grip of a bad case of indigestion; so bad it was that he had summoned a physician, who was somewhat anxiously bending above him.

"Bad heart," he said in aside to Gustave, and when I heard it I felt a little mean about what I had thought of the judge for saying the same thing. But—the following day, when I heard that the judge had been seen motoring past the Dirks's place the night before—again I questioned, questioned with a horror and cold loathing behind my suspicions, a shrinking and a fear within my heart.

Billy did not go back to New York that morning. Dick Codman dissuaded him. I heard them talking as I set the table for our breakfast, which was a jolly affair because of every one's nervous, easily started laughter.

"You quitter!" I heard Dick Codman say. Then Billy's sullen "I haven't told you why I wanted to get out—"

"Shucks!" said Dick Codman. There was a good deal of scorn in that remark. And Billy stayed.

That day, until six forty-five, was a fairly calm affair. It was one of those summer days that are weary, and hold in them a hint of fall. The rain of the night before had brought down yellowed leaves, and these had pasted themselves to the landing and porch floor, and in the stream were more being whirled away. The downpour, which had been more steady than ferocious, had colored the creek with the tone of its clay banks, and mud oozed up through the boards where the dock was moored to land. As is often the case, when the rain has not quite decided to stay at home for good, the air was heavy still.

At six o'clock I joined Dick Codman on the landing. He was sitting on a wide seat of the biggest punt, evidently quite absorbed in watching water-bugs. "Come on out and talk to me," he invited. I joined him, but for the most part we were quiet. The night had left every one tired. I began to feel peaceful and sort of loose-souled, as if my conscience had run down like a watch. Nothing troubled me; I didn't think; I only watched water-bugs zipping across the surface of the creek, making their sharp angles, jerking this way and that so quickly that one thought of lightning.

The shadows on the water, which looked green and slimy, the heaviness of the air, and the quiet, all combined to lull. Dick suggested going out in our motor-boat.

"Oh, no," I protested, "it chugs and smells and invariably stops where you have the very dickens of a time fixing it!"

At that moment I heard a motorful of people come clattering up on the porch, and my decision veered. It was Midgette's week to be waitress, and I'd done it all afternoon since she had gone off to sleep.

"Your turn," I called to Nan, "I'm going out boating."

Dick added a "Come on!" to Billy, who had just appeared in the boat-house door. Billy hesitated, and then nodded. He was pretty well covered with mud, and he looked tired. I was sorry for him, even while my rage soared against him. He ignored me, as he had ever since he had seen Gustave kissing my hand.

"Hot," he said as he mopped his forehead.

"Awful. Been walking?" This from Dick.

"Yes. I tramped over the land near Nathan's place, that spot where the Beasley boy hangs out so much, where we saw him string up Frank Lethridge's hand.

"Probably saw Nathan fixing up a blind for his camera or hanging a rope to work his affair with. Snaps 'em that way sometimes. Quite a mechanic, you know. I thought at first he'd seen some one stringing up Frank, but now I realize that he only echoed something harmless—"

"U-m—" grunted Dick.

Then Billy went on expanding; told what he knew; explained what he thought, and—it sounded logical. We had put off by that time, and were headed down-stream, the down-stream route being a better one for motor-boating. The thing pulled badly, and was hard to steer. I had to give it up, since it took two hands to hold true, and one of mine was not in very good working order.

"What the Sam Hill is the matter with it?" asked Dick Codman.

"Weeds around the propeller, I guess," said Billy as he gave the wheel an immense jerk, and so brought us back to straight going. "Sometimes they tangle"—he talked in jerks; I could see it was beginning to be more than difficult—"around the—propeller. Well stop down here, find—out."

I smiled knowingly. "Told you so," I said. "We always do stop, crawl out, and get under."

"All right, Mrs. Kill-joy," answered Dick. And then: "Why don't you pull up by the dock the kids built by the bridge?"

"I will," answered Billy. "Darn the thing! I don't see what the dickens is wrong. Well—look at that!"

We looked. Couldn't help it. What he referred to was the constant pull to the right that the boat insisted on giving. "Something big around the propeller," he went on. "Wonder whether that Beasley boy's been fooling with it—" Just then I saw Dick Codman turn white. He had been leaning over the edge of the boat, where now and again I saw something black come up through the water and prick through the ripples our boat's going made.

"You know," he said, turning to Billy, "I think we'd better start Miss April home before we begin repairing this. It may take a long time. Foot-path by the creek, isn't there?"

"Half-way up," answered Billy, "though here's some low land that she couldn't walk to-day—probably under water. She could take the road"—he stopped speaking for a minute since the boat demanded all his attention, —"but," he continued, "this won't take us—long. Darn this thing—I'd *like* to know—here, take the wheel, Codman—"

Dick did, and Billy leaned over the side of the boat, grappling near the propeller.

"Got it," he said, tugging hard, "but, my gosh, it sticks!" and then—he brought *it* up. It was hair—long, dusky-black hair—which curled around Billy's fingers and clung to his hand.

"My God!" gasped Billy.

The boat swerved, and then jerked back into its course. I saw Dick Codman set his chin, and Billy's hand begin to shake. He tried to get rid of the hair, but it clung perniciously. He didn't speak, but I saw his color fade. I felt my lips grow stiff, and those particularly sensitive muscles around the mouth begin to twitch. It seemed as if he would never reach the landing. "April," said Billy as he ran alongside the roughly built pier, "do you want to stay? Don't you think—you'd better leave us—to find—what's wrong?"

"No," I answered, "I'll stay." Dick helped me to step out and tied the boat.

Together they began to pull "it" out of the water.

I looked at the boat and then I looked at Billy. His face stands out as a more horrible thing than that tragedy on which I had gazed. His horrified eyes, his fading color and his futile trying to moisten dried lips, will ever remain for me as the picture of that day.

What he saw was Gloria Vernon; Gloria Vernon, tied and bound, and gagged; Gloria Vernon, with half of her face scraped raw from rubbing against the bottom of a boat. The first layer of skin was gone, leaving little pricks of scarlet; and the water, or horror, had turned her face the green, gray-white that had fixed itself upon her to stay—with death.

Her eyes protruded, and one lid had been torn away—I looked at this, and then quickly turned my gaze on the men. "I won't help by fainting," I thought. "I must not—*must not*—"

The men were struggling to loosen her. Strips of cloth wound around her, were then tacked again the boat; the cloth that gagged her ran back of her neck, crossed, and was taken around to hold her face close against the water-slimed surface of the Lily.

"Pretty well done," said Dick Codman.

"How—" began Billy, and could not go on.

"God knows," Dick answered as he steadied the body while it slipped to the dock. I looked away again. My gaze rested on one of the strips of cloth which had bound her. Dully, I realized it meant something. Jane sprang up in my mind, and then I knew. The pieces, the strips used to bind her, had been torn from Jane's lost frock.

"The Echo?" asked Billy, unsteadily.

"No," answered Dick.

"He's strong as a horse," said Billy, "and after last night—" Again he couldn't finish.

"No," Dick said again. Then he pocketed one of the strips, voiced some directions, and the rigid body of that once beautiful girl was lowered in the boat, now righted and ready to go on.

"The boat wasn't out to-day," said Billy, as we pushed off.

"No," Dick answered. Then he asked how I felt. I think I said: "Very well, thank you," but I am not quite sure. Things surged, rose, and fell around me; the pound of my heart made hearing difficult. I remember going up, seeing some small boys in swimming. So strange how little things fasten. I did not know at the time, that we had seen a soul as we went by, but afterward, all tangled in the memory of sunlight, green-oily shadows of the willow-shaded creek edges, the hot, still air, and the muddy water, were voices—the high, shrill voices of America's youth, saying: "Fellers! There's a lady in that there boat—" and with them, I saw the lithe, small bodies seeking the shelter of the creek.

I think Billy sat by me, I know he did—I seem to feel his arm around me. Dick Codman, or somebody, said I was a sport. I said: "Not at all," quite as one would say "Don't mention it," or "Pray, don't bother."

The day, the hour, stands out indelibly; the yellowed leaves which the rain had brought down, swirling on the faster currents of the creek; water-bugs shooting here and there making their cubist patterns on the still surfaces; green fields that lined the creek, so buoyant, so freshly, cheerfully alive after the long, slow rain; two cows drinking, and—*in the bottom of the boat*—I did not look, but I saw, saw *everything,* in the faces of those two men.

"They said she was in New York," said Billy.

"Who?" Dick Codman asked.

"Every one. She—did start. She was seen starting."

"When?" Dick asked. They went on talking. I heard them dully. I wondered whether their voices bothered Gloria. I looked down at her, and then hid my face. And then I felt a bump, and knew that we had hit the landing. "In here—" said Dick. I was helped out. I saw them take the body in the boat-house.

"And now," said Dick, "the telephone, and then—the deluge—"

CHAPTER XXII.

THE TRIAL

I CANNOT DESCRIBE the week that followed Gloria Vernon's murder. It was too horrible. With the exception of Gustave, we were all badly shaken. He was only dull, heavily wondering, seemingly half awake, looking as if he had been suddenly shocked from a long, troubled sleep. One could see in his eyes the memories of nightmares, his surprise that they had been—that he had let them be.

A strange development that somewhat shook us out of our morbid introspection and into alert questioning was the suspicion that fastened on the judge. A detective from Philadelphia put him in prominence, and seemed to take pleasure in doing it. The judge's nature, which combines choleric explosion, and over-pompous dignity, led certain people to enjoy belittling him. He had always shown a contempt for the mob, and the mob had honestly enjoyed it. But now, with a breath of suspicion, the mob plainly revealed another American characteristic, that entire and sudden shift of alliance, that veering to the extreme other side. I saw it in faces and I heard it in the snickers that followed the judge wherever he went.

Therefore, when the court opened, a month later, Gustave appeared under a heavy cloud, the judge was arraigned openly, and lawyers grew loud—or soft—as they pleaded for their victims.

The things that came out were extraordinary, but told nothing. They were like bits of a picture puzzle, lying separated on a table; each one had some sort of a picture scrap on it, but each one, alone, meant nothing.

"You were aware that the deceased was not in New York?" This from Gustave's lawyer to the judge.

"I knew that she was not," he replied, after a spluttering cough and an anxious look toward Nathan, who, imperturbable, and with as little expression as a stone wall, sat well to the front of the courtroom.

"How did you know?"

"I saw her."

"Where?" asked Gustave's lawyer, a Mr. Beagle by name.

"In the cabin," answered the judge.

"What cabin?"

"A cabin that Rudolph Loucks allowed my younger brother to put up on some of his wooded land. It lies past the pine woods and a rough piece of rocky land on the hill behind the Loucks house."

"Why were you there?"

"I often walked there. I go there because my brother sometimes lived there—association, sentiment—" He broke off and coughed so hard that his neck grew red.

"Why was she there?"

"She was going to meet some one," answered the judge silkily. Gustave turned white, his lawyer frowned, and for a moment testimony was stopped.

"Is your brother dead?"

"No."

"Where does he live?"

"New York."

"Occupation?"

"Artist."

"Does he ever come here?"

"Rarely," replied the judge.

"Are you on good terms? Is your relation in every way amicable?"

"Entirely," responded the judge. "He is much my junior. I have for him that affection which, ah, might be called paternal, as it were. I, ah, was, ah—his guardian, his adviser and guide—until he left here."

"When?" asked the lawyer. The judge named a date which I do not recall. It was several years gone.

The lawyer then asked Mrs. Harkins to take the stand. She was in the back of the court-room. Necks craned around, whispers rose, dresses rustled as she made her way forward, and as she did I began to understand why the judge drank, and to pity him. I imagined that any one who disagreed with her would have to tiptoe about doing it. She was one of those awful women who are always conducting vice crusades, and positively enjoy rattling off statistics about dance halls, illegitimate children, underpaid factory hands, and child labor in the South. I'd rather meet a lion than one of that type any day.

After she took the stand she surveyed the court, which withered. Then she was requested to narrate something—anything about the judge's relation with his brother, and whether it was likely he would kite off into the woods for sentiment. Of course these questions were veiled, but their substance was that.

"A most impractical young man!" she said, after which she clamped her hammer-jaw shut, and gave a quick, backward jerk to her head. When she let her voice out again she informed us that Joseph Harkins was a person of little refinement, and that what she had endured while he lived with them was unthinkable. He was an artist and his work had made dirt and disorder. He was fond of low company, spending much time with Nathan Greenleaf at his cabin. He was constantly with Nathan Greenleaf's nephew. Once in a while he took her husband off, but—another firm wag of her head—not often. When he left she had to admit she was relieved. He had been in the gas office; Rudolph Loucks, because of his friendship with the judge, had been good about giving him a position, but he had given it up.

Then she rambled on a little while longer, and then, unwillingly, retired. Questions came after that about when the judge's brother, Joseph Harkins, had left Rudolph Loucks's employ. It seemed he had left after Rudolph's death. There was a titter around the court at this.

Where was Nathan's nephew? was the next question.

Nathan responded, giving an address, which he said was near Canal Street. He had been there, and described it, and the fact that he had wandered around lower New York was proved by his evident knowledge of landmarks.

"Was your nephew here the night that Rudolph Loucks was stabbed?"

"Shot," corrected some one from the back of the room.

"Shot," the lawyer said, some irritation appearing on his face. "Was he here?"

"Yes, sir; he went for the doctor. I was took with pleurisy. I had it bad."

"He was with you?"

"Yes, sir. Doc Smith'll tell you so," answered Nathan. "Ask him!"

Evidently that avenue did not lead where the representative of the law would have it, and he veered off.

The judge's lawyer, whose calm achieved remarkable results, succeeded in tangling Gustave in a maze of questions, none of which seemed vital as he put them separately. Gustave knew she was not in New York; he had met her regularly; she told him she pretended that she was in New York to avoid the unwelcome attentions of a bothersome suitor, a man whose jealousy had alarmed her; this man was to be in town for only a short space, until Friday, she thought, when she would return to Mrs. Beasley's. Gustave did not know his name, nor had any one seen a stranger. Gloria lived at the cabin during that time.

But she had gone to New York? Yes, she had started. Who saw her start? In here came a medley of testimony, some of it given with such nervous eagerness that it was amusing.

It was found that Gloria had gone to New York; had arrived there; but the following day she had been back. Connections were bad, a train could not have brought her so quickly; it was thought some one motored her back.

Had she friends?

Gustave was cited as the only one generally known.

How had Gustave come into possession of the strip of pink-checked gingham which had done so much to harm his chances of being proved innocent?

Gustave did not know. But—people were around there who had no business there. Some one had crept in the night that a cat had had a fit all over the place. This was described.

Why had the judge written the note to Gloria Vernon that had turned suspicion upon him? Why had he written: "Unless you leave quickly something will happen to you!" The judge answered, because Miss Vernon had taken an intense, almost insane dislike to Miss April Barry, and meant to do her harm if possible. He was trying to protect her, he asserted. How did the judge know of this dislike?

The judge hemmed and hawed, and then he said that he "had been up to see the Beasley man, who was sick—the fellow who farms—out past Greyson's hill; they had been talking—"

"Who is 'they'?" asked Gustave's lawyer.

The judge spluttered.

"Miss Vernon and myself," he shouted. No one believed him.

"Why not 'we'?" asked the lawyer.

"I erred; I refer to Mrs. Beasley, and Miss Vernon," wheezed the judge.

Mrs. Beasley then testified she had never been in the room with Miss Vernon while the judge called. "Yes, sir, he come often," she answered in reply to a question. "I don't recollect that him and my husband ever spoke afore. He says he done it fer sympathy."

"Beautiful thing, sympathy!" said Gustave's lawyer dryly. There was a ripple of mirth.

"Why," went on Mr. Beagle, who spoke nervously, and in his way affected his listeners quite as much as the heavy and more restrained tones of the judge's lawyer —"why did you buy strychnin from Jason Humphrie's drug-store the night before the Beasley's dog was poisoned?"

The judge did not answer promptly; finally he said: "Rats"—his voice weak and close to failing.

"Where did you put it?"

"In—in the cellar."

Mrs. Harkins, called upon to testify, was asked: "Does the judge go down cellar often?"

"*Very*," she replied. There was a positive hurricane of nervously pitched laughter. "Silence!" boomed the judge of the district. Then Gustave's lawyer suggested that perhaps the judge went down to drink something himself—something that was not poison—for *rats*. He paused before his reason for the material that the judge had bought. And then he went on, speaking more quietly than was his wont. The Beasley dog, it seemed, had been poisoned with strychnin.

There was counter-question about this; couldn't the dog, in wandering, have come across some of the poison left out in the judge's yard? Why didn't his own dog come across it, too?" asked Mr. Beagle. This seemed unanswerable. "No," he went on. "The judge was there that evening, and that evening the dog was killed; killed for some reason—killed so that some one could come and go to the Beasley house without being troubled—so that some one could ruthlessly murder a girl—a girl who had given her life to soothing the sick and—" a great deal more of the same, and then the court adjourned.

I walked home between Billy and Dick Codman. The rest, with the exception of Gustave, trailed behind. Gustave was boarding at the jail. He had actually been sport enough to joke with us about it as we said good-by to him that day. "The beds aren't much," he said to me, "but the food is better than I'm used to." And then, the warden drawing near with a huge key and an expression that meant "go," we withdrew.

Jane had not spoken to Gustave, but she had gone with us, and somehow I know that both of them really saw no one else. I wondered whether, as the physical appeal of Gloria was dead, his madness was dying. I knew that he had been ashamed of it, and that usually argues a short-lived growth.

No man who has to apologize to his own soul after every kiss, goes on kissing forever.

I am quite sure that Gustave's stay in that bleak, little cell did not harm him. Perhaps he saw some things that had happened, as they were. Certainly he was most healthily humble, and the very fact that he did not speak to Jane at all, and avoided her eyes, made me certain that his heart was calling to her continually, and that he saw no one else.

"I wonder how it will end?" I asked, as we trudged home that day. The dust was heavy, and the growth at the roadside was powdered thickly with it. "Gustave," I said, "mustn't be convicted. He didn't—I *know* he didn't!"

Dick Codman grunted a reflective "Um—" and I felt the irritation which arises from being tied and unable to help some one who needs it. "I can't see," I thought, "why Billy puts so much faith in him," for at that time mine had entirely evaporated.

"He's going to fix it up, April," said Billy, and then: "I wish we'd motored; you're tired."

"He isn't guilty?" I asked sharply, turning to Dick.

"Oh, no," said Dick easily,

"Then why," I demanded; "why can't you do something?"

"Maybe I will, next week," he answered. "We'll see. We'll see."

"The judge?" I asked.

"No—don't think it's the judge."

"Can't you tell me what you think?" I asked.

"No," he replied. "No, I couldn't do that. Thank Heaven, we're nearly home—nearly home—" suddenly he stopped, looked down the road, and took out a pistol. He took aim, fired carefully, and then told Midgette to be quiet; that she made him nervous.

"Oh, but"—she said between long gasps —"what—you make *me* nervous, Dick!"

He took her hand, pulled it through his arm, and said: "Come on, we'll go down and see what I bagged."

He had hit a mirror; the mirror frame was gone and could not be found, but fragments of the mirror lay on the ground, shining brightly.

"Well, well," said Dick; "guess I hit some of Nathan's bird photograph scenery. Too bad—" and at that moment Nathan appeared. I thought he seemed disturbed, but when Dick explained that he would make good, and that he was sorry, Nathan brightened.

I didn't understand it—Dick's having done that, but I didn't give the matter much thought. Nathan said he could easily get another mirror. He explained that he used it at night, back of a lantern, for moth catching. I went on, helped Nan get dinner, and forgot it. I even remember I complained about Dick's slowness, and his having done "nothing at all; positively *nothing*, Nan!" I was stupid.

CHAPTER XXIII.

THE MAN WHO SAW AN ANGEL

BILLY SENT FOR his motor, and it arrived in time to help us to and from town. We spent much time there, as the case continued, growing more exciting, more involved with each day's testimony.

All sorts of things were said against the judge; all sorts against Gustave. The judge's trying to warn people against old Nathan was held against him as a serious charge, and his acceptance of this made another black mark to his discredit.

"Look at that old woodsman," said Gustave's lawyer with something that approached a sneer; "doesn't he *look* like a murderer? Do faces tell us anything, friends? Look at his face!"

"If I could tell you," blatted out the judge, and then, with a change of color, shrunk back in his chair, shaking as if he had the palsy.

"Do tell us!" said Mr. Beagle. But the judge had an attack of "indigestion" which ended up that matter for the moment. However, the feeling that he had tried to involve old Nathan Greenleaf in the affair made many and bitter murmurs against him.

It was Saturday that Gus Dirks appeared. I shall never forget it. His entrance was dramatic from its very awkwardness; he wore his Sunday clothes, in which he was not at ease, and his collar, a high, stiff, celluloid affair, almost eclipsed his chin, which was of the sinking variety. His stiff-soled shoes made him clatter as he made his way up the narrow aisle—an aisle which had grown more slender each day as chairs were brought in to accommodate the growing crowds.

Outside, the autumn was making her coming felt; locusts shrilled loudly to fade off into nothing; bees hummed; the air was loaded with the drone of insects. It made one sleepy. I remember that my head bobbed from side to side, and that once I almost slipped off.

It was not from boredom that I longed to sleep, but from neglect of sleep. At night I could not seem to find the land of dreams; instead, I saw the boat—the pink-gingham strips lying in tangled heaps on the roughly built dock, and the green-white pallor of Gloria Vernon's face.

"You're tired," said Billy, as Gus Dirks made speech possible by his going up to the witness stand. "You poor child!" I slipped my hand in his. We had long since "made up," and when you do, you know what scraps are for.

"Not very," I answered, as I imperfectly subdued a yawn, and then the judge of the district, whose name was Llewellyn, rapped for silence, and we all looked at the human carrot.

"My name's Gus Dirks," he announced, his voice shaking a trifle from nervousness. "I live a piece away up the crick. Maybe you've saw my truck farm up thataways. I'm going to tell what I seen of these here goings on, and it is fer that reason that I have appeared in this here court to-day." He stopped, and you could hear people rustle a little as they leaned forward. Every one was listening so hard that you could hear them; the silence beat and was broken only by one big, bluebottle fly which was buzzing, kicking, and flopping up and down against a dirty window-pane. I can see that window now—the cobweb in the upper part of the sash, and the dirty shade, which was torn and run up on the bias.

"Go on," said the judge.

"It's this way; that there feller"—he pointed to Billy—"was with her; that there nurse of Beasley's what was killed, he was with her."

There was another rustle in the courtroom. Some one sobbed—some one, I suppose, who did not know Billy from Adam. There was a lot of hysteria in the air. A lot of tense interest that came from nothing but the average mob's interest in the gruesome.

"Who?" asked Gustave's lawyer.

"That there feller," said Gus Dirks, again pointing to Billy.

"Stand up," said some one else. Billy did. I clung to his hand so hard that my knuckles were white. His chief worry seemed to be about me; he whispered: "Don't worry, dear, this is nonsense," and then faced the crowd. There was a scrape of chairs from the back of the room, for people were mounting them. I heard a surging murmur. Some one back of me said: "I thought so—I says to Aunt Mandy that some one that *wasn't* accused would be the one who done it—I says—" triumphant, the voice. I wondered what difference it made to them, how they could care.

I gripped Billy's hand even more closely, and hated the crowd—hated them all. And then the surging murmurs quieted, the scrape of chair legs on the bare floor was heard and silenced, and Gus Dirks went on:

"Well," he said, as he ran his hand around his collar, trying to ease it, "it was this way. I was down by the crick layin' in wait fer them pesterin' boys that swim and roile the water so the cows won't drink—layin' there low, a waitin'. It had been hot, if you recall; that there week was a scorcher, and I guess mebbe *that* was the reason I went to sleep; leastways, I *think* mebbe—"

"Go on!" shouted Judge Llewellyn. "No one cares *how* you went to sleep! You went to sleep, and when you woke—" the judge leaned forward, his face tense, and his eyes agleam.

"Yes, sir," said Gus, "that was it. I went to sleep and slep' clean through supper-time an' all, and when I woke it was dark. I heard a splashin', and I wondered where I was. Then I recollected, and I thinks, half awake: 'Well, I got them danged kids *this* time, and I'll cowhide 'em good, too!' I meant to. They make me a lotta trouble; the cows won't drink."

"Let that go," some one broke in. Gus blinked, some one in the back of the room laughed, there was a rap, a sharp call to order, and he went on.

"What was the noise?" asked Judge Llewellyn.

"It was a boat—a motor-boat," answered Gus Dirks. "When it come alongside to where I was a layin' they shut off the motor. He done it," he asserted, pointing to Billy. Then he grew suddenly alert and a mean smile played across his usually expressionless features. "*He* done it," he said loudly again. "He was in that there boat with her. I knowed her afore, and I seen her after it happened. I never miss seein' a corpse. I enjoys a viewin' of 'em."

"Did he speak?" asked some one, I do not know who; everything about that time was hazy for me.

"Yes, sir; him and her, they talked."

"What did he say—now be careful, my man—*what did he say?*"

"He says: 'As fer money, I'll give yuh *that;* but you knowed I was as good as married to another woman. It was *you* who told me to come up to the cabin that night, you who started this here; and now, when—' "

Billy stood up and simply shouted: "*It's a damned lie!*" and after he was reprimanded sharply, sat down, looking foolish. Gus went on:

"She says," he stated, " 'I'll expose you! You'll pay for this, you—' " and he strung out some epithets that sounded as if they had come from Gloria. These were silenced, and then the court-room went mad. Some fat woman with beads on her waist wept so loudly that they had to take her out. She kept moaning: "My Gawd! My *Gawd!*" I found afterward that she was exhibiting some pickle company's products in a local store, and had never been near the town before, and didn't know a soul in it.

After her exit, again there was some sort of order, and the case went on. For obvious reasons they asked where the body of Gloria Vernon was buried, and it was found that it had been cremated. This had been her wish, and it was disclosed by an aunt of hers who lived in New Rochelle. At this news Dick Codman spoke; and it was the only time I ever knew his enthusiasm to rise so high that it broke the wall of his silence. He simply said: "Smart! Darned smart!" as he looked toward Gus Dirks.

I did not think so.

I thought very little, to be truthful; my whole soul, being, heart, were given over to and wrapped in horror and forming a blind prayer. But dimly I heard the rest of the questions and answers. The coroner testified to Gloria Vernon's looks in a way that showed his carelessness; which he shared with an examining physician, a carelessness that now proved to be criminal negligence. There was a moment's excitement when, after the coroner had described Gloria Vernon after the murder, he rolled over in a faint.

Some one admitted that Billy and I had had a disagreement at that time; some one else had seen Billy talking to her; another some one had seen him walking by the creek the very day of the murder, plastered with mud, haggard, and looking miserably unhappy.

I spoke up, and told why he looked that way; said that, it was my fault; that we had quarreled; but that I knew he was innocent of this charge. I heard myself growing more and more incoherent, and, gasping, I stopped, Billy's arm around me, my head against his shoulder. My excitement had made things swim before me, and because of that I closed my eyes. When I opened them I encountered old Nathan's gaze. His eyes seemed to tell me that it would be all right.

There were mutters of: "Poor little thing!" and "Now, ain't that sad!" then again the sharp tap, a request for silence, and questions —more questions. After these had been asked and answered, for perhaps thirty minutes, old Nathan was called to witness. Then came more craning of heads, more whispered speculations, and the queerest and most counting bit of testimony that that day had held.

"It's like this," he drawled, "something I seen this morning fixed it fer truth to *my* thinkin'. It's like this—" he paused. I know he longed to spit, and after shifting his ever-present cud of tobacco, went on with: "I ain't sayin' nothin' against the testeemony of Gus Dirks. Him and me have been neighbors, an' *good* neighbors, fer nigh forty-some years, I reckon. But—now lookee here, you ask Gus; didn't he see the Angel Gabriel real plain wunst when he was chasin' a white leghorn down in the north lot?"

Gus admitted it; admitted it with a holy, uplifted, and curiously solemn look gracing his insignificant face. That look, which would have made another man splendid, only turned his poor little face more silly than it was naturally.

"He come to me," said Gus, "a wavin' a sword. He says: 'Keep off the creek! Danger lies there!' I says 'Yes, sir,' and then he says: 'I am the Angel Gabriel!' and cut and run."

There was laughter—laughter that bewildered and hurt the poor little man and his pride in that which was his reality. He looked foolish and stunned beneath it. I hated it, and the way that people who wouldn't hurt a dog—physically—will walk up to any one's pet belief and kick it, sneering as they do so.

"Where did Gabriel go?" asked one of the lawyers.

"I dunno"—this sullenly—"I was a prayin'."

"Good occupation," said Judge Harkins's lawyer; "but he who remains to pray often loses his train. You lost this one, and Gabriel's first stop. And now, Mr. Greenleaf—"

He questioned Nathan for a moment; Nathan answered at random, seemed to have lost his thread, and then suddenly he gripped it again and turned to Gus.

"Gus, he has fallin' fits," he announced. "Just ask Gus, ain't that true?"

Gus nodded heavily—nodded in a manner that bespoke a distinction, humbly owned.

"Yes, sir," went on Nathan; "he's had these here fallin' fits ever since I've knew him, and that's forty some years, if I count correct. Now after these here fallin' fits Gus don't *always* know what he sees and hears. Ain't that true, Gus?"

Poor, stupid Gus nodded.

Nathan did not go on, he looked at Gus steadily, and the crowd breathed an "Ah!"

"Get Gus to tell 'em about some of his dreams," drawled Nathan smoothly. "Tell 'em about how wonderful he planned to drain the crick and make a place in the sand to raise melons. Tell 'em how an angel come to him and says if he prayed regular it would dry up. Tell 'em—"

Gus did.

For that moment—for several after that Billy was cleared. And then, Gus Dirks, sensing what had occurred, grew irate, spluttered, asserted that what he had seen *had* happened.

"That there feller," he said, "had a dark four-in-hand tie on. I seen it by the moon that slid up and shone bright while I was still a layin' there. He had a tie-pin shaped like a almond"—I shook; that shape of pin was the one Billy usually wore—"she was wearin' white. She picked up a dress with checks in it. She says: 'Bill, what you got this here for?' He says: 'Mebbe I'll use it.' He didn't tell her what for."

"What color was the dress?" asked some one.

"I ain't sure. I think pink."

I looked at Nathan in despair. His ruse had failed. I thought we were gone, until Nathan spoke again. When he did my heart leaped and then missed a beat from relief.

"I've more to say," he announced. "I think I know who done it. And it wasn't that there young feller who's sweet on Miss Ap*rile*. I notioned it, and this morning I seen what proved it. Leastways, to *my* thinkin', it proved it."

"Go on, omit details," said some one.

"It's this way," said Nathan loudly.

I leaned forward, breathing fast. Nathan spoke well. I felt myself relax. "They must believe him," I reflected; "they *must!*" It seemed incredible that any one should doubt him. He spoke so simply and with such evident sincerity.

What he said was this:

CHAPTER XXIV.

A GRIM REHEARSAL

"BEASLEY'S WOMAN DONE it," old Nathan asserted.

There was an incredulous silence after this, and then an outbreak. A few of the natives dared to cackle a little behind their hands, for stupid Mrs. Beasley did not seem the sort to whom you could moor such a crime. Undaunted, seemingly entirely undisturbed, Nathan went on, when asked to substantiate his statement: "We all know farmer Beasley," he announced. "We—some of us know that he wasn't always none too good to *her*, but she had washed and cooked and done all for him till this young woman arrived and *wouldn't let her go in the room!*

"I met her one day a wanderin' by the crick. First time I recollect ever having saw her outside of their farmyard and not a workin'. I asks her what she was doin'. She says: 'I dunno'—dull like. Then I says: 'That there nurse you have up to your place, I reckon she helps yuh?' And the look she gimme—well—"

Nathan paused, tugged at his whiskers, looked up at the ceiling. When he spoke again his drawl was intensified; the waiting for facts stimulated the crowd, and the hysterically minded began to gasp audibly.

"This morning," went on Nathan, "afore sun-up, I went down to the crick to see whether the lines I'd left out over night had caught anything. I had 'em moored a good ways down the crick; one of 'em near the boat landin' that belongs to the bungalow. While I was fussin' around here tryin' to untie, I hears a noise, and when I looked up I seen Beasley's boy a tackin' somethin'—a bundle of rags I found later—on the bottom of a rowboat.

"He held it down, and then he'd grunt like he does when he's a playin' his echo games. Well, after mebbe ten minutes of this, he stops jiggling them rags in the water, and begins to tack 'em on. Steady and secure, a laughin' all the while, like he does. And I seen it—"

"What?" asked Judge Llewellyn.

"What happened that there night of the murder. How they done it."

"Go on," prompted a man, I did not notice who.

"If you recollect, it was a threatenin' night. The wind blew from the south, and rain begun about four; I don't remember exact, not hearin' it start, since I aim to sleep on my good ear so's to git undeesturbed rest. That there night—" Nathan paused, and then he talked with emphasis. He whispered the rest more quickly than he usually spoke—whispered it, but so that it carried all over the court-room and left every one shaking.

"It was a dark night," he said; "the wind moaned over Greyson's Hill. Linda Beasley went up-stairs early, but she couldn't sleep. Habit took her to her room where her husband slep'. Sometimes she had hated him, often he was cruel to her, but she had cooked fer him, washed fer him, done all fer him, for all the years she could remember easy. She's laid by his side to sleep, been driven by him to work, an' he was—her man.

"Well, she went to that there room. She says: 'Is he restin' easy?' And Gloria Vernon, she reesponds: 'Yes, Miss Beasley, he's restin' comfortable, an' goin' to sleep. Ef you was to come in now you'd deesturb him likely.' So Beasley's woman she went on up to the attic, which was the only place left for her to sleep, since the nurse had the best room, and her husband the other.

"Well, I reckon she set on the edge of her broken-down cot lookin' at the candle flame and seein' nothin'. Mebbe she picked at the candle drip, like you and me does when we ain't thinkin' of anything easy thought out, and then somethin' flared in her brain, and she begins to laugh like her son laughs. Then she tiptoes downstairs soft and hunts Hiram.

" 'Hiram!' she calls, and, he come. 'Hiram,' she says, 'look!' And then he up and switches a gunny sack over a clothes-pole. Then that same way she learned him to tie it over, and to hold it. She learns him like that—"

There was a murmur from the court that meant assent.

"Well, then she goes back," continued Nathan; "she calls 'Miss Vernon, would yuh kindly step this way a minute? Yer needed down-stairs.' Miss Vernon comes down. The gunny sack goes over her head. Hiram holds her, laughin' fit to kill, fer he thinks he's playin' a grand, new game, and then they haul her down to the crick—"

"Nonsense!" said some one loudly. Nathan smiled. When he again spoke his whispers had departed.

"There's a gunny sack with 'Fairview Farm' wrote on it in my cabin," said Nathan. "I found it the morning after the murder in the underbrush by the path that leads to Beasley's. I didn't think nothing of it then—that there dress that Miss Vernon was tied with, that was lost by Beasley's woman. It belonged to Miss Jane Hoyle, who sends her wash up to Beasley's farm. Hiram will use a gunny sack like I says if you give him one. He will tack a bundle of rags on the bottom of a boat. Yesterday I found a nurse's cap in the high grass near Beasley's pigpen. That ain't sayin' much, but mebbe it come off in a struggle?"

"Mebbe it blew off the clothes line," said some one.

"Mebbe," said Nathan; "mebbe."

"How do we know this is true—that what you say of the Beasley boy is true?"

"Come out and see," said Nathan. "Come out and see—"

And all the State militia couldn't have held that court together after that. People bolted for the doors and started running toward Greyson's Hill. People rented all the teams in town; horses that were ready for the grave struggled out toward our place, drawing wagons that were loaded past capacity. Flivvers sneezed their way up the street that led out of the village. The few good cars that belonged in the place were forced to make their weary way behind carts and vehicles of every description.

The judge and his elaborate equipage were moored behind a garbage wagon, driven by an individual known to the county as "Smelly Burch." The minister sat on the rumble seat of a very noisy motor-cycle which belonged to a disreputable person who ran a dubiously considered dance hall. Caste was forgotten, ignored, swallowed up in mystery, and the wonder that it made.

When we at last arrived we found perhaps two hundred and fifty people swarming over the place, and more coming at every minute. Some one was despatched to find the Echo, and when he was found, and brought to his trial, there were probably three times as many people crowding, pushing, and jostling each other in their efforts to see. I had gone up-stairs with Nan, and we, with Jane and Laurence, looked out of a window directly over the landing.

When the Echo was brought up there was absolute silence, pounding, tense silence. Then some one handed him a gunny-sack bag, held up three oars, and—we saw it happen—that which Nathan had said would happen.

Nathan surveyed it with satisfaction, but did not speak. Instead he made his usual cut-plug offering, this time to the creek, and moved out of Hiram Beasley's way.

The boy was moving surely now, intent in every move. He muttered as he looked around, and when he saw a roll of carpet that some one had tied up with some little girl's hair ribbon, he grunted with satisfaction.

Then he dumped it in the creek, jumped in himself—the water is only shoulder-deep there—and the struggle ensued. That struggle made one hide one's head and gasp. Laurence, of course wept. When I heard a hammer I looked out again—the Echo was completing the job.

"That must have been hard work," said Jane in an undertone. "He *never* did it alone."

"Oh, of course not," I replied. And then I thought of something—something that was so simple that I wondered the others hadn't seen it; but for various reasons I kept silent.

About that time Judge Llewellyn asked whether Mrs. Beasley had been in court that day. It seemed not, and it proved that she had been there only one day, when a neighbor had consented to stay with her husband, and another had induced her, after much pleading, to make the trip.

"She don't go out much," said the neighbor, who was now looking on, and was, I feel sure, convinced with many, that Linda Beasley was the murderer of Gloria.

After a half-hour, or a little more, Linda Beasley appeared. She looked baffled, and I felt sure that no one had told her of the suspicion. "Yuh wanted me?" she asked.

"Have you ever seen this?" asked Frank Beagle, holding up the gunny-sack bag that Nathan had produced.

"Yes, sir; it belongs to our farm. That there Fairview on it is the name of our farm."

They told her bluntly, cruelly, of what she was suspected. She quailed, and then sank into her usual dull apathy. Questions flew back and forth. She denied the charge.

"Were you out that night?" Judge Llewellyn questioned.

"Yes, sir."

"Why?"

"I was a huntin' Hiram."

"Did you find him?"

"No, sir."

"Well, of course he couldn't have done this alone. He hasn't wit enough for that." That question, I felt sure, was meant to test and trap her. She tangled in it.

"He would," she contradicted, maternal pride overstepping caution. "Hiram, he ain't so dumb as people think; he helps me real nice."

"If you wanted him to help you, to do anything for you, he would?"

"Yes, sir."

"He is devoted to you?"

"How?"

"I say, he is influenced by you, cares for you?"

"Yes, sir; I reckon."

"Can any one else teach him to work—to do things?"

"Yes, sir; sometimes. But nobody can do it like me."

"You liked Miss Vernon? Now think carefully about this answer."

Fumblingly she admitted she had not liked Miss Vernon. They probed her skilfully; before she knew it an emotion that might be called a half-awake jealousy exhibited itself. The fact that she had felt more than a mild aversion to Gloria Vernon came out when she flared, after telling of her exclusion from the sick room; flared, and then, after a return to her usual level, said: "He was my man."

And so it rested.

Judge Harkins, William P. Watts, Gustave Gerome, Linda, and Hiram Beasley, all of them suspected, and from convincing evidence, of the murder of Gloria Vernon. The next day was not a happy Sunday.

Nathan alone seemed cheerful. He spent the day in the woods, using his photographs, and stringing up a mirror which he said he was going to use that night to catch a certain sort of moth which he thought was hovering around.

He had a great deal of trouble adjusting the mirror. The angle seemed to bother him, and it would not stay up. We could see it reflect on the hillside.

"My, he's having lots of trouble with that," said Nan.

"Isn't he," agreed Dick, and then he suggested that he and I go walking. As we neared Nathan we heard him singing an ancient song, the first words of which are: "Old Dan Tucker, he got drunk—"

"Doesn't seem to bother him," said I.

"No," Dick answered; "doesn't bother him—look here, do you think I have any chance with Midgette?"

"Midgette's dad appeared yesterday," I said; "they fell on each other's necks and wept. It was really touching. She says she's going back to him after this is settled, and that she'll never leave him. Something has made her decide to stick it out with us until the open season for murders closes, and we can clear out."

"She told me she'd promised to stay with you all," said Dick, a fatuous look on his face. I didn't say so, but I had never known Midgette to be really influenced by a little thing like her word of honor before. "And," continued Dick, "I could hang out here. Evidently there's a good opening for my sort of activity."

"Then why don't you take advantage of it now?" I asked. The idea of his thinking of Midgette, when Billy was suspected, enraged me; and he hadn't seemed to accomplish anything.

"Heavens, woman," said Dick, "I don't beat a drum when I work! Hello, Nathan, going to catch a moth to-night?"

"I'm settin' out to," Nathan responded.

"Go to it," said Dick, and then we wandered on.

"Don't be so impatient," said Dick. "To-morrow may show developments." I didn't answer, since my patience with Dick was worn so thin that it threatened to snap.

Monday did show developments, remarkable developments; and Tuesday the clear-up, a clear-up that held some sorrow and a great deal of relief.

I can see Nathan now, again on the stand, again telling what he knew of affairs at the Beasley farm; admitting with pride the horrible truth which so terribly involved poor, dull Linda Beasley and her son.

CHAPTER XXV.

THE VERDICT

MONDAY MORNING FOUND Gus Dirks again in court. Gus, with tears running down his sun-dried cheeks. Having attended a camp-meeting during the interval, he was all for truth. The revivalist had exhorted against deviations from exact truth; Gus, it seemed, had deviated.

In his new anxiety to escape the slow cooking promised by the revivalist for liars, Gus was coming across with the facts. These again involved an angel, but without wings.

"He come to me often, but mostly exhorted silence," said Gus, between loud sniffings and futile moppings of his nose. "And this time he come to me, he described what I described, making me repeat it after him three times. He says I was to let on I seed what I told of, but this here preacher yesterday, *he* says—"

So, Gus rambled on, showing how the last argument had convinced him, and how the fear of hell had made him disregard the injunctions of an angel.

We found out that the angel had appeared to Gus again, telling him that he had accused the wrong man; that Gustave Gerome was the guilty one, and it was he whom the angel would see avenged.

"He told me afore," said Gus, "to pin it on the feller that was always with her. Twice I seen that there feller with her, and so I thought—"

And again more ramblings and at greater length.

"Would you know Gabriel's voice if he appeared on Main Street?" asked Mr. Beagle.

"I guess," said Gus.

"Anything peculiar about it?"

"He says 'joynal' instead of 'journal,'" replied Gus.

"Little old New York," sang out some one. There was a laugh.

"I recollect this," he went on, after some queries, "because I couldn't get the sense of what he was sayin' right, and had to say

151

'How?' He says: 'In the joynal of heaven this will be reecorded to your credit.' I didn't understand fer a while."

"Some one," said the judge's lawyer, after permission was granted for him to speak, "knows of this crime—how it was committed, by whom. Quite naturally, some one is afraid to offend a character so dangerous; quite naturally, again, he wants to see the crime righted, the innocent freed, and the murderer punished."

He went on at length. He talked well, and it looked pretty bad for Gustave; and then some child had to pop in, just at that point, produced of course by one of Judge Harkins's friends, and this child said she had seen Gloria and Gustave together—"that there man," she called him. The "murdered lady" had been crying, it seemed—the child had seen her after death —and the murdered lady had said: " 'I do love you; you know it; but—I am *afraid* to see you any more! Afraid for you, of what may happen!' That there man," the child went on to say, "had replied real fierce like: 'It would be easier to *kill* you than to give you up now! Gloria, you *know* how I feel, you know I *must* have you—I'll go mad without you. If you won't see me, I'll—' " Then Gustave had taken Gloria in his arms, and the child, who had been hunting moss to sell to the town florist, hurried off.

During this recital a local lawyer whom Linda Beasley had employed wagged his head solemnly, as if each wag pounded the facts in, fastened them to truth.

And in spite of Nathan's clever supposition, which the Echo had so well exhibited, the Beasleys were regarded as out of the count. Two o'clock saw all evidence against Gustave mustered and in line. It looked pretty black.

His infatuation prejudiced folk against him; Frank Lethridge's locket, and threats against Frank Lethridge almost made him twice a murderer.

Nathan admitted having heard Gustave threaten to kill any one who harmed Jane; Jane had to admit that he had ceased to care for her. I think Gustave felt that more than any testimony that was given. He started to protest, but gave it up, and after that hung his head.

His changing love, his fierce championing of the moment's amour, his hot temper, which had so plainly shown through both affairs, made his escape seem hopeless. The judge appeared as an angel in comparison; and, in comparison, the evidence against him was slight.

Country folk of all around had seen Gustave and Gloria together. Many of them had heard fragments of the hot discussions which all seemed to involve Gloria's anxiety to be rid of his society. Children who had been hunting berries appeared with damaging contributions to swell the evidence against Gustave. Two women who had been walking home from church and who had sat down by the roadside to rest repeated a fragment of conversation that they had heard as Gloria and he had gone by.

Both Gloria and Gustave were used to city life. They could not, any more than I, sense the repose that makes country people when they relax almost a part of the landscape. I did not wonder that Gloria and Gustave had so often been overheard. I could imagine those women at the roadside, sitting beneath bushes, well-shaded by them, and as silent as that which gave them shade, as they watched the passers-by; noting what she wore, what he wore, what they said, and how they said it.

At four the jury went out, and at six we were admitted to Gustave's cell. He rose as we entered—Jane, Laurence, and I —tried to make a jest, and failed.

"I guess," he said, "I'm it."

"It is too terrible," said Laurence, who was hunting around for his handkerchief, which for once in its history had escaped his cuff. "I declare I am entirely unnerved, but you must be brave! You must be brave—everything *is* against you, but you mustn't give up hope."

Gustave paid no heed to his remark; he had turned to Jane.

"You know I didn't do it, don't you?" he asked.

"I know you didn't," she said, her eyes filling.

"This way of going would be none too good for me, no better than I deserve," went on Gustave; "but I didn't—"

"I know," Jane said again.

"I suppose I should not say it," said Gustave; "I know I have lost the right—but I always loved you, Jane, even when I treated you the most cruelly."

Jane put out her hand. He looked at it, at her, and turned away. Then I saw her go to him, put her arms around his neck, and heard him sob. Laurence, who was mopping away his easily arriving tears, planted himself with me before the door, and we tried to make some sort of a screen, the warden having just appeared with a group who wished to view the prisoner. I had one more view of Jane's swiftly moving, adorably tender hands, and then I became absorbed in a signet ring I always wear, and the initials on it blurred before my gaze.

We left a little while after that, Laurence weeping all the way home. Jane did not; she stared stonily ahead, and when she spoke, spoke too conventionally, too carefully. I saw that she was building walls within herself against all the loneliness and terror that she felt was to be hers. No one slept that night, and we heard Jane pacing to and fro during all the long hours of her vigil.

Laurence kept calling the court-house for a report from the jury, but there was none. Nan sat gazing miserably ahead. Dick and Billy played rum. I tried to read, but I cannot remember a word of it. And so the night passed slowly.

At ten o'clock the following morning the jury gave their verdict Gustave Gerome was found guilty of manslaughter in the first degree.

CHAPTER XXVI.

CODMAN EXPLAINS

AT FIVE MINUTES past ten Dick Codman came into the court-room, followed by two officers, who had between them, handcuffed and terrified, the man whom I had seen sitting on the edge of the creek the day that Frank Lethridge was drowned.

"Here," said Dick Codman, striding up the aisle, "is the murderer of Frank Lethridge and Gloria Vernon, and the man who knows who murdered Rudolph Loucks!"

Oh—the bedlam!

Judge Harkins fainted, Jane began to sob deeply, brokenly; Laurence bleated out a prayer of thanksgiving, and the court went wild. When it had somewhat silenced, Dick Codman held up a paper. "I won't read it," he said; "but you can. Just tell the assembled court the name of this periodical."

"The New York *Joynal-Gazette*," said the man.

"Gabriel!" shouted Gus Dirks.

Gabriel staggered and almost fell. I saw Jane hurry over to Gustave, and his arms close around her. I heard Laurence's sob—the first, of course, to arrive; Nan's hysterical bleating about her feeling that it *would* be righted; the howls of the mob; Billy's soothing voice, the feel of his arm.

Oh, that day! Everything whirled, and the precipitate was a gorgeous medley of relief, tears, laughter, love, and pain.

A little funny, perhaps, to turn the corner of the porch, and then to have to back out of a scene that involved Laurence and Nan; to hear Laurence in a kiss-free interlude loudly asserting that Nan needed a strong, courageous man to care for her. But not funny to find Jane and Gustave, his hand on a fold of her skirt, or her sleeve, and to hear his unconscious repetition of her name, half aloud, half pleadingly. It seemed as if his lacerated nerves found in that name peace and courage to go on; felt through her the breeze that brought cool promise of another land.

The second night after Gustave's release we heard the story of the start of it. Dick Codman told it in his easy, drawling voice and his very matter-of-fact manner. Even Midgette screamed only three times. After the third, Dick Codman laid his hand on hers, forgot to remove it, and she stopped. I think exhibitions of that sort are disgusting, and so Billy and I sat back in the shadows— But to go on.

Nan said: "Do tell us all you know, Dick. I'm interested."

Dick stood up to hunt a match, poked up the fire a bit—it had been a gray, damp, cold day—and then, after sitting down and puffing at his pipe for a few moments, he began:

"Hunger and fear started it. Of course you all know that hunger, hate, and fear make all the crimes. This started on money-hunger and fear, and it lived on anarchy—throve on it."

Dick leaned forward, stirred the fire anew, and then, his face well lit by the roaring blaze, told the tale. Always I will see that fire-lit room as I remember it then; the shadows and brightness of it, the tense, listening group.

"Judge Harkins's younger brother, Joseph," said Dick, "was a dreamer, an impractical, paint-loving, artistic, erratic dreamer. The judge, starved for love, disillusioned, childless, woman-nagged, fastened all his affection on the boy. And, in spite of the quality of his offering, the thing he gave was a pretty heavy burden for young shoulders to bear. The judge demanded character, pine-straight character, in a boy who was ruled, as much as any sapling, by the strongest wind.

"The judge was a business success, not a creator. He admired creators, but didn't reflect that money-sense and artistic achievement seldom go in one package; so he expected this younger brother to work for the money which was to take him to Paris, where he planned to study under Guernierre.

"I suppose he thought he was doing the thing which was best for the boy—anyway, he got the youngster a job in the Water Company his friend Rudolph Loucks headed; and the kid started his pegging. Days were long and ledgers stupid. I suppose this Joseph felt the call to his colors more than forty times a day—as a drunkard feels his thirst.

"Paris, I suppose, became farther and farther away," continued Dick. "You can picture the boy's hopelessness as he looked at his scanty savings, and realized what the trip would cost, the living take—the dreamed-of years of learning nearing the impossible—while his employer and his brother wallowed in money, a small part of which would have given him his chance at—"

"Heaven," finished Nan.

"Heaven," agreed Dick. "After working hours, he wandered these hills, and here—perhaps on this very spot—he came across a woodsman who hated the moneyed people of the world because one of them had taken off his wife.

"They became close friends, and I think that in all the vitriol that their words flung Joseph found a sort of peace until Nathan's nephew came back from the city, where he had learned as well as worked, and he sneered at words and spoke grandly of action.

"Harry Greenleaf was the sort who flourished south of State Street, Chicago, not so very long ago. When he wanted things, he took them, and he had at his tongue's end the patter of the most idle and discontented class on earth—the class that we are beginning to deport.

"Joseph Harkins was persuaded; some of the things Rudolph Loucks did backed Harry Greenleaf's theory that Rudolph not only had no right to more money than they, but had less right. 'It's yours—*yours!*' Harry Greenleaf would shout. 'Yours and mine! Some day we'll take it, teach those parasites of the poor that we—' and so on.

"Then one day the paint call grew too strong, and Joseph Harkins had a chance to divert a little of the money that belonged in the coffers of the Water Company. On the spur of the moment he took it, in the way an impetuous, unbalanced youngster might, afterward feeling all the horror of what he had done. He spent it, tried to get enough to put it back; couldn't. Took more—you know that old story; every one knows it; it's a part of life.

"He didn't know how to retrieve, so he began a blackmailing scheme. 'Put your money under this rock'—whatever sum he wanted—directed this at Rudolph Loucks, with a threat of death; directed it for money, so that he might pay Rudolph Loucks what he owed him!

"Practical, wasn't it? That was what made Rudolph afraid when he heard the hoof-beats behind him on the road that wild, stormy night. That was what made him tie the girl's hands, fearing that if he were hurt she might be implicated, charged with it. No slate altogether black, is there?"

"Wasn't he afraid to go out alone?" asked Nan.

"No. He carried a pistol, and he rather liked the spice, I think. He had to use a lot of seasoning to get a sensation," answered Dick, "for he had made himself immune to the usual sensations of usual men."

"Why didn't he resort to the law?" asked Laurence primly. "I think that was a matter for the police."

"Rudolph had too many black spots of his own to hunt the police," replied Dick. "I think he supposed it was a relative of some one whom he'd wronged. Perhaps he was afraid of what the search might reveal, or perhaps he liked the new interest. He was a strange man—a very strange man. He was not a coward, for he paid no attention to the demands, and left no money to insure his safety.

"On the night of the murder Joseph Harkins started for New York, where he was to meet Judge and Mrs. Harkins. He was a miserably unhappy young man, for he had had word, just that afternoon, that the Water Company's books were to be audited. Plans went through his head about disappearing, but the lack of money, his usual state, made all these impossible. Every gate was closed, and he was up against a fight with no armor or any other means of defense.

"He brooded all the way over to the junction, shrinking every time any one looked at him. In the station he met Harry Greenleaf, who had driven over that day with a load of firewood Nathan had just cut. Harry was warming up before his return trip.

"Somehow, Joseph Harkins confessed—and Harry offered a solution. He judged that Rudolph wouldn't be so brash in the face of a forty five, and he asserted that Rudolph would have no mercy if he discovered the shortage, which was undoubtedly true.

" 'This is your only chance,' said Harry Greenleaf. 'Squeeze him, or he'll squeeze you; and it'll be the pen—you can wear a mask—'

"Joseph went back with him; drove behind Nathan's team, and was seen by no one. After Harry had put up the team they made their way to town. At the foot of Greyson's hill they paused, considered walking the rest of the distance, decided they would not.

"Sleighs whirled by them, returning to town, for the storm was growing bad. These sleighs and the cold made Harry sneer over the division of the world's goods and decide that what was needed must be taken by force.

"That led them to use the sleigh of the Norwegian draftsman, gag him, take him through an adjoining building, an easy-to-open, empty storage place, to the third-floor room of the disreputable hotel on the flats, from which Vera Struthers had been coaxed by Rudolph Loucks.

"Without knowing he had her, they followed him, having learned, by the judge's telephone—the house was closed, but Joseph had a key—that he had gone to his bungalow.

"After they again started, Harry Greenleaf decided he would not become involved. 'My uncle's sick,' he said; 'has a hell of a cold. I'll go get a doctor. You go on. You can deal with him, and it's your matter, after all. Got a pistol?'

"Shaking, Joseph admitted that he had one that he had gotten at the judge's after telephoning; and then, letting Harry Greenleaf get out of the sleigh, he went on alone.

"Now, no one knows what happened," said Dick, after Midgette's third small squeal made his hand cover hers; "but you can judge—"

Nan sat forward. Her plot sense was asserting itself.

"He followed him into the field," she whispered, "the wind blowing the handkerchief away from his mouth, revealing his shaking lips. A thin, pitifully shaken boy, forced by circumstances to his lowest hell. In the center of the field Rudolph Loucks turned—waited. He spoke, after a laugh—a sneering laugh."

" 'To think,' he said, 'that it was you, Joe—you weak, shuffling—' and so on—"

"No, he didn't," cut in Jane. "How would he know?"

"He might have gone over the books that evening," said Nan, "or known the cut of the boy's coat, his hat, his walk—I'll venture he knew, and *laughed,* and that that piece of arrogance from the class that Joseph had learned to hate brought his death."

"I'll venture he said, 'Come here and fight like a man!' " said Gustave; "and the boy turned weak, and in a frenzy of fear shot him down."

"He was shot in the back," said Dick.

"Perhaps," Nan cut in, "all the hell of fear was upon him. Perhaps every breeze brought to his fevered hearing the sound of footsteps; perhaps Rudolph refused to help him, quelled him, laughed, and carelessly turned away, swaggering like a conqueror; and then, desperate, hunted, sick from fear and loss, the boy followed—followed until he was near; and then he screamed, as a woman might—and fired!"

"No one will ever know about that," said Dick. "Not unless Joseph is found, which I doubt. What is known is the fact that he got away."

"How?" asked Midgette. "And why were Gloria Vernon and Frank Lethridge killed? You do explain things so wonderfully, Dick—so *wonderfully!*"

CHAPTER XXVII.

THE SORDID STORY

"JOSEPH HID IN the attic of his cabin in the woods," said Dick, "the one that Gloria Vernon knew and used. Somehow, he escaped detection. The small town police force were flustered by the affair, and he slipped off before the bigger and more capable men arrived."

"How?" asked Midgette, in her softest voice.

"Nathan hid him in a load of spruce-trees he had just cut. These he took over to Bridgeport, which is forty miles away. Here, Joseph, who is small, masquerading as a shawl-wrapped country woman, took the train for New York, where he was supposed to be all the while."

"Didn't the judge's wife—" began some one.

"She'd gone to visit relatives in Vermont the night before the murder. Only Harry Greenleaf, Nathan, and the judge knew where Joseph Harkins had and had not been in the interim. The judge had taken his wife to her home, and then, returning, had changed his hotel. That made that purely unconscious action of his another shield.

"However, precaution really wasn't necessary. Joseph encountered no suspicion. Harry Greenleaf's innocence was established by his own capable handling of the situation; for, on leaving Joseph, he had immediately gone to the doctor's, asking him to come out to see, old Nathan, who had what the boy thought a cold.

" 'Lucky if *you* aren't sick after your walk to town,' said the local M.D. 'How long did it take you to make it, young man?' Harry thought about an hour and a half, he wasn't quite sure.

" 'Plucky!' said the doctor, and then he loaded him up with Scotch, told him to get warm before he started, after which they drove off toward the country. Now, that walk in the driving snow made Harry Greenleaf a little hero. People liked his devotion to old Nathan, prattled of his taking care of him during Nathan's attack of pleurisy and pneumonia which developed that night.

"Harry saw in this attitude and his uncle's reputation for gentleness a screen for an enterprise which he wished to establish in silence, an enterprise which was to level ranks, wipe out hurts and injustices, by—fear and death!

"Well, you can see the rest: the old woodsman's unwillingness to comply; the glib persuasions of the younger man; the hurt in the old man that had made him think much money and sin were synonymous; finally you can see him coming around, and how, once converted, his unsophisticated yet cunning brain would never waver.

"It was his sort who made the early Christians—I mean the sort who could he so filled and dominated by an idea or an ideal that they would suffer anything, suffer anything *to be,* for the great and ultimate good.

"Nathan at first only protected the bomb-maker, but soon he was helping. Seems strange to think of that old man doing that, perhaps after he'd been tramping in the woods and there had spent half an hour trying to get a baby bird to cling to a high branch that meant safety."

Then he leaned over to the table, picked up a sheet of paper, and drew scrawls and meaningless lines as he went on, his narrative growing short-clipped, staccato.

"The judge knew," he said as his pencil moved jerkily, "but for obvious reasons he couldn't blow on the gang. Frank Lethridge thought Nathan a moonshiner, went to poking in the creek in spite of the warnings the judge gave him. He was caught in the trap, put on top of the box that held tools, by Harry Greenleaf.

"This was tied on a rope which ran down in deep water, and there through a heavy root. The rope then hid itself in underbrush, ran from that over a tree-bough, so that the pulling could be easily done by weight if the work were hard.

"Frank Lethridge was caught in the trap as he triumphantly fumbled over the thing he'd been hunting so long. Then he was pulled out of his boat, into deep water, and held there until the bubbles stopped rising and the surface was still. So far—all right; but at that moment some one came along—perhaps Gustave in a boat, or a farmer's boy—anyway, the murderer had to drop the rope and hide.

"The Echo came forward after the boat had slipped away, pulled wildly, following the lead he'd seen, broke the hand off where the trap had weakened it—the arm and hand slipped under the root, but not the body—and then went bounding off with his find. I suppose Harry Greenleaf had a bad moment or so, don't you?"

We nodded.

"Frank kissed me that day," said Jane, "so that Nathan, who was looking on, should think us sweethearts and not suspect. Then he went on, pretending he was going home, but intending to take the road on the other side of the creek—as he did—and—" Her voice faded.

"Gloria?" asked Gustave.

"Killed by Harry, as you know, because she was his amour and loved some one else. She was Vera Struthers of the flats, whom Rudolph Loucks had tried to ruin. She, from that experience, was another one who was ripe and ready for the cult that harms the man who controls. She lived with Greenleaf in New York until it got hot for her—there was some suspicion—then they hurried her up here; the judge, at Nathan's request, suggesting her to the town's doctor for the case.

"Nathan controlled every move of that old man. Knew where his brother was, you know, and threatened to disclose it. Always scared of his life, that old codger. That day April found him poking here he was hunting for letters from Joseph, thinking some of the anonymous blackmailing ones might still be around. That shows how rattled he was, for the place had been pretty well combed years before."

We were silent for a few moments. I was picturing Harry Greenleaf's vigil. I saw him creeping through the woods, with the soft tread he had learned as a country boy; coming upon Gloria and Gustave, watching, watching—laughing silently when he saw her go white, her eyes widen, darken, in a fear that was almost mad. It was he who had worn Jane's frock, he who made Gustave think Jane followed them; he who kept the country folk quelled by his ghostly appearances and made the bungalow an unpopular place for night parties. Most of the important work was done at night, and then—as the dawn broke—hidden in a box, sunk in the creek, by Nathan.

Perhaps the most picturesque bit of the affair was the meetings in the room of the voiceless husband of Linda Beasley. Here, in the shadows, which were brought to being by a wavering candle-light, Gloria and Harry talked. For the most part in lowered tones, but once and again, as when Linda thought she'd heard her husband's voice, theirs would rise over some altercation.

I can visualize it entirely.

The law-abiding citizen who lay on the bed, chained and made harmless by his infirmities, listening to talk that must have set even

his flesh to creeping horribly. Perhaps he'd watch the brutal ca-
resses of Harry Greenleaf, see through Gloria's response a shrinking—the new shrinking. Seeing in Gloria's eyes a wonder
about—how much he, this master and lover of hers, *knew.*

"You came from New York to-day?" she would ask.

"Yes. Some people moving to Franklinsburg—" Part time he
drove a moving van which plied over the Lincoln way. "Nathan
signaled not to stop. That crowd's made hell for us."

The affair was discovered by Dick through Nathan's signals.
After he'd read a message that flashed "Start two tomorrow," he
shattered the glass with his mighty good shot, to find that it was a
better, stronger glass than was necessary for moth catching, and the
sort of glass that is manufactured in only one place. He located this
and the buyers, from which list he selected Harry; but Harry bought
under a *nom de plume*, and Dick selected him because of the address to which the glass was to go. It was on Broome Street, near
Pitt, and that caught Dick's attention because the rents of that
quarter and the expense of the mirror did not tally.

Some one probed him as he told of that—or tried to.

"The very usual or the very unusual," he explained, "almost
always lead somewhere. The real normal, the middle ground, is
seldom attained by a nervous, fear-cramped man."

"How do you go about these things?" asked Nan.

"I'm not a Sherlock Holmes," he answered. "You'd laugh at
some of the steps that take me into the heart of crime; they are so
simple. All of you thought Gloria Vernon a strange person to be a
nurse. I did too—nothing remarkable in that—only I took the
trouble to find out, by probing Mrs. Beasley about the way her
husband was cared for.

"I saw in Nathan's eyes the light of a fanaticism; I talked to him
of government. I saw in the judge a certain gentleness, this was
revealed in his fears for April's safety, and his decency—except in
one case, when he was ordered to poison that collie—to animals. I
knew that he sent large checks to his brother in New York. I knew
something made him drink. All these things—" then Dick waved
his hands, settled back, and went on with his puffing of a short brier
pipe, his eyes half closed, his face benign and peaceful.

I knew that he had gone down to the post-office; there he had
seen the postmistress address a package for Nathan.

"Write on 'em real plain," said Nathan; "write photeegraph
plates from Nathan Greenleaf, so they'll know." After he left, Dick
flashed a bit of authority, went back of the screens, and inspected

"the plates." He said that they were the prettiest bombs he had ever seen, and that some of them had been used by the chap who had used the Gamble paper; he had only recently seen some of that display. Dick said that that made the rest very simple, the solution only natural.

Obviously, people around the bungalow were a bother; people on the creek, and the constant use of the boats, disturbed the industry. So the ghost occasionally appeared on the hillside, when Nathan flashed a "safe" message. Harry Greenleaf, of course, was Gus Dirks's "Gabriel," carefully sandwiching orders between hints about the crops, and so avoiding the suspicion possible even in that dull mind.

It was he who put the poisoned cat in the bungalow that night to cover noises; for the judge had grown so uneasy that he demanded a search for his brother's letters in the old storeroom.

None were found, and the judge, relieved, declared a sort of truce. It was he who stole the judge's check, filled it in, and so made the confusion about the writing. It was he who left the note in Frank Lethridge's car the day he was murdered, which read, as Billy conjectured: "Keep away from the creek."

He didn't want to kill Lethridge. He only wanted to kill one person, and that person was Gloria. The law, he thought, would torture Gustave, whom he planned to implicate, more cleverly than he could. And so he planned it—and after it Nathan taught the trick to the Echo.

Poor old Nathan! I was, in spite of the hideous truth, sorry for him, and I was not sorry to see him go. The shock ended him, and the valvular defect that he had gone around with for so many years saved him from prison—or worse. He died in the court-room after the truth came out; and he had contributed to it.

"Yes, sir," he had admitted, "my nephew and Gloria, who was Vera Struthers, they met at Beasley's, in the room where he lays. He couldn't talk, and they kep' her out." Then he swayed. "Men will die," he shouted, his voice hoarse and his color beginning to fade—"men must suffer, men must kill! Until—until—*men learn—to live!*" Then he fell, and was not conscious again.

I hurried to the front of the room, bent above him, and laid my hand on his forehead. He felt my touch, and murmured a name. That name, his last word, I found afterward, was his wife's. When I remember that, together with what Nathan lost, I am more gentle in my judgment of him.

" 'Mary' meant love, for Nathan," I said that evening, as Billy and I sat out in the end of the big punt. "I wish he had not lost Mary, and that he could have been as gentle as I am sure he wanted to be, deep inside."

"April is love for me," said Billy, and then: "when?"

And we fixed a date which involved Billy, myself, and a clergyman, two witnesses, a ring, and a fee.

CHAPTER XXVIII.

THE END—WHICH IS THE BEGINNING

AS I SAID, the resolve is interesting; but it is the thing which doesn't resolve that holds. Little things like the true reading of Judge Harkins's note slipped from my consciousness after being answered. It was, "I'll get you some dry," and it was a promise made to Rudolph Loucks, made when he and the judge had met at a lecture given by the local clergyman at his home.

The magazine the divine took, the only subscription in town, you will remember, was afterward sent by him to Rudolph Loucks because of an article he wanted Rudolph to see, and in that manner found its way to the dark corner of the storeroom.

But Nathan's going on grips the question mark in me. For the gentleness of Nathan was real, in spite of the horror of what he did, the warnings he wrote on our bungalow walls, the fear he tried to fix in us on that first day with—blood from a chicken. It was he who caused the unusual noises, sneezed in the cellar that absurd afternoon of the crowded bath-tub, and—he who shielded us from Harry's more vicious forms of attack.

It is the unanswerable that makes conjecture. I thought of him a good deal, and I did of Joseph Harkins and the judge. "I hope," I said to Billy, on the afternoon before we left the bungalow for good, "that old Nathan has left the twisted side of him here, with his ailing heart and world-worn body."

Billy hoped so, too.

"I can imagine him taking pictures of the little angels," I went on, "hiding behind a cloud, as he hid in trees here, to catch them off-guard and at play!"

"So can I," Billy agreed.

Then he sat down by me, on Nan's trunk, which was waiting to be taken to the station. We were out on the porch of the bungalow, looking down on the creek, that creek that had made possible so many horrors.

167

"Heard that Joseph Harkins was identified in a morgue in Cincinnati," said Billy.

"Who identified him?" asked Jane, who came out carrying a hat which she had just shoe-blacked.

"The judge," replied Billy.

"H-m!" said Gustave, who had followed, having come to be Jane's second shadow.

"Don't believe it," asserted Jane. "He's gone abroad, hasn't he?"

"Yes."

"Well, can't you see him—meeting that boy? Trying to step from the bitterness of all his wasted hopes? To forget his own failure to do the right, and the boy's crime? I can see him"—Jane twirled the hat and inspected her work—"sitting opposite Joseph at a boulevard café, listening to studio gossip and for the voice of some one from home—some one he knows, who may at any moment intrude—"

"That old soak?" sneered Gustave, who had never forgiven the judge for the headache his hospitality had given him.

"He is capable of feeling," I asserted. "It was he who wrote Midgette about loneliness, after she had left her father—he wrote of loneliness too graphically; it was a confession of his—"

We were all silent, thinking of Midgette's wedding, which we had witnessed that afternoon. In the strange way that weddings have, it had left us sad. Perhaps it brought to us the seriousness of the step which we were all about to take.

"Dick was frightened," said Laurence, who arose from the bosom of a porch swing I'd thought to be empty. "I, for one, *cannot* comprehend that sensation."

Gustave snorted, and I realized that his old balance was returning.

"Fright, personal fright, and divergence from truth I cannot sense," Laurence continued ponderously. No one applauded this, Nan having gone to town to buy a few new things for a trousseau.

I *could* understand divergence from truth. I had let Linda Beasley and her boy bear suspicion—more, conviction—when I knew that they weren't guilty. The boy had moaned from a tree-top all that night, but to shield Billy—to shield Billy I had acted a lie in my silence. I am ashamed of it, and I suppose the sensation is healthy. I wonder if there are many of us who are so tall they cannot stoop?

"Strange ending," said Jane, "and yet"—her eyes traveled to Gustave—"no other was possible for me."

"Nor for me," said Billy.

"Beginning," I corrected.

Gustave and Jane went off toward the hillside path.

"Boating?" asked Billy.

I shook my head. I couldn't bear the creek, for at that time what it had made was far too close. But now—since I am shielded, happily entrenched behind love, the grocer's orders, sock darnings, and a real three-story house, I can look back on the whole affair and even see its humors.

And yet, when I do, I always think of a windy, wet, blowing day in March—that day when our summer plan was made; and after that I seem to see a bomb slipping into almost still-water, so gently putting out that it hardly made a ripple. And then—I hear my friend, the boy whom I met at Le Monte-Dore, hear him say: "Look at the little beggar! A bit calm, isn't she? But she'll make some jolly hell when she 'up and busts,' to quote you Yankees—some jolly hell, you know!"

But our particular bomb, which was started by Nan and furthered by Jane, Midgette, Dick, Gustave, Billy, Laurence, and myself, went a little better; it manufactured both extremes—the nicest coming last!

THE END

RAMBLE HOUSE's

HARRY STEPHEN KEELER WEBWORK MYSTERIES

(RH) indicates the title is available ONLY in the RAMBLE HOUSE edition

The Ace of Spades Murder
The Affair of the Bottled Deuce (RH)
The Amazing Web
The Barking Clock
Behind That Mask
The Book with the Orange Leaves
The Bottle with the Green Wax Seal
The Box from Japan
The Case of the Canny Killer
The Case of the Crazy Corpse (RH)
The Case of the Flying Hands (RH)
The Case of the Ivory Arrow
The Case of the Jeweled Ragpicker
The Case of the Lavender Gripsack
The Case of the Mysterious Moll
The Case of the 16 Beans
The Case of the Transparent Nude (RH)
The Case of the Transposed Legs
The Case of the Two-Headed Idiot (RH)
The Case of the Two Strange Ladies
The Circus Stealers (RH)
Cleopatra's Tears
A Copy of Beowulf (RH)
The Crimson Cube (RH)
The Face of the Man From Saturn
Find the Clock
The Five Silver Buddhas
The 4th King
The Gallows Waits, My Lord! (RH)
The Green Jade Hand
Finger! Finger!
Hangman's Nights (RH)
I, Chameleon (RH)
I Killed Lincoln at 10:13! (RH)
The Iron Ring
The Man Who Changed His Skin (RH)
The Man with the Crimson Box
The Man with the Magic Eardrums
The Man with the Wooden Spectacles
The Marceau Case
The Matilda Hunter Murder
The Monocled Monster

The Murder of London Lew
The Murdered Mathematician
The Mysterious Card (RH)
The Mysterious Ivory Ball of Wong Shing Li (RH)
The Mystery of the Fiddling Cracksman
The Peacock Fan
The Photo of Lady X (RH)
The Portrait of Jirjohn Cobb
Report on Vanessa Hewstone (RH)
Riddle of the Travelling Skull
Riddle of the Wooden Parrakeet (RH)
The Scarlet Mummy (RH)
The Search for X-Y-Z
The Sharkskin Book
Sing Sing Nights
The Six From Nowhere (RH)
The Skull of the Waltzing Clown
The Spectacles of Mr. Cagliostro
Stand By—London Calling!
The Steeltown Strangler
The Stolen Gravestone (RH)
Strange Journey (RH)
The Strange Will
The Straw Hat Murders (RH)
The Street of 1000 Eyes (RH)
Thieves' Nights
Three Novellos (RH)
The Tiger Snake
The Trap (RH)
Vagabond Nights (Defrauded Yegg-man)
Vagabond Nights 2 (10 Hours)
The Vanishing Gold Truck
The Voice of the Seven Sparrows
The Washington Square Enigma
When Thief Meets Thief
The White Circle (RH)
The Wonderful Scheme of Mr. Christopher Thorne
X. Jones—of Scotland Yard
Y. Cheung, Business Detective

Keeler Related Works

A To Izzard: A Harry Stephen Keeler Companion by Fender Tucker—Articles and stories about Harry, by Harry, and in his style. Included is a compleat bibliography.

Wild About Harry: Reviews of Keeler Novels—Edited by Richard Polt & Fender Tucker—22 reviews of works by Harry Stephen Keeler from *Keeler News*. A perfect introduction to the author.

The Keeler Keyhole Collection: Annotated newsletter rants from Harry Stephen Keeler, edited by Francis M. Nevins. Over 400 pages of incredibly personal Keeleriana.

Fakealoo—Pastiches of the style of Harry Stephen Keeler by selected demented members of the HSK Society. Updated every year with the new winner.

Strands of the Web: Short Stories of Harry Stephen Keeler—29 stories, just about all that Keeler wrote, are edited and introduced by Fred Cleaver.

RAMBLE HOUSE's LOON SANCTUARY

A Clear Path to Cross—Sharon Knowles short mystery stories by Ed Lynskey.

A Corpse Walks in Brooklyn and Other Stories—Volume 5 in the Day Keene in the Detective Pulps series.

A Fair Californian—Novel by Olive Harper about a young woman's quest for gold — a quest that turns into something completely unexpected.

A Jimmy Starr Omnibus—Three 40s novels by Jimmy Starr.

A Niche in Time and Other Stories—Classic SF by William F. Temple.

A Shot Rang Out—Three decades of reviews and articles by today's Anthony Boucher, Jon Breen. An essential book for any mystery lover's library.

A Smell of Smoke—A 1951 English countryside thriller by Miles Burton.

A Snark Selection—Lewis Carroll's *The Hunting of the Snark* with two Snarkian chapters by Harry Stephen Keeler—Illustrated by Gavin L. O'Keefe.

A Young Man's Heart—A forgotten early classic by Cornell Woolrich.

Alexander Laing Novels—*The Motives of Nicholas Holtz* and *Dr. Scarlett*, stories of medical mayhem and intrigue from the 30s.

An Angel in the Street—Modern hardboiled noir by Peter Genovese.

Automaton—Brilliant treatise on robotics: 1928-style! By H. Stafford Hatfield.

Away From the Here and Now—Clare Winger Harris stories, collected by Richard A. Lupoff

Beast or Man?—A 1930 novel of racism and horror by Sean M'Guire. Introduced by John Pelan.

Black Beadle—A 1939 thriller by E.C.R. Lorac.

Black Hogan Strikes Again—Australia's Peter Renwick pens a tale of the 30s outback.

Black River Falls—Suspense from the master, Ed Gorman.

Blondy's Boy Friend—A snappy 1930 story by Philip Wylie, writing as Leatrice Homesley.

Blood in a Snap—The *Finnegan's Wake* of the 21st century, by Jim Weiler.

Blood Moon—The first of the Robert Payne series by Ed Gorman.

Bogart '48—Hollywood action with Bogie by John Stanley and Kenn Davis

Butterfly Man—1930s novel by Lew Levenson about a dancer who must come to terms with his homosexuality.

Calling Lou Largo!—Two Lou Largo novels by William Ard.

Cathedral of Horror—First volume of collected stories by weird fiction writer Arthur J. Burks.

Chalk Face—Curious supernatural murder thriller by Waldo Frank.

Cornucopia of Crime—Francis M. Nevins assembled this huge collection of his writings about crime literature and the people who write it. Essential for any serious mystery library.

Corpse Without Flesh—Strange novel of forensics by George Bruce

Crimson Clown Novels—By Johnston McCulley, author of the Zorro novels, *The Crimson Clown* and *The Crimson Clown Again*.

Dago Red—22 tales of dark suspense by Bill Pronzini.

Dark Sanctuary—Weird Menace story by H. B. Gregory.
David Hume Novels—*Corpses Never Argue, Cemetery First Stop, Make Way for the Mourners, Eternity Here I Come*. 1930s British hardboiled fiction with an attitude.
David&Son: Peregrine Parentus and other tales—Collection of tales and memoirs by Avram Davidson and Ethan Davidson, some published for the first time. Introduced by Grania Davidson Davis.
Dead Man Talks Too Much—Hollywood boozer by Weed Dickenson.
Death in a Bowl—1930's murder mystery by Raoul Whitfield.
Death Leaves No Card—One of the most unusual murdered-in-the-tub mysteries you'll ever read. By Miles Burton.
Death March of the Dancing Dolls and Other Stories—Volume Three in the Day Keene in the Detective Pulps series. Introduced by Bill Crider.
Deep Space and other Stories—A collection of SF gems by Richard A. Lupoff.
Detective Duff Unravels It—Episodic mysteries by Harvey O'Higgins.
Devil's Planet—Locked room mystery set on the planet Mars, by Manly Wade Wellman.
Dime Novels: Ramble House's 10-Cent Books—*Knife in the Dark* by Robert Leslie Bellem, *Hot Lead* and *Song of Death* by Ed Earl Repp, *A Hashish House in New York* by H.H. Kane, and five more.
Doctor Arnoldi—Tiffany Thayer's story of the death of death.
Don Diablo: Book of a Lost Film—Two-volume treatment of a western by Paul Landres, with diagrams. Intro by Francis M. Nevins.
Dope and Swastikas—Two strange novels from 1922 by Edmund Snell
Dope Tales #1—Two dope-riddled classics; *Dope Runners* by Gerald Grantham and *Death Takes the Joystick* by Phillip Condé.
Dope Tales #2—Two more narco-classics; *The Invisible Hand* by Rex Dark and *The Smokers of Hashish* by Norman Berrow.
Dope Tales #3—Two enchanting novels of opium by the master, Sax Rohmer. *Dope* and *The Yellow Claw.*
Double Hot & Double Sex—Two combos of '60s softcore sex novels by Morris Hershman.
Dr. Odin—Douglas Newton's 1933 racial potboiler comes back to life.
E. R. Punshon novels—*Information Received, Crossword Mystery, Dictator's Way, Diabolic Candelabra, Music Tells All, Helen Passes By, The House of Godwinsson, The Golden Dagger, The Attending Truth, Strange Ending, Brought to Light, Dark is the Clue, Triple Quest*, and *Six Were Present*: featuring Bobby Owen.
Ed "Strangler" Lewis: Facts within a Myth—Authoritative illustrated biography of the famous American wrestler Ed Lewis, by noted historian Steve Yohe.
Evangelical Cockroach—Jack Woodford writes about writing.
Evidence in Blue—1938 mystery by E. Charles Vivian.
Fatal Accident—Murder by automobile, a 1936 mystery by Cecil M. Wills.
Fighting Mad—Todd Robbins' 1922 novel about boxing and life
Five Million in Cash—Gangster thriller by Tiffany Thayer writing as O. B. King.
Food for the Fungus Lady—Collection of weird stories by Ralston Shields, edited and introduced by John Pelan.

Francis M. Nevins—Two omnibus volumes of novels featuring his legal sleuth Loren Mensing: *Publish and Perish / Corrupt and Ensnare* and *Into the Same River Twice / Beneficiaries' Requiem*.

Freaks and Fantasies—Eerie tales by Tod Robbins, collaborator of Tod Browning on the film FREAKS.

Gadsby—A lipogram (a novel without the letter E). Ernest Vincent Wright's last work, published in 1939 right before his death.

Gelett Burgess Novels—*The Master of Mysteries, The White Cat, Two O'Clock Courage, Ladies in Boxes, Find the Woman, The Heart Line, The Picaroons* and *Lady Mechante*. Recently added is A Gelett Burgess Sampler, edited by Alfred Jan. All are introduced by Richard A. Lupoff.

Geronimo—S. M. Barrett's 1905 autobiography of a noble American.

Gordon Eklund—*Second Creation, Retro Man* and *Stalking the Sun*: three volumes of the author's best short stories.

Go Forth and Multiply—Anthology of science fiction tales of repopulation, edited by Gordon Van Gelder.

Hake Talbot Novels—*Rim of the Pit, The Hangman's Handyman*. Classic locked room mysteries, with mapback covers by Gavin O'Keefe.

Hands Out of Hell and Other Stories—John H. Knox's eerie hallucinations

Hell is a City—William Ard's masterpiece.

Hollywood Dreams—A novel of Tinsel Town and the Depression by Richard O'Brien.

Homicide House—#6 in the Day Keene in the Detective Pulps series.

Hostesses in Hell and Other Stories—Russell Gray's most graphic stories

House of the Restless Dead—Strange and ominous tales by Hugh B. Cave

Inclination to Murder—1966 thriller by New Zealand's Harriet Hunter.

Invaders from the Dark—Classic werewolf tale from Greye La Spina.

J. Poindexter, Colored—Classic satirical black novel by Irvin S. Cobb.

Jack Mann Novels—Strange murder in the English countryside. *Gees' First Case, Nightmare Farm, Grey Shapes, The Ninth Life, The Glass Too Many, Her Ways Are Death, The Kleinert Case* and *Maker of Shadows*.

Jake Hardy—A lusty western tale from Wesley Tallant.

James Corbett—*Vampire of the Skies, The Ghost Plane, Murder Begets Murder* and *The Air Killer* – strange thriller novels from this singular British author.

Jim Harmon Double Novels—*Vixen Hollow/Celluloid Scandal, The Man Who Made Maniacs/Silent Siren, Ape Rape/Wanton Witch, Sex Burns Like Fire/Twist Session, Sudden Lust/Passion Strip, Sin Unlimited/Harlot Master, Twilight Girls/Sex Institution*. Written in the early 60s and never reprinted until now.

Joel Townsley Rogers Novels and Short Stories—By the author of *The Red Right Hand: Once In a Red Moon, Lady With the Dice, The Stopped Clock, Never Leave My Bed*. Also two short story collections: *Night of Horror* and *Killing Time*.

John Carstairs, Space Detective—Arboreal Sci-fi by Frank Belknap Long

John G. Brandon—*The Case of the Withered Hand, Finger-Prints Never Lie*, and *Death on Delivery*: crime thrillers by Australian author John G. Brandon.

John S. Glasby—Two collections of Glasby's Lovecraftian stories: *The Brooding City* and *Beyond the Rim*. Introduced by John Pelan.

Joseph Shallit Novels—*The Case of the Billion Dollar Body, Lady Don't Die on My Doorstep, Kiss the Killer, Yell Bloody Murder, Take Your Last Look.* One of America's best 50's authors and a favorite of author Bill Pronzini.

Keller Memento—45 short stories of the amazing and weird by Dr. David Keller.

Killer's Caress—Cary Moran's 1936 hardboiled thriller.

Knowing the Unknowable: Putting Psi to Work—Damien Broderick, PhD puts forward the valid case for evidence of Psi.

Lady of the Yellow Death and Other Stories—More stories by Wyatt Blassingame.

Laughing Death—1932 Yellow Peril thriller by Walter C. Brown.

League of the Grateful Dead and Other Stories—Volume One in the Day Keene in the Detective Pulps series.

Library of Death—Ghastly tale by Ronald S. L. Harding, introduced by John Pelan

Lords of the Earth—A novel of meddling dabblers in the occult invoking the ancient powers of Atlantis. J.M.A. Mills' sequel to *The Tomb of the Dark Ones.*

Mad-Doctor Merciful—Collin Brooks' unsettling novel of medical experimentation with supernatural forces.

Malcolm Jameson Novels and Short Stories—*Astonishing! Astounding!, Tarnished Bomb, The Alien Envoy and Other Stories* and *The Chariots of San Fernando and Other Stories.* All introduced and edited by John Pelan or Richard A. Lupoff.

Man Out of Hell and Other Stories—Volume II of the John H. Knox weird pulps collection.

Marblehead: A Novel of H.P. Lovecraft—A long-lost masterpiece from Richard A. Lupoff. This is the "director's cut", the long version that has never been published before.

Mark of the Laughing Death and Other Stories—Shockers from the pulps by Francis James, introduced by John Pelan.

Mark Hansom Novels—*Master of Souls, The Ghost of Gaston Revere, The Madman, The Shadow on the House, Sorcerer's Chessmen* & *The Wizard of Berner's Abbey.*

Max Afford Novels—*Owl of Darkness, Death's Mannikins, Blood on His Hands, The Dead Are Blind, The Sheep and the Wolves, Sinners in Paradise* and *Two Locked Room Mysteries and a Ripping Yarn* by one of Australia's finest mystery novelists.

Mistress of Terror—Fourth volume of the collected weird tales of Wyatt Blassingame.

Molly and her Man of War— Romantic novel with a difference, by Arabella Kenealy.

Money Brawl—Two books about the writing business by Jack Woodford and H. Bedford-Jones. Introduced by Richard A. Lupoff.

More Secret Adventures of Sherlock Holmes—Gary Lovisi's second collection of tales about the unknown sides of the great detective.

Muddled Mind: Complete Works of Ed Wood, Jr.—David Hayes and Hayden Davis deconstruct the life and works of the mad, but canny, genius.

Murder among the Nudists—1934 mystery by Peter Hunt, featuring a naked Detective-Inspector going undercover in a nudist colony.

Murder in Black and White—1931 classic tennis whodunit by Evelyn Elder.

Murder in Shawnee—Two novels of the Alleghenies by John Douglas: *Shawnee Alley Fire* and *Haunts*.

Murder in Silk—A 1937 Yellow Peril novel of the silk trade by Ralph Trevor.

Murder in Suffolk—A 1938 murder mystery novel by the mysterious 'A. Fielding.'

My Deadly Angel—1955 Cold War drama by John Chelton.

My First Time: The One Experience You Never Forget—Michael Birchwood—64 true first-person narratives of how they lost it.

My Touch Brings Death—Second volume of collected stories by Russell Gray.

Mysterious Martin, the Master of Murder—Two versions of a strange 1912 novel by Tod Robbins about a man who writes books that can kill.

Norman Berrow Novels—*The Bishop's Sword, Ghost House, Don't Go Out After Dark, Claws of the Cougar, The Smokers of Hashish, The Secret Dancer, Don't Jump Mr. Boland!, The Footprints of Satan, Fingers for Ransom, The Three Tiers of Fantasy, The Spaniard's Thumb, The Eleventh Plague, Words Have Wings, One Thrilling Night, The Lady's in Danger, It Howls at Night, The Terror in the Fog, Oil Under the Window, Murder in the Melody, The Singing Room.* This is the complete Norman Berrow library of locked-room mysteries, several of which are masterpieces.

Old Faithful and Other Stories—SF classic tales by Raymond Z. Gallun

Old Times' Sake—Short stories by James Reasoner from Mike Shayne Magazine.

One Dreadful Night—A classic mystery by Ronald S. L. Harding

Pair O' Jacks—A mystery novel and a diatribe about publishing by Jack Woodford

Pawns of Destiny—Psychological drama by Kay Seaton.

Perfect .38—Two early Timothy Dane novels by William Ard. More to come.

Prince Pax—Devilish intrigue by George Sylvester Viereck and Philip Eldridge

Prose Bowl—Futuristic satire of a world where hack writing has replaced football as our national obsession, by Bill Pronzini and Barry N. Malzberg.

Red Light—The history of legal prostitution in Shreveport Louisiana by Eric Brock. Includes wonderful photos of the houses and the ladies.

Researching American-Made Toy Soldiers—A 276-page collection of a lifetime of articles by toy soldier expert Richard O'Brien.

Reunion in Hell—Volume One of the John H. Knox series of weird stories from the pulps. Introduced by horror expert John Pelan.

Ripped from the Headlines!—The Jack the Ripper story as told in the newspaper articles in the *New York* and *London Times*.

Rough Cut & New, Improved Murder—Ed Gorman's first two novels.

R. R. Ryan Novels — *Freak Museum, The Subjugated Beast, Death of a Sadist, Echo of a Curse, Devil's Shelter* and *No Escape*. Introduced by John Pelan.

Roland Daniel Novels — *Ruby of a Thousand Dreams*, *The Girl in the Dark*, and *A Roland Daniel Double: The Signal and The Return of Wu Fang*.

Ruled By Radio — 1925 futuristic novel by Robert L. Hadfield & Frank E. Farncombe.

Rupert Penny Novels — *Policeman's Holiday*, *Policeman's Evidence*, *Lucky Policeman*, *Policeman in Armour*, *Sealed Room Murder*, *Sweet Poison*, *The Talkative Policeman*, *She had to Have Gas* and *Cut and Run* (by Martin Tanner.) Rupert Penny is the pseudonym of Australian Charles Thornett, a master of the locked room, impossible crime plot.

Sacred Locomotive Flies — Richard A. Lupoff's psychedelic SF story.

Sam — Early gay novel by Lonnie Coleman.

Sand's Game — Spectacular hardboiled noir from Ennis Willie, edited by Lynn Myers and Stephen Mertz, with contributions from Max Allan Collins, Bill Crider, Wayne Dundee, Bill Pronzini, Gary Lovisi and James Reasoner.

Sand's War — More violent fiction from the typewriter of Ennis Willie

Satan's Den Exposed — True crime in Truth or Consequences New Mexico — Award-winning journalism by the *Desert Journal*.

Satan's Secret and Selected Stories — Barnard Stacey's only novel with a selection of his best short stories.

Satans of Saturn — Novellas from the pulps by Otis Adelbert Kline and E. H. Price

Satan's Sin House and Other Stories — Horrific gore by Wayne Rogers

Second Creation — The first volume of selected short stories by Gordon Eklund.

Secrets of a Teenage Superhero — Graphic lit by Jonathan Sweet

Sex Slave — Potboiler of lust in the days of Cleopatra by Dion Leclerq, 1966.

Sideslip — 1968 SF masterpiece by Ted White and Dave Van Arnam.

Slammer Days — Two full-length prison memoirs: *Men into Beasts* (1952) by George Sylvester Viereck and *Home Away From Home* (1962) by Jack Woodford.

Slippery Staircase — 1930s whodunit from E.C.R. Lorac

Star Griffin — Michael Kurland's 1987 masterpiece of SF drollery is back.

Stakeout on Millennium Drive — Award-winning Indianapolis Noir by Ian Woollen.

Strands of the Web: Short Stories of Harry Stephen Keeler — Edited and Introduced by Fred Cleaver.

Summer Camp for Corpses and Other Stories — Weird Menace tales from Arthur Leo Zagat; introduced by John Pelan.

Suzy — A collection of comic strips by Richard O'Brien and Bob Vojtko from 1970.

Tail of the Lizard King / Kaliwood — Two novellas by Adam Mudman Bezecny paying homage to the sleaze genre.

Tales of the Macabre and Ordinary — Modern twisted horror by Chris Mikul, author of the *Bizarrism* series.

Tales of Terror and Torment Vols. #1 & #2 — John Pelan selects and introduces these samplers of weird menace tales from the pulps.

Tenebrae — Ernest G. Henham's 1898 horror tale brought back.

The Alice Books — Lewis Carroll's classics *Alice's Adventures in Wonderland* and *Through the Looking-Glass* together in one volume, with new illustrations by O'Keefe.

The Amorous Intrigues & Adventures of Aaron Burr — by Anonymous. Hot historical action about the man who almost became Emperor of Mexico.

The Anthony Boucher Chronicles — edited by Francis M. Nevins. Book reviews by Anthony Boucher written for the *San Francisco Chronicle,* 1942 – 1947. Essential and fascinating reading by the best book reviewer there ever was.

The Barclay Catalogs — Two essential books about toy soldier collecting by Richard O'Brien

The Basil Wells Omnibus — A collection of Wells' stories by Richard A. Lupoff

The Beautiful Dead and Other Stories — Dreadful tales from Donald Dale

The Best of 10-Story Book — edited by Chris Mikul, over 35 stories from the literary magazine Harry Stephen Keeler edited.

The Bitch Wall — Novel about American soldiers in the Vietnam War, based on Dennis Lane's experiences.

The Black Dark Murders — Vintage 50s college murder yarn by Milt Ozaki, writing as Robert O. Saber.

The Book of Time — The classic novel by H.G. Wells is joined by sequels by Wells himself and three stories by Richard A. Lupoff. Illustrated by Gavin L. O'Keefe.

The Broken Fang and Other Experiences of a Specialist in Spooks — Eerie mystery tales by Uel Key.

The Case in the Clinic — One of E.C.R. Lorac's finest.

The Strange Case of the Antlered Man — A mystery of superstition by Edwy Searles Brooks.

The Case of the Bearded Bride — #4 in the Day Keene in the Detective Pulps series.

The Case of the Little Green Men — Mack Reynolds wrote this love song to sci-fi fans back in 1951 and it's now back in print.

The Charlie Chaplin Murder Mystery — A 2004 tribute by noted film scholar, Wes D. Gehring.

The Cloudbuilders and Other Stories — SF tales from Colin Kapp.

The Collected Writings — Collection of science fiction stories, memoirs and poetry by Carol Carr. Introduction by Karen Haber.

The Compleat Calhoon — All of Fender Tucker's works: Includes *Totah Six-Pack, Weed, Women and Song* and *Tales from the Tower,* plus a CD of all of his songs.

The Compleat Ova Hamlet — Parodies of SF authors by Richard A. Lupoff. This is a brand new edition with more stories and more illustrations by Trina Robbins.

The Contested Earth and Other SF Stories — A never-before published space opera and seven short stories by Jim Harmon.

The Corpse Factory — More horror stories by Arthur Leo Zagat.

The Crackpot and Other Twisted Tales of Greedy Fans and Collectors — The first retrospective collection of the whacky stories of John E. Stockman. Edited by Dwight R. Decker.

The Crimson Butterfly — Early novel by Edmund Snell involving superstition and aberrant Lepidoptera in Borneo.

The Crimson Query — A 1929 thriller from Arlton Eadie. A perfect way to get introduced.

The Daymakers, City of the Tiger & Perchance to Wake — Three volumes of stories taken from the influential British science fiction magazine *Science Fantasy*. Compiled by John Boston & Damien Broderick.

The Devil and the C.I.D. — Odd diabolic mystery by E.C.R. Lorac

The Devil Drives — An odd prison and lost treasure novel from 1932 by Virgil Markham.

The Devil of Pei-Ling — Herbert Asbury's 1929 tale of the occult.

The Devil's Mistress — A 1915 Scottish gothic tale by J. W. Brodie-Innes, a member of Aleister Crowley's Golden Dawn.

The Devil's Nightclub and Other Stories — John Pelan introduces some gruesome tales by Nat Schachner.

The Disentanglers — Episodic intrigue at the turn of last century by Andrew Lang

The Dog Poker Code — A spoof of *The Da Vinci Code* by D. B. Smithee.

The Dumpling — Political murder from 1907 by Coulson Kernahan.

The End of It All and Other Stories — Ed Gorman selected his favorite short stories for this huge collection.

The Evil of Li-Sin — A Gerald Verner double, combining *The Menace of Li-Sin* and *The Vengeance of Li-Sin*, together with an introduction by John Pelan and an afterword and bibliography by Chris Verner.

The Fangs of Suet Pudding — A 1944 novel of the German invasion by Adams Farr

The Finger of Destiny and Other Stories — Edmund Snell's superb collection of weird stories of Borneo.

The Gold Star Line — Seaboard adventure from L.T. Reade and Robert Eustace.

The Great Orme Terror — Horror stories by Garnett Radcliffe from the pulps

The Hairbreadth Escapes of Major Mendax — Francis Blake Crofton's 1889 boys' book.

The House That Time Forgot and Other Stories — Insane pulpitude by Robert F. Young

The House of the Vampire — 1907 poetic thriller by George S. Viereck.

The Illustrious Corpse — Murder hijinx from Tiffany Thayer

The Incredible Adventures of Rowland Hern — Intriguing 1928 impossible crimes by Nicholas Olde.

The John Dickson Carr Companion — Comprehensive reference work compiled by James E. Keirans. Indispensable resource for the Carr *aficionado*.

The Julius Caesar Murder Case — A 1935 retelling of the assassination by Wallace Irwin that's more fun than Shakespeare's version.

The Kid Was a Killer — Caryl Chessman's only novel, based on his own experiences.

The Koky Comics — A collection of all of the 1978-1981 Sunday and daily comic strips by Richard O'Brien and Mort Gerberg, in two volumes.

The Lady of the Terraces — 1925 missing race adventure by E. Charles Vivian.

The Lord of Terror — 1925 mystery with master-criminal, Fantômas.

The Man who was Murdered Twice — Intriguing murder mystery by Robert H. Leitfred.

The Melamare Mystery — A classic 1929 Arsene Lupin mystery by Maurice Leblanc

The Man Who Was Secrett — Epic SF stories from John Brunner

The Man Without a Planet — Science fiction tales by Richard Wilson

The N. R. De Mexico Novels — Robert Bragg, the real N.R. de Mexico, presents *Marijuana Girl, Madman on a Drum, Private Chauffeur* in one volume.

The Night Remembers — A 1991 Jack Walsh mystery from Ed Gorman.

The One After Snelling — Kickass modern noir from Richard O'Brien.

The Organ Reader — A huge compilation of just about everything published in the 1971-1972 radical bay-area newspaper, *THE ORGAN*. A coffee table book that points out the shallowness of the coffee table mindset.

The Place of Hairy Death — Collected weird horror tales by Anthony M. Rud.

The Poker Club — Three in one! Ed Gorman's ground-breaking novel, the short story it was based upon, and the screenplay of the film made from it.

The Private Journal & Diary of John H. Surratt — The memoirs of the man who conspired to assassinate President Lincoln.

The Ramble House Coloring Book — Twenty illustrations to color in, each adapted from one of Gavin L. O'Keefe's cover designs.

The Ramble House Mapbacks — Recently revised book by Gavin L. O'Keefe with color pictures of all the Ramble House books with mapbacks.

The Secret Adventures of Sherlock Holmes — Three Sherlockian pastiches by the Brooklyn author/publisher, Gary Lovisi.

The Secret of the Morgue — Frederick G. Eberhard's 1932 mystery involving murder and forensic science with an undercurrent of the malaise that's driven by Prohibition.

The Sign of the Scorpion — A 1935 Edmund Snell tale of oriental evil.

The Silent Terror of Chu-Sheng — Yellow Peril suspense novel by Eugene Thomas.

The Singular Problem of the Stygian House-Boat — Two classic tales by John Kendrick Bangs about the denizens of Hades.

The Smiling Corpse — Philip Wylie and Bernard Bergman's odd 1935 novel.

The Sorcery Club — Classic supernatural novel by Elliott O'Donnell.

The Spider: Satan's Murder Machines — A thesis about Iron Man.

The Stench of Death: An Odoriferous Omnibus by Jack Moskovitz — Two complete novels and two novellas from 60's sleaze author, Jack Moskovitz.

The Story Writer and Other Stories — Classic SF from Richard Wilson

The Strange Thirteen — Richard B. Gamon's odd stories about Raj India.

The Technique of the Mystery Story — Carolyn Wells' tips about writing.

The Tell-Tale Soul — Two novellas by Bram Stoker Award-winning author Christopher Conlon. Introduction by John Pelan.

The Threat of Nostalgia — A collection of his most obscure stories by Jon Breen

The Time Armada — Fox B. Holden's 1953 SF gem.

The Tomb of the Dark Ones — Adventure in Egypt where ancient forces are roused from æons of slumber. A J. M. A. Mills novel from 1937.

The Tongueless Horror and Other Stories — Volume One of the series of short stories from the weird pulps by Wyatt Blassingame.

The Town from Planet Five — From Richard Wilson, two SF classics, *And Then the Town Took Off* and *The Girls from Planet 5*

The Tracer of Lost Persons — From 1906, an episodic novel that became a hit radio series in the 30s. Introduced by Richard A. Lupoff.

The Trail of the Cloven Hoof — Diabolical horror from 1935 by Arlton Eadie. Introduced by John Pelan.

The Triune Man — Mindscrambling science fiction from Richard A. Lupoff.

The Unholy Goddess and Other Stories — Wyatt Blassingame's first DTP compilation

The Universal Holmes — Richard A. Lupoff's 2007 collection of five Holmesian pastiches and a recipe for giant rat stew.

The Werewolf vs the Vampire Woman — Hard to believe ultraviolence by either Arthur M. Scarm or Arthur M. Scram.

The Whistling Ancestors — A 1936 classic of weirdness by Richard E. Goddard and introduced by John Pelan.

The White Owl — A vintage thriller from Edmund Snell

The White Peril in the Far East — Sidney Lewis Gulick's 1905 indictment of the West and assurance that Japan would never attack the U.S.

The Wonderful Wizard of Oz — by L. Frank Baum and illustrated by Gavin L. O'Keefe.

The Yu-Chi Stone — Novel of intrigue and superstition set in Borneo, by Edmund Snell.

They Called the Shots — Collection of authoritative articles by Francis M. Nevins exploring the action movie directors of the late silents through to the late 1960s.

Time Line — Ramble House artist Gavin O'Keefe selects his most evocative art inspired by the twisted literature he reads and designs.

Tiresias — Psychotic modern horror novel by Jonathan M. Sweet.

Tortures and Towers — Two novellas of terror by Dexter Dayle.

Totah Six-Pack — Fender Tucker's six tales about Farmington in one sleek volume.

Tree of Life, Book of Death — Grania Davis' book of her life.

Trail of the Spirit Warrior — Roger Haley's saga of life in the Indian Territories.

Twelve Who Were Damned — Collection of weird menace tales by Paul Ernst.

Two Kinds of Bad — Two 50s novels by William Ard about Danny Fontaine

Two Suns of Morcali and Other Stories — Evelyn E. Smith's SF tour-de-force

Two-Timers — Time travel double: *The Man Who Mastered Time* by Ray Cummings and *Time Column* and *Taa the Terrible* by Malcolm Jameson. Introduced by Richard A. Lupoff.

Ultra-Boiled — 23 gut-wrenching tales by our Man in Brooklyn, Gary Lovisi.

Up Front From Behind — A 2011 satire of Wall Street by James B. Kobak.

Victims & Villains — Intriguing Sherlockiana from Derham Groves.

Wade Wright Novels — *Echo of Fear, Death At Nostalgia Street, It Leads to Murder* and *Shadows' Edge*, a double book featuring *Shadows Don't Bleed* and *The Sharp Edge*.

Walter S. Masterman Novels — *The Green Toad, The Flying Beast, The Yellow Mistletoe, The Wrong Verdict, The Perjured Alibi, The Border Line, The Bloodhounds Bay, The Curse of Cantire* and *The Baddington Horror.* Masterman wrote horror and mystery, some introduced by John Pelan.

We Are the Dead and Other Stories — Volume Two in the Day Keene in the Detective Pulps series, introduced by Ed Gorman. When done, there may be 11 in the series.

Welsh Rarebit Tales — Charming stories from 1902 by Harle Oren Cummins

West Texas War and Other Western Stories — Western hijinks by Gary Lovisi.

What If? Volume 1, 2 and 3 — Richard A. Lupoff introduces three decades worth of SF short stories that should have won a Hugo, but didn't.

When the Bat Man Thirsts and Other Stories — Weird tales from Frederick C. Davis.

When the Dead Walk — Gary Lovisi takes us into the zombie-infested South.

Whip Dodge: Man Hunter — Wesley Tallant's saga of a bounty hunter of the old West.

Win, Place and Die! — The first new mystery by Milt Ozaki in decades. The ultimate novel of 70s Reno.

Writer, Volumes 1, 2 & 3 — A *magnus opus* from Richard A. Lupoff summing up his life as writer.

You'll Die Laughing — Bruce Elliott's 1945 novel of murder at a practical joker's English countryside manor.

You're Not Alone: 30 Science Fiction Stories from *Cosmos Magazine*, edited by Damien Broderick.

RAMBLE HOUSE

www.ramblehouse.com   fender@ramblehouse.com
10329 Sheephead Drive, Vancleave MS 39565

I *always look for the* 'RAMBLE HOUSE' *when I want a* PLEASANT BOOK*!*

Your troubles are at an end when you choose a Ramble House novel. No more doubts! No more disappointments! A Ramble House novel will give you hours of happy reading. Next time, just say to your librarian, "A Ramble House, please!"

www.ingramcontent.com/pod-product-compliance
Lightning Source LLC
Chambersburg PA
CBHW030336030726
47499CB00003B/791